THE WINTER TREE

THE WINTER TREE

GEORGINA LEWIS

LONDON
VICTOR GOLLANCZ LTD
1985

First published in Great Britain April 1983
by Victor Gollancz Ltd,
14 Henrietta Street, London WC2E 8QJ
in association with Arrow Books
Second impression July 1983
Third impression May 1985

27795426

The characters in this book are entirely imaginary and
any resemblance to any living person is coincidental.
The village of Lanissick is purely fictional; the county, of
course, is not.

I wish to thank Viggers and Hodgson (Publishers) of
Chesham, Bucks. for their kind permission to quote from
the *Ringer's Notebook and Diary*.

British Library Cataloguing in Publication Data
Lewis, Georgina
    The winter tree.
    I. Title
    823'.914[F]   PR6062.E/

ISBN 0-575-03258-8

Photoset in Great Britain by
Rowland Phototypesetting Limited, Bury St Edmunds, Suffolk
and printed by St Edmundsbury Press
Bury St Edmunds, Suffolk

For Robin

This is the song the stars sing,
(Toned all in time)
Tintinnabulous, tuned to ring
A multitudinous-single thing,
(Rung all in rhyme).

From "New Year's Chimes" by Francis Thompson

Chapter One

THE BADGER

THIS MORNING THE sky opened again. For all these years, no more than a glimpse: a distant figure crossing a field, a curl of tobacco smoke in the lane, the casual mention of a name in conversation. Then this morning to see him again, so close that we could have spoken.

He stood in dappled shadow under the trees, half in light and half out of it, looking across at us. Oh, he saw us, I know that he did, for he nodded in his old familiar way and smiled a shadow of that rich smile of his. He looks older now, and tired. And yet his smile still has power to shake the heart and bring the old pain back, vivid and sharp and grievous.

The child frowned and pulled at my sleeve. 'That man. Who is he, Abbie?'

As we looked across at the still figure, the branches above him moved and lifted a little in the wind. A puzzled look came into the clear young face beside me, as if she were listening to music a long way off and couldn't quite catch the strain of it; and my heart held still a moment to see that look of Hester's born again. I wondered whether he saw it too, and if the memories came flooding back for him, the way they did for me.

Later tonight she will ask me again. 'Who was that man, Abbie? Do you know him?'

And I shall have to answer. 'His name is Joseph,' I shall tell her.

'But who is he?' she will persist. 'Did he know my mother?'

'Yes,' I shall say. 'Yes darling, he knew your mother. Long before you were born.'

7

And later still, after supper, she will fasten down the window-catches for me and stir the fire. Then turning out the light, she will sit down beside the flaming coals and say, 'Now, Abbie. Tell me about him. Tell me about Joseph, and about my mother.'

And then there will no longer be any escape for me.

Already the wind is beginning to rise behind the village, picking up its power from the ancient mound of stones up on the hill. The child hears nothing but the wind; she is too young to remember. But I can hear a twist of music carried there, the distant cadence of a violin. The violin is my father's, playing as he always played, late into the night in the woodshed at the far end of the orchard. Mother used to say that he played far away from the cottage so that he could be in peace but I think, looking back, it was because she couldn't bear to listen, so sad and filled with longing was the music.

It is on wild, dark nights like these that those old days come back so piercingly clear. The sounds of the present mingle with the sounds of childhood, and I am lost in the past. The rattling of the sashes in the rain when the weather is rough, the wind snorting and bellowing off the hill, the window-panes creaking and shuddering as if a wild thing were trying to get in at them. Then I am once more a child of seven, curled up in the big bed with my little sister Lissie, the covers up round our ears for fear that the Old Ones from the mound would get us. We are listening, half-sleeping, half-waking, to Father playing his violin in the dark at the top of the orchard, so that it sounded at one with the wind from the hill: tunes full of the soul's sadness, wild and plaintive. Father always played on stormy nights, accompanying the wind as if it got into his soul. I think he had no fear, only a deep sense of unity with the elements and he would make up the music as he went along, or 'natural' as he called it, for not a note of music could he read. Lissie and I would lie in the dark and listen. It held us, in an odd way, in a grip of calm. In later life I never was able to listen to sad

8

and powerful music without it evoking the memory of Father playing to the tormented wind.

Suddenly it is summer again, and warmth comes rushing back into memory. The wind from the hill is no longer sad but light and kind, and the fluid days roll into one another. There is the scent of wood smoke, and there are wasps in the fruit trees. There are the bent backs of Father and my brother Perran in the orchard cutting grass for hay, and Joseph – ah, Joseph – come to help them for the afternoon. Wind-fallen apples thud into long grass, gnats hover in clusters above a stream, the baby's cheeks are brown and rosy, touched by the sun. There is the feel of warm bark beneath my hand up in the orchard on the morning of the day that Hester came to change our lives. And there is the look of Joseph's face when he first saw her standing in the doorway.

But before that. Even before Hester came. I remember a day shortly after I was eight, and what now seems a very young Father taking us aside, Perran, Lissie and me. He perched us girls on his knees: Lissie on one and me on the other, like two birds ready for flight, with six-year-old Perran between us; and he frowned at us severely as was his habit when embarrassed, and coughed softly to clear his throat.

'Now,' said Father awkwardly, smiling at us through his eyebrows with a kind of false jollity. 'I've got two girls in my family, and that's enough.'

We waited respectfully for him to continue, hoping perhaps it was a penny for sweets, as from his behaviour we were evidently to expect some sort of a present. He coughed again and went slightly red, looked fierce, and pinched Perran's cheek kindly. He seemed at a loss as to how to begin. Then he said loudly, 'We've – ah, we've got a surprise for you soon.' So we knew it was a treat. We looked at him expectantly.

'Yum-yum!' said little Lissie. Father frowned. I wondered why. Perhaps it wasn't sweets.

'Buns, is it Father?' I asked brightly. 'Or a cake?'

Father coughed again, went deeply scarlet, and then said recklessly, 'You're going to have a baby soon.' He paused and passed a hand across his forehead. 'At least, your mother is.'

We stared at him aghast. I tried hard to hide my disappointment. A baby? Of what use was a baby? I'd far rather have had the sweets. There was a long pause while we thought about the information.

'Harry Tregulla got a baby,' Perran said helpfully. 'He've got a baby boy. Harry's missus is going to call 'en Toby because she said he's full of water like a jug.'

Father received this fascinating news in silence for a bit, and then he said, 'Your mother and me's hoping ours will be a boy.' He frowned at us again, then rummaged in his pockets. 'Here's a penny each for you,' he said, and brought them out after all: three huge round coins that clinked together enchantingly. Then he ruffled our heads and put us all down and went up to the orchard to play his violin.

Soon after that Mother disappeared upstairs for a few days and Father looked after us and cooked us half-raw porridge for dinner and potato soup for supper and took Mother up little trays of the strawberries he grew in the garden.

Next time we were allowed to see her we trooped soberly up the stairs with our best clothes on and our faces scrubbed and shining. Mother was propped wanly up in the bed holding the new baby, and looking rather transparent. The baby was pale and asleep. It looked dreadfully fragile. I hoped for its sake it wasn't a girl.

Lissie flung herself onto the bed and wanted to kiss the baby. Mother said no but allowed her to stroke its tiny hand and little crumpled cheek. Perran and I stood respectfully to attention beside the bed and looked at it asleep in Mother's arms.

'A boy,' whispered Mother, her strained face softening into a tired smile. 'And your father's awful pleased.'

The baby hiccuped, and its tiny mouth curved into a tremulous arc.

'Smiling!' said Lissie, stroking its forehead under Mother's watchful eye. 'Babby smiling.'

'That's wind,' said Perran scornfully, 'not smiling. I know from Harry's baby. They do that when they've got a wind in their stomach.'

Mother nodded gently and said he was probably right, but I began to feel more impressed. If it smiled it was real.

'What's it called?' asked Perran frowning. 'You got to call 'em sommat.'

Mother smiled again and stroked the baby's cheek with her thin hand. 'We thought to call him "Thomas",' she said.

Hester's arrival just over a year later seemed to upset our household very little at the time, although now the event stands out very clearly, like a shaft of sunshine across the haze of childhood. She was due to arrive in the evening, and we had spent the day up in the orchard. The lingering autumn was full of warmth and rosy kindliness. Joseph had come up from his cottage to help Father cut the grass and gather the last of the season's apples, and we had had our dinner out under the trees in the late sunshine.

Thomas was tied up in his little chair, for he'd almost learned to walk and was set fair to trample all over the dinner and jab his pudgy fingers in the butter. I remember that Mother tied him into his chair with an old pyjama-cord of Father's round his waist. We all laughed at him and he chuckled back, screwing up his baby nose in delight and not minding a bit. Mother put a hunk of cheese in one of his hands and a tomato in the other, and he sat there looking from one to the other of us and grinning widely while the tomato seeds slipped down his chin. He was a great, strong, healthy baby. His hair was curly and very white, standing out in snow-coloured tufts about his head. Later on there were freckles across the squat nose, but at thirteen months there were none; only the fading brown patches which were the result of lying idle in the summer sun, with nothing else to do but sleep and eat and learn to laugh. And what a laugh he had: a great wide grin, in which presently appeared a few white pearls. A lovely child was Thomas, full of sunshine.

In the evening Joseph came to have supper with us, a thing he did occasionally, for his mother had died the year before when he was twenty and he lived all alone in his cottage, except for his hens. He seemed vastly old to me, and very strong. He carried Lissie and me, both together, round the orchard on his shoulders. We shrieked and squealed in delight and pleaded for more until Mother said firmly, 'Abigail! Elizabeth! Leave Joseph alone, you'll hurt him!' And Joseph grinned and pitched us both, laughing helplessly, into the pile of hay. Ah, Joseph! How young he seems to me then, looking back now. He never did seem quite so young as that again, not after that day; the day Hester came.

I'll never forget the evening she arrived. After a shave and a good wash to get rid of all the dust and bits of mowing-grass, Father left on the train to go over and fetch her from Truro, where she had apparently been deposited from up-country somewhere by one of his sisters. The year was drawing in and, following the sunny day, the evening seemed fresh and nippy. After supper we all sat round the fire: Joseph and Perran and Lissie and me, and Mother with the baby, waiting for them to come. Mother had kept Thomas up late especially so that Hester should be able to meet us all on her arrival and not feel a stranger to anyone the next morning.

The wind had got up during the evening, and the windows began their usual rattling and banging. Shortly after Father left it began to rain, filling the cottage with a faint roaring sound and pattering gustily on the windows. It made the living room seem very cosy.

We sat there before the fire, watching the patterns of the flames. Joseph was smoking his pipe and whittling a whistle for Perran, who was watching him with interest. Lissie sat perched on the arm of Mother's chair playing with the baby's hands. She was wearing her best dress and a long ribbon for the occasion, not entirely sure of what was to happen but excited all the same. From time to time she would start to wriggle and squirm in her dress where the stiff material scratched and tickled her skin. Mother chided her gently and she settled again, thumb in her mouth, huge blue eyes peering up at us from above the thumb, until Mother told her that at four she was too big a girl to suck her thumb and to leave that to the baby, for if she was that tired she had better go to bed. The thumb came out of her mouth at once and Thomas's thumb went into his. Lissie and Mother played finger games with him, for being up so long after his usual bed-time he was fractious and inclined to grizzle.

The wind sighed in the chimney and Joseph puffed on his pipe. My thoughts were up on the hill, for I always felt the Old Ones were likely to be about on wild nights. The wind moaned in the chimney and a stray shower of rain splattered down and hissed for a moment on the coals. Perran sat, still as a cat watching a mouse, following the movements of Joseph's fingers. The firelight flickered across his square boyish face and threw all our shadows dancing on the walls. I watched the grotesque shapes jumping and listened to the wind battering at the windows and thought how safe we were inside and that nothing could ever harm us.

'Lissie,' said Mother patiently, 'stop wriggling, my sweetheart, there's a lamb. Father will be home directly with Hester and I want you to look nice and not crumple your dress.'

'Hester?' said Perran. 'That's a silly name.' He scowled into the fire. 'I wish she was a boy and not another silly girl, with all they things she's bringing.'

'What things?' I asked, with interest. No one had told me about her bringing things.

'Oh hush, Perran,' said Mother. 'You must all be very kind to Hester, my darlings, for she's got no parents left any more and she's very sad about it, and she's going to come and live with us for always.'

There was a long silence while we all thought about it. Then I remembered the things. 'What things?' I asked. 'Mother, Perran said she's bringing things with her.' We all began to talk at once. The little room was full of sound, and the noise of the wind and rain outside was quite drowned by the racket we were making.

'Children, please!' said Mother, and Joseph said, 'Come on now!' in stern tones and order was restored. 'Now,' went on Mother, 'she's only bringing a few bits of clothes in a bag, and the cage with the bird in it, and maybe a few things her mother left her . . .'

'A bird!' shrieked Lissie. 'A bird? What is it, a parrot?'

'Hush darling,' said Mother. ''Tis only some sort of a pet of hers, I believe, nothing fancy or foreign. She's the same age as Abbie is Hester, and she's to be your sister, Abbie, and share your bedroom and your clothes too if necessary, and you're all to love her and be very kind to her, and never ever talk of her parents.'

Perran stared. 'Why not?' he demanded.

Mother paused momentarily, and then she said, 'Because it would upset Hester, and it's rude to talk about anything that might upset other people. You know that, Perran, don't you? We've told you that before, haven't we?'

Perran scowled into the fire and said nothing, and I knew they were both remembering the week before when Perran had got into awful trouble with Father for calling out, 'Puss! Pussy, here Pussy!' in a loud voice after our vicar's wife who had just lost her cat in an accident in the lane, and he had been soundly walloped for it when it was reported to Father. From the look on his face the memory of the walloping still lingered.

'Why is she bringing the bird here?' I asked by way of changing the subject for him. 'I wonder – does it talk, do you suppose, Mother?'

'I believe there's some kinds that do,' Mother said. 'I expect it belonged to her mother or father, and now that

14

she's coming to live with us she's bringing it with her.'

Then we were all clamouring once more, as to why Hester should be bringing the bird and the bag and no doubt the clothes too. The baby began to cry because of all the noise we were making and Mother told us again to hush. She started to sing little snatches of song to soothe Thomas, fingering his curls and stroking his forehead to quieten him, when suddenly there was a bang and a clatter from the front gate and the sound of Father's voice telling someone in the front porch to hurry up and not linger about in the cold and the rain. Then the door opened upon us all and there they were before us: Father, his figure damp with rain, the familiar sight and sound of him; and beside him the girl Hester, she who was to be my sister. We all turned our eyes from Father to look at her, and in the split second before I did so I glanced at Joseph's face.

There was a curious stillness about him. His face was set with a kind of shock as if his heart had ceased beating for a moment and then started up again with a lurch. There was hunger in his look, and pity, and a sort of terrible anger I had never seen in his kind face before. I shook myself and turned my eyes to look at the girl who had had such an extraordinary effect upon him.

She stood there in the doorway looking round at all of us sitting there so cosily in the firelight: at Mother holding the baby, at Lissie playing on the floor with Father's slippers and at Perran staring at her with eyes round as buttons; at me; and, lastly, at Joseph standing there with his soul written clear upon his face. It was indeed a strange moment, like the past and the future all rolled into one. As for Hester, I never saw anything like the hunger in her eyes as she stared back at us all.

We had expected her to be beautiful, I think, or at least pretty, but she was neither. She was small, as sparsely made as a bird, with wrists and ankles so thin that she was more like a child of six in size than a girl of my own age. The firelight flickered across her face and caught in her eyes, strange empty eyes, of a curious amber colour. She had her brownish hair tied back behind her neck with a bit of stringy ribbon that looked rather like an old bootlace. On top of a limp dress of some dirty green material she wore a shabby and buttonless grey coat which looked as if it did little to keep her warm. She caught and held the lapels of it together under her chin with a small hand, the nails of which were chewed and torn and badly in need of a wash. She looked ill and tired and thoroughly bewildered, like the frightened bird that crouched on its perch in the rusting metal cage at her side.

'Well!' said Mother, coming to her senses after the shock. 'Come in, my love. I'm glad you got here safely.'

Hester came forward into the living room with Father's large hands pushing her shoulders from behind, and Mother took her into one arm and kissed her rather awkwardly upon the cheek while her other arm encircled Thomas's fat little body and anchored him to her lap. Perran took the bird-cage from Hester's hand and we girls relieved her of her bag and coat. Father placed her carefully on the edge of the sofa beside me.

'Well now,' said Mother kindly, 'did you have a good journey from your aunty's, Hester? I believe tis raining now, isn't it? Dear me, and what a shame.'

Hester said nothing. She looked round at us all once again with vacant bewildered eyes. Then suddenly her face crumpled up and she began to cry. Her mouth opened in an oddly silent gape and tears coursed down her dirty cheeks, but she made no sound at all. The tears dripped and soaked into the thin collar of her dress and we all stared at her fascinated, Father, Mother, Joseph, Perran, Lissie and me; even the baby, thumb in his mouth, regarded her solemnly over the back of his fat fist.

'Er, would you like something to eat, my sweetheart?' asked Mother with embarrassed concern. 'I've got a pasty put by for you, and a nice bit of cake. A drink of milk, Hester? Surely you'd like a drop of milk?'

There was no response from the figure on the sofa beside me. Nobody knew quite what to do. Mother and Father exchanged a look of momentary panic. Then Joseph spoke up unexpectedly.

'Take her to bed,' he said. 'Take her upstairs. She's too tired to do anything but sleep tonight.'

'But,' said Mother, floundering helplessly for words and a handkerchief for Hester, 'the child must have something to eat first, Joseph! She must be awful hungry.'

Father scraped his foot awkwardly and nodded towards Joseph. 'Lad's right,' he said. 'You'd do better to leave her be, Susan. She needs her bed worse than food right now.' He began to cough and clear his throat a little. 'You can feed her in the morning.'

'Well, if you think so, Garfield,' said Mother doubtfully. She picked up Thomas, who had fallen asleep in her arms, his white curly head fell back against her shoulder and his thumb sagged in his mouth. 'I'd better just tuck this one down first.'

And then we all stared unable to believe our eyes, for Joseph had taken two strides across the room to the sofa and scooped up the small figure that was Hester into his arms, and, straightening up, held her against his breast for a moment before turning to Mother. 'Where's the child to sleep?' he asked. 'I'll carry her up and Abbie can make cocoa for her and put her to bed.'

'Oh, upstairs, Joseph,' said Mother, hurriedly disguising her astonishment. 'Can you manage her on the stairs, my 'ansome? Tis rather narrow up there. Shall Garfield go first with the candle, Joseph? Then you can see your way. You come behind, children, with Hester's things. I dearly hope the bird don't screech at night and keep us all awake.'

And so it was that the strangest of processions started out up the stairs, our feet scraping with unusual care on the wooden treads: Father in front with a candle to light the way for we had no lights at all upstairs, then Joseph, so young and strong, with the silent figure of Hester in his arms, then Mother with the sleeping baby on her shoulder. Behind Mother came Perran carrying the bird in the cage, followed by Lissie with thumb in mouth, and me last of all,

17

carrying Hester's bag, for though mine was the honour of making her cocoa, I was going to see this first. Together we all trooped up the narrow staircase and turned into the big bedroom where Mother tipped Thomas gently into the cot. He rolled over silently and never stirred.

Mother went straight to Hester's bed, which was all clean and neat and ready for her, and stood aside. I saw her glance at the grubby little figure with its dirty hands and face and filthy clothes, and I winced for her at the thought of the spotless sheets. 'She should really have a wash first,' Mother was muttering doubtfully. 'She's awful dirty, Joseph . . .'

'Abbie,' said Joseph to me, taking no notice at all, 'turn back the covers, will you?' and I did so. Carefully he laid her down and bent with awkward hands to take off her boots. Mother leapt forward to help and then she shooed us all out. Before I went to make the cocoa (which was still beside her, untouched, in the morning) I caught a glimpse of Joseph straightening himself by the side of the bed. The candlelight fell upon his face and there was an odd look there that I had never seen before, save once, and that once was when he had taken Perran and me out for a walk, years and years before, and we had found a poor, dead badger, caught in a trap.

Chapter Two

THE ROSE

THE NEXT MORNING Mother set about bathing Hester. The child had been fast asleep when we woke up that morning; it must have been a Sunday for the bells were ringing from church as we had our porridge round the table, watching Mother feeding the baby with his little spoon and the blue dish that had been a christening present from one of Father's many sisters. Lissie and I had crept out of our big bed and come downstairs in our nightgowns and huddled round the stove in the morning chill. By the time the bells stopped we had dressed, and Hester was awake. Mother brought her downstairs with an old checked blanket round her dirty clothes and sat her at the table, putting a bowlful of steaming porridge before her. Father had gone up to church to ring for the service and Perran was out in the orchard somewhere. Hester sat there looking round at the three of us and the baby over her bowl of porridge with suppressed alarm, like Goldilocks regarding the three bears. Mother put Thomas into my arms. 'Hold him for me, Abbie, there's a lamb,' she said and went to fetch the sugar. Thomas flexed his fat brown legs and jiggled up and down in my lap, waving a spoon in the air and grabbing handfuls of my hair and crowing, and Hester's strange amber eyes watched him, transfixed.

'Thomas, Thomas,' sang Lissie to him, unwilling to be left out. She tickled the back of his fat neck to distract him from my hair. He turned round and beamed at her, white pearls gleaming in his gums, and dropped the spoon.

'Sugar, Hester, on your porridge?' Mother asked her. Hester nodded silently. It occurred to me that we had not yet heard her speak. Mother sprinkled sugar and added a drop of milk hot from the stove and Hester began to eat, while we all looked on in silent shocked amazement.

She ate like a little savage, her chin almost in the bowl, shovelling the hot porridge in with desperate haste until Mother threw up her hands in horror, afraid she would burn herself.

'No, no, Hester!' cried Mother. 'You can't eat like that, child – slowly, for heaven's sake!' She stood behind her and held the spoon with her hand on top of Hester's grubby little one and showed her how to do it. The child blinked and gazed steadily at the porridge with a sort of blankness in her eyes until it was all gone. Then Mother put the spoon down for her in the dish, Lissie and I licked our lips and heaved a sigh, and Thomas twirled a finger in a white curl and cuddled up to me. Hester looked up at Mother with those strange eyes of hers, and spoke at last.

'I like porridge,' she said. She had a soft, small voice with a different sound to it from ours, a kind of up and down quality that gave her words a rhythm of their own. 'I like porridge,' she said again, and Mother smiled. She loved to feed people. I wondered perhaps if she had been afraid Hester would be a fussy child.

'Would you like some more, Hester?' Mother asked.

She nodded gravely and Mother refilled her bowl. This time, after a start of shovelling, she remembered and ate slowly, although it was obvious she was very hungry and longing to gobble. Altogether she got through three bowls of porridge (and Mother's helpings were generous ones) before she refused more. She shook her head at bread and butter, looked strangely at a piece of toast and indeed, all she ever really seemed to want to eat even years later was porridge. Perhaps, said Mother to me later, it was all she was used to getting.

After breakfast and a pause for the porridge to 'go down', Mother set about The Bath. She fetched the big tin tub from the kitchen and put great pans of water on the stove to heat. We all had baths like this so it was nothing strange to us, but poor Hester began to look quite terrified. Mother bustled about collecting soap and a face-cloth and a towel, a clean dress of mine, a jumper and some bits of underwear. Then it was time for Thomas's morning nap so, while the water heated, Mother heaved him off my lap, kissed his fat cheek and went upstairs with him to tuck him down. Then she came back, filled a bucket from the rain-water butt by the back door and stood it at the ready, and the fun began.

She spread a large rag rug across the floor in front of the stove and put the tub upon it. Then she poured the water in, steaming hot and smoky, while Hester's eyes grew rounder and rounder and more and more terrified by the minute. Then she added cold to get the temperature just right, and tested it with her hand.

'Abbie,' said Mother to me, 'undo her hair,' and I slipped off my chair and moved towards Hester. Like lightning she wriggled away and shot to the far end of the kitchen, trembling, her eyes huge in her small face. 'Oh dear,' said Mother with a sigh, 'perhaps she's never had a bath,' and it did begin to look rather that way. 'There's only one thing for it,' said Mother. 'You'll have to get in first, Abbie, to show her that it's safe.'

'Me?' I said aghast. 'I had one yesterday!'

'Well, one of you will have to,' said Mother. 'Lissie then. She dearly loves a bath.'

Lissie's blue eyes gleamed and she began to throw off her clothes with relish. Unfortunately Hester was still hiding in the depths of the kitchen and missed the enthusiasm. 'Call her in Abbie,' said Mother. 'She'll have to see it all.'

I went round into the kitchen and there was Hester crouching in a corner between the pantry and the sink.

'Come on, Hester,' I said persuasively, holding out my hand. For answer she dived past me, clutching the blanket round her, shot out of reach and would have jumped clean out of the window I believe, had it been open. Unfortunately, Mother had not had the presence of mind to bolt the kitchen door. In a trice Hester was out of it and running down the path towards the garden gate, the checked blanket clutched about her neck, brown hair flying in the wind. With a shriek like an owl sighting its prey Mother was after her, apron strings flying like wings, with Lissie and me close behind. We both began to giggle, which slowed us up somewhat, but Mother was hot in pursuit.

By some extraordinary stroke of luck there were two familiar male figures standing at the gate: Joseph going past on his way home from church, for he still had on his Sunday-best suit with the waistcoat, and his green silk tie, in which he looked very staid and dignified and personable; and Father coming home, in his rather battered tweed suit that smelled faintly of the woodshed and turpentine. Joseph was in the process of lighting an after-church pipe, the peculiarly haunting aroma of his home-made tobacco drifting across the gate to us as we ran up the path. Perran once told me that he made it up himself in some mysterious process of his own invention out of tobacco leaves and treacle and a pinch of dandelion leaf.

Into the midst of them flew Hester and her blanket, shrieking and wriggling to get past and out of the gate. I'm sure she would have been off down the lane too, and straight on to the railway station, if Father and Joseph hadn't stopped her. Father took a grab at her, missed, and got a handful of the blanket. Mother, panting up the path towards them with bits of long hair dangling down from her bun, was beaten by Lissie (half-undressed) and me. We slipped round Mother's skirts and got there first.

By this time Hester was out of the gate. In a trice Joseph leapt forward. The pipe was knocked out of his mouth. It fell onto the grass by the gate and lay on its side, smoke rising gently from its bowl. Joseph had grasped the struggling blanket firmly round its middle as we reached the gate; he held on tight with his strong arms, and lifted it clear of the ground. Lissie and I let out a cheer and Perran, emerging from behind the cottage, looked on in amazement.

'Bring her in, will you, Joseph?' said Mother breathlessly, catching at her hair and trying to recover her dignity, and Father held open the gate. Joseph marched in, holding the kicking bundle aloft with no apparent effort at all, and carried it round the back into the steamy kitchen. Father picked up Joseph's pipe and we all followed them, like a flock of fascinated chicks.

Once inside, Mother closed the door and bolted it this time. Joseph surveyed the scene. Seeing the steaming bath water, he gave a nod and a smile and deposited the kicking bundle on the floor. The blanket fell away and Hester stood up out of it in her grimy clothes and faced us all. Her face was pale and dirtier than ever and her arms trembled at her sides. The uproar, which had seemed hilarious to us while it was happening, now seemed rather sad and not at all funny. We stood round watching her rising up like a drowning sea-nymph out of waves of blanket and suddenly she looked small and terrified and somehow rather tragic.

Joseph turned to Mother. 'I'll be off now,' he said quietly. 'You've got your hands full here.'

'Yes, all right, Joseph,' Mother said, putting up her long strands of fallen hair and patting them into place again. 'Come and have a bit of dinner with us, though, won't you? Come back when we've bathed the child.' Father let him out and went with him. He nodded through the window and smiled assent and waved, and I locked and bolted the door behind them again. I rubbed at the steamy glass with my hand and saw them meandering in the direction of the vegetable garden, Father waving his arms across the lines of newly-planted spring cabbage, Joseph puffing at his pipe and nodding, and Perran at their heels.

Mother checked the security of the back door and then turned to Hester. 'Now Hester, watch, my darling,' she said gently. She crossed over to Lissie and calmly proceeded to take off her remaining clothes and to fold them in a neat pile, while Lissie stood obediently still and was undressed down to her little pink, round shape.

'Hair too, I'm afraid, my pet,' said Mother, and off came Lissie's ribbons, to be added to the pile. I tested the water for Mother with my hand and Lissie clambered in. She

23

sighed happily with pointed delight and, to Hester's obvious astonishment, sank down into the steaming water and said 'Oh, lovely!' three times with commendable emphasis.

Mother picked up a jug and carefully soaked Lissie's hair. The look of bewilderment grew in Hester's face, and when Mother picked up the soap and began to lather Lissie's hair, she let out a muffled squeak of horror and backed away.

'Lovely! Lovely!' said Lissie helpfully from the tub, and smiled seraphically while Mother worked her hands across her head and back in the lather.

'Rinse, Mother?' I asked, and brought the bucket. Mother added hot water to the bucket, dipped the jug, and poured it over Lissie's hair. The water streamed across her face and down her flat pink chest in rivulets and she smiled away happily enough to convince a hundred spectators, let alone one.

At last it was finished and Mother got her out and dried her and she pranced around the kitchen, naked and shining with cleanliness. Then, while I helped Lissie to dress, it was Hester's turn.

We all held our breath. Mother calmly held out her hand and, avoiding her eye, said, 'Now, Hester.' Nothing happened. Hester stood there shivering among the folds of discarded blanket, and refused to move.

'Come along, my pet,' said Mother brightly. Hester shook her head.

'Go on, Hester,' said Lissie eagerly. 'It's lovely in the bath. You'll like it, my 'ansome, you will. You just try it. Go on!' Hester shook her head again and pressed her lips into a firm line. Lissie patted her on the back with a small pink hand, like Mother did Thomas after meals, and said eagerly, 'I dearly love a bath.'

Still Hester refused to move. Mother sighed. It was a difficult situation. Suddenly I had an idea. 'Hester,' I said, bending towards her, 'shall I get your bird? Perhaps he'd like to watch you have your bath. Shall I get him? Would you like that?' Her eyes came round to look at me and she nodded slowly. It was a hopeful sign.

'Go and get him quick, Abbie,' said Mother. 'Has he got a name, Hester?' She began to pour more hot water into the tub, slowly so as to avoid alarm. Hester nodded, said nothing, but watched Mother's every move with wary eyes. I slipped out of the living room and up the stairs to the bedroom we children all shared, and peered into the corner of the room by Hester's bed. The disreputable bird crouched on its perch and glared balefully at me from a single bright eye; the other one was strangely white and cloudy. I picked the cage up and nervously carried it downstairs, depositing it on the floor in front of them.

'There!' said Mother brightly. 'Now he can watch you have your bath, my love. He's a nice bird, isn't he? A lovely bird.'

I carefully moved the cage and put it beside Hester. Her eyes fell on it. Relief and gratitude flooded her face. The dingy creature gave a muffled squawk and fluffed its wings a bit, then settled down sulkily further up on its perch.

Mother caught at Hester's hand. 'Come on, my poppet,' she said gently, 'tell us the bird's name and then we can all say hello to him.'

'Jacky,' said Hester shyly. 'He's called Jacky. He's a jackdaw. He's mine, Jacky is.'

'That's nice,' Mother was saying. 'That's a nice name for a jackdaw, Hester. He's a lovely bird, isn't he? You must be some proud of him.' She went on talking softly about the bird while the whole time she was gently drawing the child towards her, until somehow she had got her out of the blanket and in front of her with her feet bare. It was fascinating to see.

Lissie and I retreated quietly to a corner of the living room. This was something that was going to need Mother's whole concentration and we settled down to watch. From outside the window we could hear Father tuning his violin and beginning to tease strains of music out of it which floated dimly in to our ears from the orchard. I wondered what he had done with Joseph. Hester, about to refuse to take off her green dress, heard it and her head shot up. The bird heard it and inquiringly turned its one good eye upon the window. Mother took advantage of the moment to undo Hester's dress and slip it off. I heard a sudden cry.

'Oh my dear life!' said Mother biting her lips, for underneath was the most remarkably dirty vest that we had ever seen in our lives, and equally dirty bloomers. Mother compressed her mouth and Lissie and I stifled a gasp. Mother shuddered. She peeled them off gingerly, took them straight over to the stove, lifted up the lid and dropped them into the fire. 'You'll not be needing those again, my lamb,' I heard her mutter. Hester was still straining her ears to hear the violin and hadn't noticed her loss.

'Now,' said Mother, regarding Hester thoughtfully. She stood there before us, trembling and naked. Her body, where Lissie's had been pink, was grey and pitifully small and thin. Her ribs stuck out like stair-treads up and down her narrow chest and her neck was filthy. There were several small red marks about her waist and I saw Mother's eye fall suspiciously upon the old dress. She bent to the green rag and picked it up with great respect. Then she crossed purposefully over to the stove. Hester let out a frenzied shriek.

'No!' she screamed. 'Not my dress! Don't burn my dress, Missus, please!'

Mother paused in the act of lifting up the lid of the stove, walked through into the kitchen as though she had made some sort of decision and tossed the dress into the sink. I wondered what she was up to. I soon knew.

'Right. Now, Hester,' said Mother briskly, 'test the water with your toe and then get into the bath.'

Hester gave the bath a terrified glance and stood quite still.

'Come along,' said Mother. 'Into the bath with you.' Hester stood her ground. 'All right,' said Mother grimly. 'Then the dress goes in the fire.'

Hester's eyes fell on her imploringly.

26

'Into the bath!' ordered Mother. Hester shook her head.

'Hester,' said Mother, 'there are fleas on your dress and on that bird too, no doubt, and I won't have fleas in my house.' She paused to let her words take effect. 'If you don't get into the bath I'll put the dress into the fire, and the bird in after it.' I wondered how on earth she could pretend to be so cruel. 'Abbie,' she said, 'please pick up Hester's dress and put it in the fire.'

'No!' Hester shrieked. 'I'll get in the bath, I will. I will! I promise. Don't burn my dress, Missus. I'll get in the bath.'

'All right,' said Mother. 'Let me see it then.'

Gingerly Hester dipped one toe into the water. She withdrew it with an expression of horror upon her face. She changed her mind and put her foot in. Then she put the other foot in. Lissie and I bent forward from the shadows like wasps attracted to the sight of jam, and heaved a sigh of relief.

'Sit!' said Mother inexorably. Carefully, Hester sat. A fleeting look of pleasure crossed her thin face and she looked up at Mother in wonder.

'Nice, isn't it?' said Mother, beaming. 'There, I knew you'd like it, Hester.' She soaped the child's thin neck and shoulders. 'And now your hair.' She released the grubby ribbon.

Oh dear, I thought, now comes the difficult bit. Hester started to protest, but her eyes fell upon me and then upon the stove. Mother damped her hair and began to soap it lavishly, and the lather turned grey and flew about like dingy snow. Each time she began to protest Mother said threateningly, 'Abbie, get that dress!' and in the end poor Hester gave up. I've never seen such bath water before or since. Altogether Mother washed her hair four times and each time the colour got lighter and the water got darker and her body grew pinker, until the water cooled and at last Mother was satisfied. When they had finished and Mother got her out on to the rug and dried her she looked like a different child.

'Clothes, Abbie!' said Mother, issuing orders like a field

marshal and I jumped to it and brought them to her, handing them one by one: the clean socks and underwear, the dress (luckily also green), the cardigan and the dry towel for her hair. 'We'll wash your old dress, Hester, I promise,' said Mother. 'You've been a good girl and when we've dried your hair, my poppet, you'll look lovely.' And she rubbed at the long hair in the warmth from the stove.

We threw away the dirty water and Mother unlocked the back door and put the old green dress to soak in a bucket of soapy water outside by the wall. Then we set to work to clear up the chaos. Hester sat before the stove and rubbed and rubbed at her hair as if her life depended on getting it dry again and I fetched my brush and comb and gave them to her.

When everything was dried and cleared away, Hester stood before us all in my old green gingham dress, which fitted her fairly well, if a bit long, and looked out at us from beneath her drying hair.

'Well!' said Mother, rendered almost speechless by the sight. She did indeed take our breath away. In place of the filthy little urchin that we had put into the bath stood a slender child, glistening with pinkness and quite radiant with colour, Her hair, which had been brownish, stood revealed as a cascade of rippling auburn the colour of marigolds; springing from a clear wide forehead it curled in tendrils round her cheeks. Her face, no longer pinched and grey, was glowing with warmth and flushed with rose from Mother's scrubbing. We gazed and gazed in silent astonishment.

'Oh!' said Lissie in wonder, and I thought suddenly: why, Hester is beautiful!

'My dear life!' said Mother in amazement, coming towards her with a hand outstretched as if in some doubt. 'But Hester, your hair is red!

'You look lovely!' I breathed. 'Doesn't she, Mother?'

And then, like the sun coming out from behind a bank of clouds, Hester smiled. The smile kindled her eyes with a swift glow, as if a lamp were suddenly alight inside her. She caught at her skirt and twirled and danced around before us with self-conscious delight. Lissie clapped hands and Mother hugged her. We all cheered and the old bird squawked to add to the noise.

And thus Father and Joseph and Perran found us when they came in to dinner from the garden. Joseph presented Mother with a bowl of eggs, so I supposed he must have gone home for them whilst Father was playing his violin. Then they came through to us from the kitchen and they stood and stared at Hester, so alight and glowing.

Father put out his hand and touched her damp hair and said, 'My, but the child's lovely,' in a startled aside to Mother. Perran stared with frank disbelief upon his freckled face and said, 'My dear life!' in a tone so exactly like Mother's that we all laughed hugely. And Joseph? He said nothing at all.

Joseph Chygowan looked upon Hester the radiant child and into his face came a kind of hush. Nobody noticed his stillness. Nobody noticed his silence. But I saw glory come into his face on that late autumn morning of my childhood.

That dinner was the last time Joseph came for a meal with us for many years. Oh, Mother asked him often enough, but he always said no thank you and invented some excuse. In the end she shrugged to herself and gave up asking. I don't think it ever occurred to her to wonder why.

Chapter Three

THE JACKDAW

HESTER APPEARED TO settle into our household with very little trouble. She shared our bedroom and my clothes and came with Lissie and Perran and me to the little stone school in the nearest village, there being no school in Lanissick itself, and soon it seemed that there always had been five children in our family. After a bit of initial teasing from the other children at school about her extraordinary lack of basic learning and her terrible spelling, Hester was more or less ignored. Once or twice Veronica Braze pulled her long red plaits and other children pinched her neck and tried to make her cry, but they never succeeded and after a while they lost interest. Hester rarely cried. A remote, closed look would come over her face and then they would leave her alone.

In many ways she seemed years older than me. I found her a strange girl: sad, as if she was steeped in sorrow through to her bones and could never quite be free of it. At times there was a poor lost look in her eyes, a slight enchantment, as if she were for ever listening to music just out of our reach. She was destined to be small and she stayed slight, although her shape filled out a bit with Mother's good food. Sometimes she sparkled and laughed and had a bit of fun with us but always there was that odd, pinched look deep at the back of her eyes.

I never could get Mother or Father to reveal the circumstances of her birth. She was the only child of Father's youngest sister, which made her our cousin, and she had the same surname as us so I supposed she must have been a love-child. Although we had almost no contact at all with

Father's family (who thought us children wild and Father more than a little eccentric) there had never been any hesitation about who would take Hester in when her mother died. Her father was an even more shadowy figure and I could never get anyone to talk about him at all. Whenever asked by the children at school, Hester would simply say 'He died', and go all quiet, in that shut-in way of hers, and you could get no more out of her. Perhaps she knew no more than we did. Lissie and I used to imagine things about him and make up stories. Lissie thought he might have been a gypsy (there were gypsies up on the hill from time to time and we were always hoping they might turn out to be Hester's relatives) but we never really knew. I don't think Mother did, either.

Father knew, but he would never say. He would just begin to clear his throat with that little dry embarrassed cough of his and go outside to pull rhubarb, or tune his violin, or potter about in the pantry with his wine jars. About this time he had begun to make the odd gallon or two of wine with fruit and vegetables from the garden and the huge jars of it stood for months around the pantry shelves.

As children, the pantry was a magical place to us, with rows of these huge fermenting jars: red and yellow and straw-coloured, with half-stained labels in Father's crabbed handwriting stuck on their sides, and all of them bubbling and gulping and giving off gusts of mysterious vapour as the yeasts went about their alchemy. Lissie kept well away, for the smell alone would set her off sneezing as she often did for weeks during the summer, but Perran and Hester and I loved it in there. For a treat we were sometimes allowed to watch Father at work among the jars, sieving and straining and racking the wines with a huge long pipe and a giant funnel. We had to stand well back with our hands well-washed and not make a sound while he worked but sometimes, on our birthdays and on Christmas Eve, we might be allowed a watered sip.

As we grew older we were occasionally allowed to go up into the tower with Father when he went to ring for the service at church. We climbed the spiral steps behind him, careful not to get our fingers in the way of his enormous shoes, until we reached the ringing room. There we sat on benches round the walls, watching with awe as the ringers took their places and pulled away in some mysterious sequence they alone seemed to understand. The ropes flickered up and down, seemingly alive in their hands, and the ringers nodded and frowned at each other within the dancing ropes. Harry Tregulla or George Pascoe would shout out strange words that meant nothing to us, and they would all mutter to themselves, their lips moving silently, as if they counted something that we had no knowledge of. Occasionally Father would shout 'Stand!' in great irritation and glower at some unfortunate member of the circle, and proceed to berate him with peculiar arguments and talk of bobs and dodges and things called snap leads as if they had been taking dogs for a walk instead of making music; but always we had to sit there silently and not move a muscle if we could help it, and certainly not to walk about. It all seemed a curious occupation to me, but Father's eyes sparkled and gleamed with apparently intense concentration, and after what had appeared to be a bit of music that pleased him greatly, would come over to us and be quite jovial, winking at Perran and promising to teach him one day, when he was tall enough to reach the ropes properly.

'What about us, Father?' Lissie and I tentatively enquired. 'Can we learn too, one day?' and Father threw back his head and laughed heartily; but the vicar looked faintly disapproving, as if such laughter were slightly out of place within the hallowed walls.

There were boards yellow with age around the ringing chamber, and lists of names and numbers under esoteric titles like 'Bob Minor' and 'Doubles' and one that I always thought said 'Grandsire's Triplets' until Perran put me right years afterwards.

Looking back, I suppose we were very lucky children. We had plenty of freedom and ran wild about the village and the heath behind, and we almost lived in the churchyard. The place was mostly deserted anyway, and full of high old elm trees which waved their branches in the blue vault overhead when the wind blew from the hill. They were a nesting place for rooks for miles around and in spring the air was full of their clamour and the old graves littered with dropped twigs. Hester was fascinated by the churchyard, and by the birds. Whenever she was missing from home I always knew that I would find her sitting under the elms up there, with the poor mangy bird beside her in its cage, shrieking and squawking and hopping about on its perch as the rooks in the trees called to it and taunted it with their freedom. Hester would sit there for hours, transfixed by the birds and, I think, desperately fighting with herself to let the jackdaw out to join them.

'Let him out then, Hester,' Perran would urge. 'Give poor old Jacky a bit of freedom.'

'I can't, I can't,' cried poor Hester. 'They'd peck 'en to bits if I did; but oh dear, oh dear, I wish I could.'

'Then don't bring him up here,' I would say helplessly. 'It only seems to upset him.'

'No,' said Hester passionately, 'he do love to watch them flying round and round. Look at him, Abbie – all excited and hopping about! He dearly loves to watch them.'

And indeed the old bird did exhibit great signs of emotion within the cage. It squawked and flapped and ran up and down the perch in great agitation until Hester called urgently: 'Jacky, Jacky! It's me – hush now,' and it would crouch low on its legs and peer at her with its one good eye, while the lid came up on the milky one and half-closed it, and the poor thing gave up longing.

'Oh, I wish I could let him go. I wish I could,' said poor Hester, caught in the ancient battle between freedom and security. 'But they'd kill poor Jacky up there, they would; they'd tear him to bits.'

Because of the fleas, Mother made it live outside in its cage and made Hester keep it in the out-house where we stored the apples on high racks well away from the floor,

33

along with the rake and the hoe and numerous rusting bits and pieces, where it was nearly always dark, except for a chink of light through a dingy window. Hester would go into it every morning with little parcels of food, and every evening she would take the bird out in the cage for a walk. She fed it on berries and bits of bacon-rind and poked worms and snails in through the bars of the cage for it to peck at, and gave it little trays of water to drink. Perran was greatly intrigued. 'Was the bird your mother's, Hester?'

'No – Jacky's mine.'

'But where did he come from?'

'I found him in our old garden and a lady gived me the cage.'

'Why don't he talk, Hester? Can't you teach him to talk? How did he get that funny eye?'

'Cat got 'en, in the garden.'

Perran would make noises of affection, and try to persuade it to walk on to his hand inside the cage, but the bird would crouch, considering, then peck irritably at his fingers. 'Let 'en out, Hester,' Perran would plead. 'He don't like it in there.'

'But I can't, I can't,' wailed Hester. 'The others would kill him if I did. Oh dear, I wish I could, but I can't!'

We spent long summer evenings in the churchyard, sitting on the lichen-encrusted box-tombs with Jacky in his cage beside us, swinging our legs and picking absently at the mossy lumps under our fingers. We would line up bits of it along the top of a tomb to make hedges and fields for woodlice-racing. We called them grammersows, and never knew the proper name for them until we went to school. Perran would arrange several of them into a line of little grey balls, and we would wait breathlessly, to see which one would unwind first. After a while they would hesitantly unfold themselves and start to wander about the mossy enclosures, going round and round the boundaries with their feelers waving in frustration, unaware of the fact that the winners would be poked into the cage for Jacky's critical appraisal. Hester would crouch over them, her face

34

absorbed, and Perran would prod his with a stick (which Hester said was cheating) and Lissie would cry a bit and hang back, unsure of the ethics of it all; even at seven her sense of motherhood was very strong.

It was a constant source of sorrow to Hester that she had no relatives of her own buried in the churchyard. She would poke about for hours among the headstones, trying to read the worn inscriptions, hoping to find our name there somewhere, while Jacky sat on his perch in the cage beside her and screeched at the sky, and Perran and Lissie and I played hide-and-seek among the graves. It never occurred to us that our games were in any way irreverent. I think we felt more awe among the tombs than ever we did in the church, for here, where no adult had set foot for years, were purlieus mystic with unfolding life, of hedges riotous with blossom, the abode of robin and of wren; and if you crouched down very small and pushed your nose into the grasses you could hear insect music and smell the black earth raw with rain.

One afternoon I found Hester kneeling on soft earth and scratching at an ancient stone. 'Look, Abbie,' she said eagerly, 'this one could be mine, couldn't it? It could be my grandfather.'

I peered closely at the name, 'No Hester, it isn't, I'm afraid. It's the wrong name.'

'No, but Abbie,' she persisted, 'it could be mine, couldn't it? I could have it for mine.' She leant forward on her knees, a finger tracing the weathered lettering, and slowly read out 'Isaac Bartholomew, dearly beloved husband of Agnes, departed this life . . ."Resteth in The Arms of The Lord" . . .' She paused. 'I never had a grandfather.'

I laughed. 'Of course you did, Hester. Everybody has one; well, two. Your mother's and your father's father.'

She shook her head firmly. 'No. I never had one.'

'Not one you knew, perhaps – but Hester, your grandpa would have been the same as mine; we're cousins.'

But she remained unconvinced and stubbornly repeated, 'No, I never had a grandfather. I'll have this one.' And, from then on, every week, winter and summer, she would go up to the churchyard and put a few straggling flower-heads on the grave of Isaac Bartholomew. It became a weekly ritual for her, and she never missed. At home she would go round the garden or the orchard, picking anything suitable that she could find. I would find her in the orchard, head aglow, knee-deep in waving couch-grass or sorrel in summer; and in the spring, among the daffodils which bloomed and nodded in their thousands. Perran and I made up an elaborate story for her about Isaac Bartholomew: we gave him wild red hair (like Hester's), a fine flowing beard, flashing eyes and a parrot. We made him a sailor who had sailed round the West Indies on a pirate ship, found buried treasure and then come home to claim his bride (Agnes). He then made his fortune mining up on the hills in the local tin-mines, and produced a vast red-headed family, of whom the only surviving member was Hester. He was a remarkably fine singer, rang the tenor bell to a hundred full peals (this was Perran's contribution) and had a fine reputation for holding his liquor and roistering (whatever that meant). He was deeply appreciative of Hester's continuing to honour his memory with regular bunches of flowers and in return kept a residential eye on the churchyard for us in our absence. Privately I thought it not unlikely that Isaac Bartholomew had been a weedy little farmhand with greasy hair and a cast in one eye, but imagination knew no bounds. Unfortunately, Perran's devotion turned to scorn after a while: 'Veronica Braze thinks it's stupid,' he said sulkily, kicking the headstone.

'Then Veronica's stupid,' retorted Hester. 'He's my grandfather anyway, not hers. She's only jealous.'

'He's not; he's only pretend.'

'He's not, he's not!' Hester would storm and break into anguished wailing. 'He's real, and if you don't believe me you can read it on the stone. Look, it says "Isaac Bartholomew, dearly beloved husband of Agnes, departed this life . . ."'

'Yes, but he wasn't *your* grandfather, was he,' said Perran

36

with laboured emphasis. 'He was somebody else's grand-father, not *yours*.'

'Whose then?' demanded Hester. 'Tell me whose! You don't know, do you? You can't say 'cause you don't know, so there!' Then she would toss her head and stamp off down the path between the graves. 'You can get your own grandfather's grave; you're not sharing mine!' and she would poke little bits of plantain and clover into a jamjar with fierce proprietorial emphasis; but she wouldn't cry. Hester rarely cried. I used to think sometimes that it might have helped to ease that strange lost look of hers if she had cried a bit now and then; but in all the time I knew her, I only really ever saw her cry the once.

Jacky always accompanied us to the churchyard, scaly feet clutching at his swinging perch as we marched up the lane. Hester would talk softly to him as we walked, or stand the cage on a tomb as we played, and let him flap his wings at the sky. Perran never gave up pleading with her to let him out. 'Go on, Hester, I want to see him fly! Let him out, go on.'

'No,' said Hester stubbornly, 'I can't.'

'He'd like it up there, Jacky would. Go on, let him go, just for a little bit. You can always put 'en back in again.' And when this failed, he turned to taunting. 'You're a cruel girl, Hester Horrid. Veronica Braze says it's cruel to keep a bird in a cage. You're cruel!'

'Oh Perran, she's not!' I said angrily. 'She can't let him out. He wouldn't come back.'

'She is cruel, she is, she is!' retorted Perran. 'She wouldn't keep him in there if she wasn't cruel!'

'Oh, I wish I could let him go,' wailed poor Hester yet again. 'I wish I could, but I can't!'

And then, quite suddenly one day, she did. She and Perran and I were taking Jacky up to the old hill for one of his constitutionals on a day that Hester said was his birthday. As we drew near the churchyard Jacky heard the rooks calling and began to hop about as usual, screeching at the sky. Quite suddenly Hester made up her mind. She took

37

the cage into the graveyard and stood it on an old box-tomb and opened the rusting metal door. Jacky stared at the sudden gap in the bars for a while with frank disbelief, hopped along the perch a few tentative inches, backed away again and stopped. Then with a scurried flutter and a whirl of fallen feathers he was out of the cage and off into the blue air. Rooks called above us from their lofty perches and we stood with our mouths open, enthralled, watching him go.

'Happy Birthday, Jacky!' Perran called gleefully. 'Have a nice time!'

'Goodbye Jacky,' I called after him. 'Goodbye!'

But Hester said nothing. She just stood there with a look of quiet rapture on her face, watching the bird surge skywards.

Three days later Perran and I found a dead jackdaw with a clouded eye in a battered heap on the grass under the tower. It was crawling with fleas and we buried it in an old cardboard box in a corner of the churchyard field. 'We won't tell her,' said Perran soberly. 'I expect she'd be upset.'

We never did.

Chapter Four

THE TOWER

DURING THE SUMMER that Perran was ten, my father and
Harry Tregulla taught him to ring. He was positioned on a
huge wooden box on the belfry floor, with Father in front of
him holding onto the rope-end and issuing instructions and
dire warnings about letting go of the sally at the right
moment and not looking upwards at the rope. Perran was
proud as a king, and learned quickly, so Father said. I'd
loved to have learned, too, but our vicar had old-fashioned
ideas and did not approve of women in the ringing chamber, perhaps for fear they would see the men in their
shirt-sleeves and fall down in a faint from shock. So Hester
and Lissie and I were barred from such delights by our sex,
and had to content ourselves playing games with little
Thomas in the orchard. Thomas at four was round and
rosy. We would run about the garden with him, hiding from
him, and rolling his ball across the grass into his fat legs, to
his everlasting delight. Then he would watch us from the
garden with his face full of disappointment as we, growing
bored, would wander off between the trees at the back of the
cottage.

It was one such day as this that I remember well. It was
late summer; the drowsy season of long grass and warmth
heavy with sun and the sound of insects buzzing and
humming in the churchyard grass. Lissie had a sneezing
attack that day and had stayed at home to play with
Thomas; Hester and I had gone up to the heath behind the
village to pick blackberries. The bushes were heavy with
them that year and we picked and ate to our hearts' content,
filling our baskets and our mouths with soft, black sweet-

ness until the juice ran down our chins and stained our clothes. We wandered about between the bushes in happy half-oblivion, content and hazy-minded with the bloom of summer upon us. We picked and picked until our baskets and stomachs were full and then, drowsy with warm fruit and sun, we made for home, as the shadows lengthened across the scrubby hillside and dropped dimly into the lanes. It must have been a practice night for the ringers, because as we came down from the hill we could hear the music of the bells high and sweet, falling about our ears.

The narrow lane wound slowly round and down and the trees began to close in overhead so that it always seemed to us here that we walked in a green tunnel. Around us the hills rose on either side and far ahead of us at the end of the tunnel we could see the grey tower of the church. We had come out of the lane on to the level land beside the church before the bells stopped and the sudden silence was heavy in the air.

'Let's wait a bit for Perran,' pleaded Hester. 'Oh Abbie, please!' Her mouth was set determinedly in her rosy face, stained streaky-purple with the juice of countless berries. 'And then, if we wait until they've all gone, we could go up the tower and get out on to the roof. Oh please, Abbie, please! I'd dearly love to go out on to the roof!'

I shrugged, not really minding. Waiting for Perran was as good an excuse as any to ward off bed-time. I nodded. 'All right, then. We'll have to wait until they've all gone home; then after a while, when things are quiet, we'll creep in. They never lock the door. Sit on the wall and make out you're resting for a bit.'

'Your face is awful dirty, Abbie,' Hester said. 'Is mine, too?' She rubbed at it with the back of her hand, making matters much worse. I produced a handkerchief and, licking it hopefully, tried to rub off the streaks from Hester's face and then from my own. My cheeks felt hot from the sun and Hester's were bright pink. My nose felt quite sore and there were new freckles all over hers.

After a while Perran and the ringers ambled slowly out of the shelter of the church and round to the lych-gate where we sat on the wall, innocently swinging our legs and inspecting the fruit in our baskets and throwing out the odd grub. Nobody took much notice of two dirty and dishevelled children. One or two of the men winked good-humouredly at us and one of the older boys helped himself to a handful of berries from my basket, but they weren't really aware of us. They were laughing and joking amongst themselves; remote, grown-up talk. They stood around with their backs to us, hands in pockets, engaged in lazy conversation.

I saw George Pascoe look across at us and wink. We liked George. He was small and strong, with thick wavy brown hair and flashing eyes like berries. He would pinch my cheek playfully without much thought, and always had a grin for us. 'What have you got there, girls?' he asked us. 'Blackberries? Cor! My missus wouldn't half like some of them for our tea. Have you got any to spare then?'

I wasn't sure whether this was a serious request or not, but Harry Tregulla laughed and told him he could go up there and pick his own instead of pinching ours, as there were plenty to be had that summer.

'Go on!' said George with mock resentment. 'They've been there before me and got all the best ones!' and then he lost interest and turned back to join in the general male discussion. Hester dropped lightly to the ground and began a sort of half-climb, half-dance up and down on the low wall beside the lych-gate, hopping up on one leg and down with two. No one was taking the least notice of her. The men were deeply engrossed in their conversation about a peal or something they were planning and Perran was arguing with David Penkevin about a football team. Hester and I abandoned our baskets and sidled away from them.

We slipped out of sight, round to the north of the church and struggled with the heavy door, our arms straining upward to lift the iron latch. The door fell inwards on its hinges, and the soft gloom inside became our world. The familiar smell of musty hymn books, polish, paraffin and old timbers met our noses and we breathed deeply in appreciation. A shaft of late sunlight glanced in through a window and struck the stone floor in a fuzzy square of yellow light. We tiptoed across to the tower door and tried the handle. 'It's not locked,' Hester whispered, her eyes shining. We looked at each other in suppressed excitement.

'Perhaps we'd better not,' I said, seized suddenly with doubt. 'What if the vicar comes, or Harry or George to lock up?'

'They won't,' she said firmly, 'they're too busy talking, and the vicar's not there tonight, anyway. Come on, Abbie! I dearly want to go.'

I sighed. 'All right,' I said reluctantly, 'but don't touch the ropes, or make any noise, or Harry and George will hear us and tell Father, and you know what that'll mean.' We crept stealthily into the narrow opening, closing the door to within a crack behind us, and began to climb the spiral steps. At the top of the short flight the door opened into the ringing chamber where, from mysterious regions above, the knotted ropes hung down, still swaying very slightly from side to side. Hanging from a nearby coat-hook a notice in red lettering proclaimed 'THE BELLS ARE UP'. I knew the reverse of it announced 'THE BELLS ARE DOWN' but it meant nothing to Hester. She slipped across to the wall where a wooden ladder led up vertically towards the ceiling. She began to climb, her hands groping at the trap-door above her. One push and a muffled thump, and the trap gave and swung open, and she had hauled herself easily up into the bell chamber itself. I followed her up the ladder, my heart beating uncomfortably.

The bells stood there in the dim light, each one tipped slightly to one side, their mouths gaping upward beside their wheels like great metal flowers seeking the sun. I looked around me fearfully, shivering with horror at the bodies of desiccated spiders hanging in their ancient webs. Beyond the bells and over to one side a small door was set into the steeple roof. Hester leapt across to it. She slid back

42

the bolts and flung it open, letting in a sudden rush of sweet warm light.

'Oh Hester, we shouldn't!' I whispered in anguished doubt. 'Whatever would Father say, or Harry or George? Oh Hester, it's dangerous. Do be careful!'

She took no notice of me. With one bound she was out of the door and on to the roof, which lay between the short steeple and the crenellated stonework of the tower. I followed her nervously, closing the door behind me. Together we peered over the low wall. Below us the countryside lay flattened. Cars crept like insects along a distant road. The tree-tops stretched for miles below us, a sea of undulating, waving green, full-leafed and voluptuous in the gold-coloured evening light.

Hester turned to me, her eyes shining. 'Oh Abbie, isn't it wonderful!' she breathed. She caught a curl of hair back from her face, and peered over again. I followed her gaze. In the lane outside the church stood the tiny group of ringers still in conference, and almost hidden from our view among the trees. The air was heavy with summer and warmth pressed down upon us. There was hardly any wind; just a small golden breeze carrying the birds. Hester caught sight of them winging about the tower on a level with us, so that for a moment it seemed that we were of their kind, mysterious airy creatures.

'Oh, the rooks!' Hester cried. 'Look Abbie, the rooks!' She leaned forward. 'It's like flying,' she called to me. 'You could call them and they would hear you from up here!'

'Be careful!' I shouted at her. 'Oh, Hester, do be careful! You're far too near the edge.'

She leaned out and waved her arms. 'It's like being one of them, Abbie. Oh, it's so real! Look, they can see us now. Hello birds!'

'Stop it, Hester!' I shouted at her in alarm. 'Stop it! Oh Hester, be careful! Please listen to me. It's dangerous! You could easily fall over. The wall isn't very high. For goodness sake listen to me!' I grabbed wildly at her clothes. The ground looked perilously distant. I caught a handful of her skirt, and held on grimly.

'Leave me alone, Abbie!' she yelled. 'Don't hold on to me. I want to see properly, and I can't if you hold me back. Leave me alone!'

I began to panic, and to think of screaming for help. Hester was leaning out over the low edge with both her arms held out towards the sky, and shaking herself like a rat caught in a trap. 'I should never have let you come up here,' I shrieked at her. 'You're being stupid, Hester! Don't you realize how dangerous it is?' I grabbed at her again and tried to pull her back, hearing the thin cotton rip in my hands. 'Stop it!' I screamed. 'Stop it! *Hester!*'

She leaned out further still and I felt the blood drain from my face as I caught another glimpse of the ground. In desperation I caught hold of her red hair and tried to pull her backwards with it, feeling sick, feeling dizzy.

Suddenly there was a thump from inside the steeple. The door was flung back, and he stood there, George did, to my everlasting relief. I still held on to her hair, pulling hard. George, or Harry, leapt forward towards us; only it wasn't George, or Harry either. It was Joseph.

With one step he had crossed the narrow space to where Hester leaned out. He grasped a hold of her shoulders and wrenched her back to safety. She turned and gasped in childish fury. 'Abbie, leave me alone!' and then her face went pale under the brown and rose, the streaks of berry juice and smears of dirt. Joseph set her squarely down in front of me. He was angry, there was no doubt of that. He stared at us for a while, breathing heavily. Then he looked down at his hands upon her arms – and then he dropped them to his sides, and his kind mouth was white with anger.

Hester bit her lip, all fury evaporating at the unexpected sight of him. She looked at him through the tangled hair across her face, pushing it aside with a small stained hand. 'I'm sorry, Joseph,' she started to say, 'don't . . .'

He pointed to the doorway set in the steeple. He said nothing, but his face was grim. I clambered meekly into the narrow gloom, and Hester followed. We trembled as we climbed downwards. We shook as we descended past the bells, back down the ladder and on to the ringing room floor. He pointed to the stairway, and we sidled past the still ropes and stepped downwards into the stair. I began to cry, terrified to think what he might say to us when we reached the bottom. And all the while he followed us, grim and silent, close upon our heels. I sniffed dismally into my sleeve, thinking of Father's anger when he found out. Hester was very silent. I glanced at Joseph's face as we reached the nave. He closed and locked the door and pocketed the key. Then he turned and stood and stared at us there in the dull light, saying nothing at all. In shifting lower to a different angle the shaft of sunlight on the floor had lost some of its brilliance and a chilly draught played faintly on our bare arms. The day's warmth was going.

Still Joseph said nothing. He turned and opened the door and saw us out, our heads bowed. We stood there in the porch waiting for his anger to strike us. 'Oh Joseph, say something!' Hester begged. Her grimy little hands caught at his sleeve and shook it imploringly. 'Please Joseph, speak to me! I can't bear it if you don't speak to me. It was all my fault. Don't be angry, Joseph.'

He took no notice of her. We watched him close and lock the door and pocket that key too, all the while waiting for the storm of his wrath to break upon us. Hester was shaking from head to foot, although the evening was still quite warm outside the church. Joseph stood there in front of us, looking down at her with his mouth set in a grim line. She caught at his sleeve again, and held on to it. 'Joseph? Oh Joseph, please say something to me. If you don't speak to me now it'll be too late ever again, I know it will. Oh Joseph, please!'

I saw him look down for a moment, at her hands upon his sleeve. 'Joseph,' I pleaded urgently, 'don't tell Father, please! We won't ever try to go up there again, not ever, I promise you. Only please don't tell Father.'

He looked at Hester. She was still holding on to his sleeve, and staring up at him with eyes wide with anguish.

'You won't talk to me, Joseph,' she was saying in a pitiful little voice. 'Oh, I can't bear it if you don't say anything at all.'

'Please Joseph,' I pleaded anxiously, 'don't tell Father, please don't!'

He seemed about to say something. He looked at Hester and raised his hand, as if about to touch her face, then lowered it again. We stood there in the evening light, the three of us, all staring at each other; and I had a sudden curious feeling, perhaps the aftermath of shock, that there was nothing in between the three of us at all: no air, no world, no space, no distance. Just for a fleeting moment we were three different faces of the same person, mere folds in the fabric that made up the world. I could have thought anything, nonsense would have been the same as sense, and they would have caught it too, and known the essence there behind the words.

Then Hester shivered. Rooks called high above us, and the instant fell away. Joseph moved, and lowered his hand with a sigh. The air was back again, the space restored. He shook his head, more to himself than us, and then he turned upon his heel and strode away.

Chapter Five

THE BOUGH

JOSEPH DIDN'T TELL Father, but for years afterwards the tower door was always kept securely locked. The next time we saw Joseph he was much the same as ever, but I think his increasing remoteness from us started then; or perhaps it had started with Hester's arrival. He never came to the cottage now, or played games with us or carried us round the orchard in the summer, or made things any more for Perran. As a child it puzzled me briefly and then was forgotten, like the many things that puzzled me in passing at that age. Perhaps it was simply that we were growing up.

Hester never appeared to want to talk about her early years. She never spoke of them, and we never asked; she seemed to prefer it that way. I don't think there was any doubt that she had been bitterly unhappy before coming to live with us. She kept no mementos of the time before and had no treasures other than the old green dress, which Mother had boiled thoroughly and washed for her; but she never wanted to wear it again and it stayed neatly folded in a drawer for years afterwards. After Jacky's departure to the sky even the bird-cage was thrown away without a second glance when the dustmen took it. It was as if her life had begun when she came to us; nothing remained of the time before.

She was strangely off-hand about Joseph after the tower episode. To me Joseph was part of the fabric of childhood, part of our world of home and village and church on Sundays. His father had been killed in the war and, after his mother's death the year Thomas was born, he lived all alone in his farm cottage, with no one for company but his

47

hens and his pipe with that extraordinary evocative smell of dandelion-leaf tobacco. Father used to go and visit him from time to time, and invite him to dinner on Mother's instructions, but he never came. When he wasn't at work on the farm he appeared to spend most of his time in his garden, pottering about amongst tobacco leaves, or in his shed working away at making chairs and gates for the rest of the village. We walked to school along deserted lanes, knee-deep in fern and ragged-robin, and returned the same way each evening. Occasionally we would pass him on his way to the fields and he would nod briefly to us, silent and remote. At church on Sundays he was there, of course, part of the rock, the earth, of home.

Years passed, and we began to grow up. It seemed a slow process at the time, but so brief now, looking back. Perran began to grow very tall. Lissie grew plumper and Thomas grew thinner and even Hester filled out and lost the awkwardness of childhood. My mother would look at her sideways now and again and catch my father's eye, and even I could see she was fast becoming a beauty. She grew a little taller and lost most of her pallor, and a soft look would be there in her eyes sometimes when she was deep in thought; but there were days in the month when she would double-up and clutch her stomach and look very thin and pale and be sick occasionally. And then, one Sunday after church, David Penkevin asked her out.

I remember how we stood, older and more dignified, in the porch after the evening service, all of us and the ringers crowding round; and some of the younger lads were climbing up on to the low wall that divided the churchyard from the field, running along it and daring each other to fall. Joseph was there with us as he always was, silent in the background, watching us with his hands in his pockets, saying nothing. That evening he stood, by chance, opposite to me, and directly behind Hester. From my place in the shadow of the porch I could see his face, and he did not realize I was watching him. He stood behind her, looking down at the back of Hester's slim neck. She had put her bright hair up that evening and caught it into a bunch of curls, and it left her neck oddly bare and vulnerable. She had bent her head to examine something on her hand and was laughing a little at some remark one of the others had made and there was Joseph behind her, looking down at the back of her neck. I think it was probably at that moment that I fully realized.

There was a silence enfolding them both. Around them there was plenty of desultory conversation: banter and chatter and laughing replies, and an older George Pascoe was still organizing the ringers for a peal; but Joseph and Hester were caught up in a timeless moment that was theirs alone.

Then David Penkevin came over and asked Hester if she would like to go to the cinema with him to see some film that had been much talked about and Hester looked up at him, flushing, and said yes, she would like to, and smiled with pleasure at being asked; not giggled like Veronica Braze would have done. Hester never giggled; I think she would have been incapable of it. I knew she had been aware of David Penkevin for some weeks, and when he had gone she turned to me. Her eyes shone with suppressed delight, her cheek warm with new power, and she cast me a glance of excitement. But she hadn't seen Joseph's face and I had.

Veronica caught hold of my arm and drew me aside to demand what David had asked Hester, and when I told her, her face clouded. She was younger than I was, and same age as Perran, and pretty in a plump, pinkish sort of way. She wore rather old-fashioned clothes that her mother and grandmother had had made by a dress-maker, the family being rather well-to-do; but the dress-maker's talent was for tailored styles, the sort of thing that suited Veronica's handsome portly mother, no doubt, but merely made poor Veronica look dowdy. I once saw her in a cotton dress looking almost pretty. But that evening she was wearing a strange grey suit that strained across the bosom and looked as if it had been handed down from her grandmother's grandma, and made her flat feet look flatter than ever. She was desperate to impress David Penkevin and on her wrist she wore a silver charm-bracelet that she kept shaking self-consciously, so that the charms jangled on their chain and her pink face grew even pinker with the effort.

I glanced back at Hester, and behind her to where Joseph had stood minutes before, but he wasn't even there.

Hester began to go out with David Penkevin quite regularly. It soon became an accepted fact that she and David were a couple. He took her to parties and dances and the sort of social events where Joseph would simply not have been at ease, and it was soon very obvious that David was serious about her.

Then, one Christmas, we had a spell of mild, wet weather followed by a day of cold so sharp that icicles hung from our out-house. Ice lay in the lanes all day and glittered on the church roof at noon. The day before Christmas Eve, Hester and I were on our way up to the mound behind the village for a walk, drawing our breath in gulps so that the freezing air stung our noses and made our teeth ache with the shock. All morning my mind had been full of thoughts of Joseph all alone in his cottage in the intense cold, so it was a relief to see him fit and well. We met him in the lane outside the church, his arms full of great piles of holly that he was taking over to the vicarage to decorate the hall for the Christmas carol party. Arms burdened, he nodded and smiled when he saw us in the lane.

'For the party!' said Hester, her face bright with delight. She fingered the holly. 'How lovely and waxy it looks – and the berries! Abbie, look!'

As usual she had no word of greeting for Joseph. It was as if he was not there at all; mere wood of the holly, bough of the tree. 'Look Abbie, the lovely shiny leaves!'

'Where did you pick it, Joseph?' I asked him. 'It's beautiful.'

'Church field,' said Joseph briefly. He smiled at me, an indulgent smile given to a playful puppy. 'There's plenty there. I'll cut you some later for yourselves if you like.'

'Oh no,' I said, 'we couldn't put you to the trouble, Joseph. You're busy.'

'No trouble,' he said. He looked at Hester. 'Shall I cut you some, Hester?'

She avoided his eyes. 'No,' she said lightly, 'we've plenty at home.' She pulled at my arm. 'Come on, Abbie, we're late.'

It seemed a curt way to take leave of him, so I lingered. 'Are you going to the carol party, Joseph?' Although of course I knew he would.

'Oh yes,' he said, 'I'll be there.' He always was.

Hester tugged at my arm again. 'Come *on*, Abbie!' She pulled away and walked on up the lane.

Up here on the higher ground by the church there was a thin sprinkling of snow. Hester danced ahead, slender against the white, her boots stamping footprints in the crisp fluff. Beneath the trees bending inward in their green gloom she danced up the lane, like a child intent on her play. She jumped up into the cold air, trying to catch hold of a bough and bring the snow down on top of us. I followed her. Turning round, I saw that Joseph was still standing there watching us. I waved and he waved back. With some haste I caught up the dancing figure. 'Poor Joseph,' I said. 'Oh Hester, you were rude to him!'

She laughed, jumped up and grasped a low hanging branch, bringing a shower of white down upon our heads. Her laughter rang out, sharp in the clear air.

'Hester!' I said. 'Don't you care about Joseph's feelings? Listen to me!' She jumped higher, missed the next branch and ran on. 'Oh Hester, stop doing that and listen to me. You're like a child!'

'No,' she said, 'I'm sixteen.'

'That's not what I meant. The way you hurt people, careless of their feelings.'

She stopped jumping and turned to me, serious, listening. She frowned, considering, and shook her head gravely. 'I don't, Abbie. I don't think so.'

'Well no,' I relented, 'not usually. But just now, with

51

Joseph. Poor Joseph! You hardly speak to him, Hester, ever, poor chap. You treat him as though he's not really there. Don't you care about people's feelings? Don't you care about Joseph's?'

'Joseph?' she said blankly. 'Oh – Joseph.' And then she brightened. 'Race you to the gate!' she said, and was off, her feet flying across the thin snow.

It was a hard climb up to the top of the hill in the biting wind but worth it when we gained the summit. Our hands stung and tingled with the exercise and the cold, and Hester's cheeks glowed pink with effort. We scrambled across the mound of ancient stones that the vicar always said had been put there at the dawn of history, even before Christ was born or the Romans came to Britain. There was a restlessness about the old hill always, so that the wind that blew there seemed to gather up an ancient power from the very stones, and it moaned about our ears with old lament. We could see for miles.

Hester gave a long sigh. 'I love it up here,' she breathed. 'Don't you feel like a bird, Abbie? Free as air; as if you could stand on one of these great stones and fly across to – oh, France, or Devon, or the moon?'

I looked at her, red hair below her green scarf flying about her face, cheeks flushed and eyes aglow, and laughed. 'Hester, you're like a young pony let out of your stable to toss your mane in the wind.'

'I'd rather be a bird than a pony,' she said thoughtfully, 'but not in a cage. I'd like to be one of the rooks, I think.' She paused. 'Don't you ever feel, Abbie, that to be a bird would be the most – I don't know – the most *real* experience that you could ever have?'

I thought about it. 'Not really. Maybe the freedom would be nice for a bit; perhaps on a warm summer afternoon, just for half an hour.'

She laughed, and then grew serious again. 'No, the bitter cold would all be part of it; shivering in a hedge on an icy morning and breaking the ice with your beak to get a drink, and pulling up worms, and dying . . .' She paused. 'Dying one day of starvation in a wintry field.'

There was a short silence. I said lightly, 'Because you couldn't find enough worms to eat to stay alive, you mean? And Joseph or Harry Tregulla would come along one morning and find your poor, stiff little feathered body?' The conversation had taken an odd turn, and I shivered. 'No,' I said, 'I wouldn't like to be a bird. I'd rather stay a human being in a safe little house, anchored to the ground.'

Hester said, 'I sometimes think that to be trapped in something, unable to get away, would be worse than anything. I don't think I could bear it.'

'What about death?' I asked her, laughing. 'You can't get out of that!'

'Oh no,' she said, quite seriously. 'Death is a kind of freedom, Abbie. I mean now, trapped in a sort of prison or cage. That would be far worse.'

I smiled. 'Then you mean like marriage,' I said, feeling witty and adult. We had lately begun to consider the state of marriage with academic detachment and a certain distant interest.

'Perhaps,' said Hester vaguely. She began to walk slowly, and I followed. 'Although perhaps with David marriage might be quite nice.'

'You don't think you'd feel trapped?' I asked her. We rounded a bend in the rough track and the bitter wind caught at us unexpectedly. 'What if you didn't like the bed bit?'

'What about you, Abbie?' She stole a sideways look at me. 'How would you feel, sleeping with a man?'

'Rather odd, I suppose. Although if it was the right man, rather nice, I should imagine.'

'But you wouldn't know, would you, about whether you'd feel trapped or not, until you were married? And then it would be too late.'

'I suppose that's where love comes into it,' I said. 'If you loved the chap I suppose you wouldn't feel trapped. How do you feel about David?'

She considered it for a moment. 'I don't think I would

53

feel trapped with David.' She bent down, frowning, then tossed a handful of snow up into the air. 'But I'm too young yet to think about marriage.'

'He's very fond of you, Hester,' I said. 'You know that, don't you?' I paused. 'What about Joseph?'

She looked startled. 'Joseph?'

'Yes,' I said, 'you heard me. What about Joseph?'

'Oh!' she said quickly, turning away. Her voice had a sudden hurt tone, as if I'd said something to wound her, but all she said was 'Oh – Joseph.'

It was now or never. 'Hester,' I asked her levelly, 'do you care anything at all for Joseph?'

She didn't answer me. Then she sighed, very heavily, and said, 'Let's go home, Abbie. I'm cold.'

I gave it up, and shrugged. 'All right,' I said, 'come on. We'll make toast and play dominoes by the fire if Mother doesn't need us. You know you love to play dominoes.'

Her face still had a tight look, but she turned back to me in a moment and nodded to herself as if she had made a decision. And then she said, very softly to herself, 'I shall marry David Penkevin if he asks me,' and then aloud, 'Come on, I'll race you home!'

We ran down the rough track, arms flying, coats flapping, boots thudding on the hard stones and crisp grass, Hester sailing down the hillside before me like one of her birds. She climbed the five-barred gate in our path with the ease of a squirrel, brushing aside the light snow in her way, and I followed breathlessly. In a quarter of the time it had taken us to climb the hill we were back in the lane, aching and glowing with freedom and the heady clarity of cold winter air. We turned into the lych-gate to get our breath back and collapsed onto opposite sides of the low stone benches, looking triumphantly at each other.

'You won,' I said. 'You always do. You know before we start who'll win.'

She laughed at me with sudden delight. 'You're too fat, Abbie! Or too old.'

'Both probably,' I said, laughing back at her, although I

was actually only a few months older. It was good to see her so glowing and alive with pleasure.

'You said toast,' said Hester. She pulled off her green woollen scarf and wound it absently about her wrist. 'I'm hungry.' She shook her head and her bright hair flew about like tongues of flame in the white air.

'It's dinner time by now,' I said. 'Perhaps we'd better forget the toast. We ought to get back; Mother will wonder where we've got to.'

'All right.' She hesitated. 'But first we've got to do the grave. It's Saturday.'

I nodded.

'We'll have to find some stuff to put on it. And get some water.'

'Won't it freeze?' I asked.

She shrugged. 'Probably. But we must go the grave, Abbie. You understand, don't you?'

'He won't mind if we don't, you know, Hester,' I said gently. 'Not in the middle of winter. He won't expect flowers.'

'I must do it,' she said stubbornly, 'I must. I've just got to. There's holly and some laurel. The berries will show up lovely and red.'

'All right,' I said. 'We can get holly from the field, like Joseph said. I'll run home for some laurel first, and then I'll help you cut a bit of holly.'

She nodded, and I left her there in the lych-gate, her head glowing against the dark beams. As I ran homewards down the lane I saw her wave at me; and then I had turned the bend, steep-banked with winter growth, and she was out of sight.

I cut a few small branches from a bush in the garden and shook the snow off them. Mother wandered out from the kitchen. 'Abbie, where's Hester?'

'Doing the grave,' I answered. 'We won't be long. I'll lay the table when I get back.'

'Don't worry, my love,' said Mother, 'it's done. You're a good girl; you look after Hester.' She glanced up at the sky.

55

'Looks like more snow on the way. I've got Thomas in here praying for it so that he can see the garden in a snow-storm. He wants to make a drawing of it; and Perran's talking about building a snow-man. They've got some hope, they two!'

I chuckled and she was gone again into the kitchen, leaving me pondering upon her words. Did Hester need looking after? I supposed she did. I shrugged it off and, waving at them through the window, ran back up the lane to find her.

She had gone from the porch. I looked for her in the lane, but she was nowhere to be seen. I ran back through the gate and searched the churchyard, but there was no evidence of her: no dark green scarf or ruddy head among the stones. I went into the church, holding my bunch of laurel. There was no sign of her there either. I even tried the tower door but as always now, since that evening four years ago, it was locked.

I looked for a good five minutes before I found her, crouched on a chair behind the organ, her face in her hands.

'Hester!' I cried in dismay. 'Whatever's the matter?' I dropped my bunch of laurel on to the floor and knelt beside her. I longed to put my arms around her like Mother did to us when we were troubled, but she would have hated it, and then I would have been embarrassed. 'Hester! What is it?' I shook her arm gently. 'Whatever's the matter? Why are you crying? Hester, answer me!'

She looked up suddenly from her arms and her eyes were quite dry. 'Why Hester,' I said in amazement, 'I thought you were crying!'

'No,' she said calmly, 'I was listening.'

I could have sworn she had been crying, but her eyes were bright, thick-lashed and luminously clear. She looked back at me, then over my shoulder into the dim height of the nave. 'I was listening,' she said again.

'What were you listening to?' I asked, bewildered. There was no sound in the empty church. I strained my ears to listen but there was nothing except the light sigh of our own

56

breathing and the siffling of snowy wind under the north door.

She gave me a brief little smile and stood up. I picked up my bunch of laurel leaves and followed her, waiting for her to explain; but she said nothing at all, as if it was the most normal thing in the world to listen to silence. Perhaps for Hester it was.

With a bottle of water and the laurel leaves we made our way solemnly to the grave. It was icy cold under the trees in the still churchyard and my fingers felt stiff and numb when I tried to flex them to unscrew the bottle top.

'The holly!' I said. 'You wanted holly to go with these.' I waved the laurel at her. 'I'll pick some, shall I?' I made for the gate into the field, then looked down. There was a branch of fresh holly lying on the ground by my feet, dark against the snow; a piece that had been freshly cut that morning. 'That's lucky,' I said. 'Look Hester, there's a piece here. Joseph must have dropped it.' It was long and leafy and I picked it up, shook it, and gave it to her; she always wanted to do the grave herself.

The smell of snow came across to us on the wind and filled our nostrils. It was in the air, the sky. Mother was right: there would be more before evening. I looked at Hester's bent head as she sorted out the green stems and broke them into suitable pieces for the jar.

'You put the water in, Abbie,' she said, and I did as I was told. She crouched down and I held the jam-jar while she painstakingly pushed little bits of holly and laurel into it. The water welled up and over the edge and splashed on to my fingers and I gasped with the sharp chill of it.

Hester stood up to survey her work. The bunch of greenery stood out against the snow and the granite of the headstone: spears of verdant life in a still world. We gazed down at the stone. 'In loving memory,' I read aloud, 'of Isaac Bartholomew, dearly beloved husband of Agnes, departed this life March the fifth, eighteen hundred and forty-eight, "Who Resteth in The Arms of the Lord".'

Hester said softly, 'So many years ago, Abbie. Years and years before we were ever born.'

'Is that all right?' I asked her gently. 'Are you happy now?'

She nodded, absently sucking a finger. There was a thin streak of blood on her chin.

'What have you done?' I asked her. 'Your finger's bleeding.'

She looked down in surprise and squeezed it until a small red globe formed on the side. 'Oh,' she said, 'I must have pricked it on the holly; it's nothing.' She rubbed at the side of the wound and held up the shimmering ruby drop for me to see. 'Look, Abbie!' She carefully transferred the shining globe on to a single holly leaf. 'Now there's another berry on Joseph's holly: a berry of Hester's blood.'

It was an extraordinary thing to say. For a moment I felt quite dizzy, as if strands of mist had caught together out of the very air and were swirling about, drifting white and low. I looked up at her and realized the strands were snow: huge leafy flakes falling swiftly out of a massive sky. She looked back at me through the falling flakes; across the faceless, unknown grandfather's grave, so calmly, like a figure in a dream, and she said again: 'A berry of Hester's blood.'

Then she turned and ran lightly away, disappearing soundlessly on the snow-muffled ground into the arch of trees.

Chapter Six

THE BRIDE

ON HESTER'S EIGHTEENTH birthday David Penkevin asked her to marry him. It had been expected for a year or so beforehand, and David was a nice enough chap: kind, charming and handsome in a boyish, healthy sort of way. As one of the ringers he was a frequent visitor at home, and my parents liked him well enough and seemed to approve of the match.

'I think he's right for Hester,' Mother would muse, half to herself and half to me, over the dishes, as she washed up and I dried and set the things aside. 'Don't you think so, Abbie? I think David will make her happy, I truly do.' Whether Hester would make him happy did not seem to concern Mother. She had a little frown between her eyes and a far-away look, as if she were trying to see into the future at a picture which, in its inevitable way, meant Hester and David and babies.

'They'll make a handsome couple, that's for sure,' I agreed wryly, 'and I certainly think he loves her.' There had been ample evidence of that: David arriving regularly to take Hester out, a long stream of cards and presents on her birthdays and at Christmas, and anonymous ones on Valentine's day. David's eyes softened when they looked at her, and he straightened his tie and cleared his throat nervously when she appeared, and was for ever touching her arm, her hand, and pulling out chairs for her to sit in. Oh, David Penkevin loved her, no doubt of that, no doubt at all; if that is what love is.

I once thought to mention my growing fears about such a match to Mother, but in truth, what could I say? They were all so happy about it: my father briskly jovial, Perran and the other ringers delighted, and Lissie shy and excited at the prospect of wearing a long dress and being a bridesmaid. So who was I to cast a doubt over all that happiness? But I did try, just once, to voice my vague apprehension.

We were in the kitchen one June afternoon that year, Mother and I, shelling peas. I was perched on the table eating half the ones I popped out of their crisp jackets and Mother was rapidly and steadily adding hers to the growing heap in the blue saucepan in front of her. She paused for a moment and stretched her plump fingers out in front of her to examine them.

'Dear me,' she said. 'All these vegetables. My hands are some stained, Abbie. I'll have to get to work with a lemon before the wedding. David won't want a mother-in-law with hands like these.' She glanced at me. 'You do like him, don't you, my love? You do think he's right for Hester?' She was tending to talk along these lines lately, as if the slight doubt was there, half-obscured.

'Oh yes, I like him well enough,' I paused. Here was my chance. 'But Mother, what about Joseph?'

She stared at me. 'Joseph?' Her mouth fell open and she gaped in frank astonishment. 'Joseph? Whatever makes you think of *him*?' She hesitated. 'Oh Abbie, no! Joseph's a born bachelor, don't you worry.' She began to chuckle to herself. 'Joseph at the altar? No, not him! That'll never be.' She sighed, and nodded thoughtfully. 'No, David's the one for Hester, I'm sure of it. Anyway, she's said yes, hasn't she, so she must love the chap. Oh yes, he's the one for Hester.'

I gave it up and wandered out to do the potatoes, leaving Mother chuckling to herself over the peas and saying, 'Joseph at the altar? That'll be the day!'

But perhaps Mother had thought a bit about my question for, later that day, I overheard her say to Hester on the quiet, 'You are sure, my love, aren't you? There's no one else is there, Hester? Sure?' And I saw Hester give that small bright smile of hers, shake her head and, stretching out her hand, look at David's ring. Then Mother's voice, very low, saying hesitantly, 'You don't – perhaps – you don't care for Joseph, do you Hester?'

And I heard her answer, just the same as she had done to me: 'Joseph? Oh – Joseph,' and in her voice was something I could not quite fathom, although the only thing I could have called it would be a kind of rawness.

'She doesn't,' Mother confided to me next day. 'She doesn't care for him, Abbie, you needn't worry. I asked her outright, I did. Last night.'

'What did she say?' I asked, knowing full well.

'Nothing,' said Mother. 'She was quite couldn't-care-less – as if she almost didn't know who he was. There! Now you needn't worry, Abbie,' and she smiled at me reassuringly, and patted my hand.

'Yes,' I said lightly, 'she's always been like that towards Joseph.'

'Then you're imagining things,' said Mother crisply, 'so don't let your imagination wander. It's your romantic mind, my girl – forget it!' And so I did.

Sometimes, for a week or so at a time, I'd even manage to forget Hester's face through the snow and her voice, like a voice in a dream, saying 'A berry of Hester's blood'. There was no doubt that she appeared happy. She ran about all day like a delighted child, opening wedding presents and filling the cottage with song. For months we were all caught up in a welter of preparations for the wedding, which was set for early March. We were to have a reception at home afterwards as there was only a handful of guests from David's side, and barely more from ours. David had a younger brother, James, of an age with Thomas; a fidgety, noisy little boy who twitched and made faces with a nervous air when spoken to. David's parents came over with the two sons to talk about the wedding plans, and while Lissie and I passed round cups of tea and David and Hester held hands self-consciously on the sofa in front of us, Thomas found some paper and a pencil and hid himself in a corner to do some quiet drawing of the assembled faces, and James kicked thoughtfully at his chair, twitched his mouth and picked at the upholstery.

There was some argument about a wedding dress. Hester longed passionately to be married in green, deep green, her favourite colour, but Mother was emphatic that it would not be at all suitable. 'Not green, Hester,' she said firmly. 'You can't walk down the aisle in green. Surely even you can see that. You'll have to wear a white dress; it's what David would want. You must wear white.'

'Why?' said Hester. 'Why do I have to wear white? What's wrong with green? Oh, I wish I could have green.'

'Because,' Mother told her, 'because all brides wear white if – if they've not been married before. You can't have a green wedding dress, Hester. Besides, it would be awful unlucky. You've got a terrible passion for green clothes; I'm sure I don't know why. Let Liss wear green as your bridesmaid, certainly, but not you, Hester. Abbie's going to make the dresses for you, so you ask her about green for Lissie. But not your dress, my lamb. That must be white.'

'Will you make Lissie's dress in green?' Hester asked me. 'I wish I could have a green dress, but Aunty Susan says no. Why can't I have green, Abbie? I'd dearly love a new green dress.'

'Because you're a virgin, Hester,' I told her frankly, 'and it's traditional that virgins wear white.'

'Oh!' she said, and went suddenly very red. I remembered Mother taking her aside the week before and asking anxiously in a low voice, 'Here Hester, you do know what happens on the wedding night and all that, don't you, my love? You do *know*, don't you Hester?' And Hester nodding vaguely as Mother bustled her away for a little talk in the parlour which we hardly ever used, except on great occasions. They had come out again half an hour later, with Hester looking rather dazed and Mother rather flushed and business-like. Mother had washed her hands very briskly at the sink and sent Hester out into the orchard to call Lissie and Thomas in to tea.

'Of course Lissie can wear green,' I told her, 'if that's what you want, but it isn't usual, you know. It's considered unlucky to have green clothes at a wedding. It's only superstition though, and I dare say it won't matter a bit.'

So I made Lissie a green dress – deepest green, the colour of holly leaves and dark water – and Hester looked at it with longing eyes all the time it was being made, until Lissie said, very bravely, 'Try it on, Hester. You can have it anyway after the wedding, if you like. I don't like green as much as you do.' So Hester put on her own bridesmaid's dress before the dark mirror in my parents' room, holding the material of it in to fit her narrow waist and turning this way and that before the glass. 'I much prefer it to the wedding dress,' she sighed. 'Oh, if only I could have had green!'

'And I prefer the bride's one,' Lissie said. I'd let her help me make the wedding dress. She sewed the hem and seams and a few other simple little parts that she could manage. She was a quiet little thing, very domesticated. She loved nothing better than cooking and cleaning and pottering about round the house, tidying up after all of us. At thirteen she was rather round and shapeless, but of so placid a nature that it was difficult to find fault with her even if we'd wanted to, which we didn't. She was still at school, of course. Her favourite lessons were cookery and needlework, and there was no doubt at all as to where her talents lay. Under Mother's watchful eye she made a splendid wedding-cake, and Mother iced it with green icing, at Hester's request. For the last week before the wedding it sat on a plate in the pantry among the wine-jars, picking up the scent of yeast.

Hester spent these last weeks before her wedding in a state of vagueness bordering on trance. She seemed to be living in a permanent dream; as if everything around her, all the hectic preparations and presents and good wishes, were all for someone else and not for her at all. I wondered if she was happy at the thought of being David's wife; and I wondered also how she would have felt if she had been marrying Joseph instead.

She hardly ever had occasion to see him now, as we had grown too old to run about the churchyard or come upon him in the lanes. We still saw him in the congregation on Sundays, but he sat right at the back and never spoke and afterwards was away before everyone else. I used to wonder sometimes why he had never learnt to ring, for most of the able-bodied men in the village could put their hands to a rope, even if they were not regular ringers. I suppose it was because Joseph was such a solitary man, preferring his own company and his pipe. Mother sent him a wedding invitation but he never replied, which hurt her feelings a little; but she shrugged, putting it down to his unsociability, I think, and forgot it.

Our childhood was behind us now. Hester's days of taking flowers to her anonymous grandfather were over. Some weeks she forgot altogether. But the night before her wedding day she remembered. I found her in the orchard, picking snowdrops and a few straggly primroses to go with them, and she asked me if I would go up to the churchyard with her to do the grave for the last time. She was wearing a faded yellow dress that had once been one of mine; it had not done much for me and I'd willingly handed it over. She looked young and fresh and oddly vulnerable in it and, with her rich hair, of the company of the narcissi under the trees. I had merely looked young.

'Come with me, Abbie?' she pleaded. 'For the last time? Please! I'll never go again, after today.'

'Surely you will,' I said. 'You'll always want to do the grave, Hester.'

'No, I won't,' she said. 'David thinks it's silly. Oh, he doesn't say so, but I know he thinks it is. Come with me, Abbie? It'll be the last time. You've never thought it silly, ever. You've always understood.'

Have I? I wondered, as I followed her up the lane. Has anyone ever understood Hester? Certainly not David, who was as unimaginative as a bar of soap from what I could tell of him. Although perhaps if he loved her enough he would be able to reach across to that far country in which she lived.

So I followed her up the lane, clutching the limp bunch of snowdrops. Already their pale stems were softening and they drooped their heads sadly and mourned. Like a yellow bride she walked ahead of me, and like a deferential bridesmaid I followed in the quieter dress with the wilting bunch of snowdrops. It was as if, in the spring evening, we walked to a fairy wedding; Hester walking to meet an immortal lover who waited for her under the churchyard trees; one who had waited there since the beginning of time. The odd fancy crossed my mind that it was death that waited for her there and I shivered, telling myself that the spring air was giving me foolish thoughts; but the feeling lingered oddly, and cast vague shadowed fingers across the warm spring day.

We made our way like this to the grave of Isaac Bartholomew, abandoned for some months now, and Hester reverentially removed a few dead remnants of the previous bouquet from the cracked vase Mother had given her to replace the jam-jar. I handed her the flowers and then went to move away, feeling that on this last day of her childhood she would prefer to be alone with her ancestor who was no ancestor. I'd only taken three or four steps when she realized what I was doing, and called out to me in sudden passion, 'Abbie, don't go! Don't leave me alone with him. I can't bear it if you go!'

I turned back at once and she was trembling. I knelt beside her and patted her hand as if to soothe a frightened child. 'It's all right, Hester! I won't go. I thought you'd like to be alone, that's all.'

'No,' she said. 'Don't leave me here with him on my own, Abbie. You put the flowers in this time; I'll get the water. But not for a minute. Wait a minute first.'

I nodded, and sat on the end of the grave, humming a little to myself until she was calm again. 'Better now?' I asked her at length. She nodded. 'What was it that upset you?' I asked.

'I don't know. Just a feeling. I often get it up here.'

'What sort of feeling? Frightened?'

'No, not frightened. It's very real when it comes, not like being afraid at all. Just very real.' She sighed. 'I'm all right now. I'll go and get the water.'

'Are you sure?'

She nodded and went off, and while I waited for her to return with the filled bottle I amused myself pulling out small shreds of moss and weed from in between the cracks. She had been away for about ten minutes before I realized that she had been gone too long merely to fill a bottle with water. I began to grow restless, and sighed with slight irritation. Where had she got to now? I waited a few more minutes and still she had not returned. Puzzled, I went to look for her.

I found her almost at once. She was standing under the elms, looking up into the sky and watching the rooks flying to and fro. Her hands were clasped behind her back and there in the still spring air she was totally absorbed. She stood beneath the trees in a patch of soft light which fell about her like a cloak, and struck her bright hair aflame. I remembered David's reverent glances and half-disbelieving looks; but I could no more see Hester belonging to David than I could the birds. She was too unreal for possession. She was like flame out of the earth standing there in the falling sunlight, with as much power and as little substance. As I watched her she moved and half-turned, holding up her arms to the birds, as if inviting them to take her up with them.

I was about to call out to her when I realized that someone else was there too, watching her silently from the flag-stoned path. He stood quite motionless, his gaze upon her, breathing in the sight of her. I stepped back un-observed into the shadows.

Hester, standing in her pool of light, lowered her arms. Suddenly she seemed to panic. She took several rapid steps back towards where he stood watching her from the path; she stumbled and began to fall. And Joseph, as I watched, held out his hands to catch her, caught up the flying shape into his arms, and held her against his breast.

For several seconds neither of them moved at all. Then Hester started, and pulled herself away. He said nothing. She stood there trembling a little before him, and for almost a full minute nothing happened. They were like two figures suspended in a dream, just standing there staring at each other, all alone beneath the churchyard trees.

I turned and went back to the grave and knelt down to fiddle with the dead flowers on the ground beside it. There was no sound but the soft whisper of grass around me, and the high call of the rooks. I sat there all alone while the sunlight faded rapidly and the shadowed evening drew on, until a slight dimness fell across the grave, and I looked up.

'Hello Joseph,' I said, rather at a loss. 'Lovely evening. We've come to do the grave.'

He nodded, being well-used to Hester's eccentricities. There was a long pause, while the wind sighed.

'How are you?' I asked lamely. 'We don't see much of you these days.'

'Very well,' he said. 'And you?'

'Yes, we're all fine at home,' I told him. 'Mother's very busy with the wedding arrangements and everything, but very well and happy. How are your hens?'

He chuckled. 'Laying well.'

'Good.' I said. It seemed a laboured conversation, and I gave it up. He didn't seem to mind. He stood beside the grave, looking out across the surrounding fields, seemingly deep in thought.

'I don't know where Hester's got to,' I said in desperation. 'She went to get some water for the flowers. There aren't many about at this time of year, but she managed to find a few.'

He looked down, and his eyes fell upon the bunch of straggling flowers. He bent and took a primrose from the limp collection, turning it carefully in his fingers.

'They're early this year,' I said helpfully. 'She found a few in the orchard.'

He nodded, looking at the primrose in his hands, then tucked it carefully into a buttonhole of his jacket. 'Signs of spring,' he said. It was an oddly warming thing to do, and I felt a rush of ease. 'Are you planting much this year?' I asked him. 'Your tobacco plants, of course?'

'Oh, yes,' he said. 'I put them in every year.'

Silence fell about us once again. I began to think Hester wasn't going to come back. I got to my feet, brushing off my skirt. Joseph looked thoughtfully up at the sky.

'It's tomorrow then,' he said, at length.

'Yes. It's tomorrow.' I hesitated. 'Joseph, do you mind?'

'Mind?' he said. 'Mind?' He looked at me. 'Oh no, I don't mind. Why should I mind? She must have what's best for her. She must have what she wants. He's a nice chap, David Penkevin. He'll be good to her.'

This was a long speech for him. I looked at him, seeing him clearly for the first time in years; a little older, new lines around his eyes, the firm line of his kindly mouth. 'But Joseph,' I began, 'you – you don't . . .'

I couldn't finish the sentence; it was no good. It was not my place. It was not my responsibility. If these two couldn't see that they were made for each other, twin souls, fire and earth, tree and trembling leaf, fashioned from the same stuff, then it was not my place to tell them so.

But all the same, he seemed to know what I was trying to say. He gave me a long slow thoughtful look with his rich gaze, then slowly smiled at me, a particularly generous, loving smile, like to a dearly favoured child offering a buttercup to mend a broken heart. 'She don't want *me*, Abbie,' he said, with a sort of low and scornful voice. And then again, 'She don't want *me*.'

I knew not what to say. I stood there staring at him wordlessly, and just then Hester came dancing through the arch of the trees towards us, the bottle in her hands. She stopped short when she saw Joseph. The space between them seemed to grow less and then expand again; although neither of them moved an inch.

A light breeze had got up, and swung about between the headstones. We seemed to be held there in a kind of pause; as if there were a pane like glass between the past and future, dividing the now from what was going to be. Within the moment was the chance to smash the glass, to say a word and change the course of things. But which one of them could say it, and what was there to be said? Today Hester was a virgin and a bride; tomorrow she would be a married woman. Tomorrow it would be too late, and today was already far gone.

Joseph said nothing. He just stood there as he always did, silently watching her. And I remembered another moment like this, on a late summer's evening when we were twelve: a small, juice-streaked face, two grubby little hands catching imploringly at his sleeve, and Hester pleading with him, while he looked down at her and answered nothing at all.

And he said nothing now, as if it were all up to Hester, the decision; if indeed there was one to be made, for I suppose she had made it weeks before. He looked across at her, across the short space that separated them, and he waited.

I got up to go, thinking that if there was any chance at all of this moment changing their lives, they would not want me there. 'I'll wait for you by the gate, Hester,' I said briefly. She nodded, her eyes on Joseph's face, and I left them staring at each other. I looked back before I turned the corner of the church. Hester was on her hands and knees before the grave, carefully arranging her wilting snowdrops. Joseph was standing beside her, watching her, neither of them saying a word; and in the warm spring air I felt a desolate cold.

I sat and waited for her in the lych-gate, while a blackbird cast its notes of fluid ecstasy across the evening; and when she came at last she was holding something in her hand, tight-closed. 'Well?' I asked her, curiously.

She bent her head, and shadow fell across her cheek. She looked down at her folded hand, and sighed.

'Well?' I said again. 'What happened? Did you finish doing the flowers?'

She looked up at me sideways with a strange expression in her eyes, a sort of listening look, as if she were straining to hear something far away and almost out of reach.

'Hester! Can you hear me? Did you do the grave? You look very strange. Are you all right?'

For answer she turned to me and held out her folded hand. 'He gave me this,' she said, and her voice was low. 'He gave me a present, Abbie.'

'Show me,' I said. 'What is it, Hester? A wedding present?' And she nodded.

'A wedding present, Abbie. But only for the bride, he said.'

She opened her fingers. Inside, drooping and torn, and stained with ichor where the pale pieces had broken apart, there lay a limp and crumpled primrose.

Chapter Seven

THE BRAKE

THEY RANG A peal for Hester on her wedding day; George Pascoe, Harry Tregulla, Perran and the other ringers. A peal for Hester, and for David Penkevin. The wedding was a wedding, as weddings go, and that was really all you could say about it. Lissie in her green dress looked plump and pleasant and proud, with well-scrubbed cheeks and shining freckled face; my mother round and Sundayish in her best blue silk and a new hat; my father in his suit, with hair freshly trimmed so close it looked as if it could be rubbed off altogether by a determined wind; Perran as usher, stern and unfamiliar; Harry Tregulla as best man, looking taller than ever beside David's slightness.

Mother sniffed and Lissie threatened to sneeze at the proximity of the bridal bouquet, then changed her mind with admirable control; Father gave away the bride and tapped absently upon invisible strings in the organ passages; David, young and fair and handsome in his new suit with the carnation in his buttonhole, fidgeted with his collar and everlastingly straightened his tie; and Joseph . . . Joseph wasn't even there.

Hester was suitably radiant, bright-eyed but pale of cheek. She seemed to me to be in a kind of trance, as if everything going on around her was enjoyable and pleasant, but nothing really to do with her. She moved down the church on my father's arm to David like an actress playing the part of a bride, and David was like one of the props: useful, undeniably handsome in his crisp white shirt and blue wedding suit, pale hair rippling smoothly back from a dependable hairline and youthful brow, part of the

71

equipment of every good wedding. He stepped smartly forward before the vicar to receive his bride. Hester moved to his side and gazed ahead of her, her luminous eyes fixed with a curious blankness upon the great rose-window ablaze with morning sunshine above the altar, and Lissie brought up the rear. The vicar intoned the words of the marriage service with severe and sober emphasis upon the sacred vows; the performers replied with voices low and hardly audible, and I waited for Mother to cry.

Lissie, shifting from leg to leg in her green dress, stood at the regulation distance, held the bride's bouquet and stifled another sneeze. David held the ring on Hester's finger while he repeated the magic words and the vicar blessed them; and there, it was done, and they were man and wife.

Mother dug me gently in the ribs with her elbow. 'Here Abbie, I didn't even cry!' she whispered proudly. 'How about that, my girl? I never can manage to keep a dry eye at a wedding, can I? But I did today!' I was not quite sure whether this was a salute to Mother's self-control or whether it was due to a singular lack of anything of emotional significance during the service, but I nodded with admiration and gave her what I hoped was a cheering smile.

After the happy couple had left the church the ringers, with a kind of desperate determination to make the day memorable, set about the peal. They gathered round the tower steps and rubbed their hands together. 'Come on, lads,' said George buoyantly, 'we'd better get up there, and see what we can do for 'em. Sorry you can't be with us, Garfield, you'll have to tell us how the striking sounds from home this time.' Father shrugged and looked as if he'd much prefer the tower if it was up to him. George chuckled to himself, caught Lissie's eye, and winked. She tiptoed shyly up to him and held out the flowers. George nodded. 'Lovely, aren't they,' he said approvingly. 'Is that the bride's bunch?'

Lissie lifted her chin. 'Bouquet,' she corrected him. 'Hester's. She's given it to me.'

'You'll be the next bride then, won't you?' said Harry Tregulla jovially. 'You'll have to marry my Toby and then I can be your Daddy-in-Law; a fine great girl like you! I'd marry you meself only I'm married already.'

Lissie giggled and scraped her toe and went pink. Then the men tensed their shoulders and flexed their arms and turned to their real business as the vicar closed the vestry door and came towards them in his cassock. They all disappeared into the tower stair with much subdued scuffling of feet on stone. Father followed them, with assurances to us that he would be home directly in ten minutes, 'just to ring a few warm-up touches with them first,' whatever that meant.

Lissie fell into step with me. I felt Thomas's hand slip into mine. I looked down at him, pale head bent earnestly over a sheet of paper. 'What is it?' I whispered. 'What have you been writing?'

'He's been drawing,' Lissie said. 'Show her, Thomas. Oh Abbie, they're awful good. He drew pictures in the service.' And he held up small sketches of a hymn book, Mother's hands, and Lissie's bunch of flowers.

There in the nave the bell-music came down dimly to us through the roof. We moved towards the door. Then we were out in the sunshine and there they stood together being photographed: the bride and groom, side by side; and over them stole a look of vague disquiet, of slight embarrassment, as if they wondered quite how it had all come about. Above our heads the bell-notes fell noisily from the tower. On the flag-stoned path around the porch a huddled group of coloured figures moved about a swirl of bridal white. Someone, Veronica I think, threw a handful of confetti, and then others were throwing it too; and there was scattered laughter, and good wishes, and shy hugs for Hester.

Mother was kissing her on a pale cheek. 'Good luck, my love,' I heard her whisper, and I saw her squeeze David's arm. 'Take care of her,' she said. 'She needs plenty of patience, does my Hester, plenty of love.' I saw David nod earnestly and shake her hand.

73

We all went back to the cottage for the wedding breakfast, as David's parents called it, all of us trailing down
the lane with the bells pealing about us, and Hester and
David leading the way, her hand upon his arm. Hester
waved and smiled at passers-by and looked radiantly bride-
like, and David gave his handsome, boyish smile. We all
crowded into the living room. Father, when he joined
us, passed round borrowed glasses of his most venerable
wine, and even Lissie and the boys were allowed a watered
drop.

The boys were a bit of a problem. The three of them made
a dive for the mysterious hollow under the table where the
food had been put out on little dishes, and nudged and
kicked each other unnervingly all through the proceedings.
They left the food alone (Father saw to that) but the
excitement of it all proved too much for them, and several
times I heard Polly Tregulla threatening Toby with a stick
if he didn't calm down a bit and behave. Harry was ringing
in the peal, or I think he would have given it to him there
and then. Thomas was the calmest of the three – his placid
nature was not easily ruffled – but Jim Penkevin, slightly
younger by a few months, was something of a handful. After
the sip of watered wine he became quite aggressive, and
spent most of his time inciting Toby and Thomas to fight.
His parents took little notice, perhaps because it was
normal behaviour for him, but I saw Mother and Father
exchange a look which plainly said they were thankful that
Thomas, at least, could be trusted to behave himself.

I got caught in a corner by David's mother and father.
His mother made veiled allusions to the peculiar colour of
the cake-icing, a thing which seemed to worry her more
than Hester's blankness. During the ensuing speeches,
when David was referred to as her husband, there was a
slightly awkward moment as Hester continued to frown in a
vaguely puzzled way, looking around her as if searching for
someone else. David, standing beside her, nudged her
sheepishly and her face cleared; but an odd expression that
looked to me like a breath of fear had been there for a

moment. Then she laughed rather suddenly and jerkily, and everyone else laughed with her.

'Tell me,' said Mrs Penkevin, sipping carefully at Father's wine, 'tell me, Abigail, why green?'

'Green?' I echoed, my eyes still on Hester who, now that the laughter had stopped and everyone was listening politely to what Father was saying in praise of paraffin for eradicating woodworm in garden-tool handles, had gone very pale. 'Sorry – what were you saying?'

'I was asking you, dear,' said Mrs Penkevin, 'why green for the bridesmaid? It seems such a pagan sort of colour somehow at a Christian wedding.'

'I don't know about that,' I said, 'it's just that it's Hester's favourite colour. She wanted a green wedding-dress too, but she had to make do with a green bridesmaid instead.'

I thought they might laugh, but Mrs Penkevin looked a little alarmed. 'Tell me some more about Hester. She's not actually your sister, is she? More of a cousin, I understand. From your mother's side?'

'No, from Father's.'

'Oh?'

'His youngest sister's daughter.'

'And her father?'

There was an awkward pause, and I said lamely, 'We don't keep in very close touch with Father's family, I'm afraid. They live so far away, you see.'

'Good heavens, child, how fascinating! I didn't realize you had relatives abroad. You must tell me more. Where are they, exactly? America?'

'Er – no,' I said. 'Up-country somewhere. Bristol, I think, or Wales. I don't know much about them really.'

'Oh,' she said, and her face fell. 'But surely you must know the family history. What happened to Hester's parents? I understand she's lived with you since childhood.'

'I'm afraid I don't really know anything,' I said. 'You'll have to ask Father to tell you about his family. Does it matter?'

She seemed to hesitate, and gave me rather a strange look. Then she said quickly, 'Well, naturally we'd like to know a little more about our new daughter-in-law. David himself seems to know almost nothing about her background. But, then, young love is blind, isn't it?' She shook her husband's arm. 'Isn't it, dear?'

David's father, who seemed to have realized at last that the ear-splitting shrieks coming from beneath the dining-table had their origin in his son, turned a preoccupied eye upon his wife and said, 'What's that, my dear?'

'Hester,' Mrs Penkevin was saying. 'I was asking Abigail about Hester. I was saying, dear, that it would be un-friendly of us not to want to know a little more about her, wouldn't it?'

'Oh yes, indeed. Pretty girl, Hester. Your cousin, Abigail, I hear? Lovely looking girl.' He sipped appreciatively at the wine. 'Quite a cracker. This wine's very good. What is it, Spanish? A Sauterne?'

'No, it's Father's own. It's parsnip.'

'Good Lord, is it really? It's very good.'

'I was saying, dear, that green seems a peculiar colour for wedding-cake icing. Don't you think so?'

'Green? Sorry dear, what are we talking about? Green icing on the cake? Yes, it looks very pretty, doesn't it. Very nice. Strange? No, I don't think so. Not at all. Rather unusual. Very pleasant. I'm a little worried about James, my dear. He's making rather a mess under the table with crumbs.'

'Oh, Mother won't mind crumbs,' I said cheerfully. 'Don't worry about that, she's used to crumbs.'

'Really?' said Mrs Penkevin with slight distaste. She began to poke about under the table. 'James? Come out of there. Where are your manners? James!'

I caught sight of Mother signalling frantically to me from the kitchen to help her cut more sandwiches, and I left them to it. And while I sliced and buttered and grated cheese, a moment came back to me. A moment earlier, outside the church, when the newly-weds were posing for the photographs. Suddenly, across the small knot of people, I had caught Hester's eye. She had given me her tight little smile and then quickly looked down. I saw her bite her lower lip very slightly, as if the thought had crossed her mind, as it had mine, that we would never again be quite so close as friends. Separated for ever from our childhood by her new estate, her closest one would be David now. I found it strangely difficult to see Hester in the role of David's wife.

A little later, across the heads of smiling faces, she had caught my eye again, and beckoned me over to them. I shook hands with David, who gripped my fingers with a clasp of deep sincerity, and smiled into my eyes. 'Good to see you, Abigail. Doesn't Hester look wonderful? I hear you made her dress – a splendid piece of work. My mother was very much admiring it.'

I nodded, and smiled back as warmly as I could manage. 'Yes, she looks lovely.'

He turned away to shake hands with equal sincerity with someone else, and Hester whispered to me, 'It really is a lovely dress, Abbie. I'm glad now that I had white.'

'Are you happy, Hester?' I asked her.

'Oh yes, I'm happy,' she said brightly. And then, in an odd, flat little voice so low that no one else could hear, 'He didn't come at all, did he?'

I stared at her, but she turned away and began to smile at something David was saying, her face composed in loveliness; but I shivered involuntarily and I felt cold, cold for them both; for the years and years of loneliness pressing in upon them both if David could not reach across to her and make her love him.

She stood there, a beautiful, well-grown woman, slender and vivid in the early sunshine; and I wondered just what the future held for her, my little lost sister, and for David, too; and it crossed my mind also to wonder how on earth anybody ever had the courage to get married at all.

For several weeks following the wedding our routine at home struggled a little adjusting to life without Hester.

Perran and Thomas and Lissie kept us busy. Lissie and Thomas went to school as usual, and Perran and I went to work, but all day the strange knowledge was with us all that Hester would not be there when we got home in the evenings. Mother said it felt quite empty at home without her during the day. She said she found herself pottering about quite listlessly until Father came home on his bicycle in the evenings from the farm where he put in a few hours a week. She pined for Hester's company, and felt a little lost without the extra chores that her presence had meant.

Personally, I missed her very much. It seemed quite strange without her. I thought of her constantly and wondered how she and David were settling down to married life. I had got myself a job at Mrs Blamey's shop in the village on leaving school, and it was an odd feeling to walk home through the narrow main street after a day of selling sweets and tobacco and baked beans and washing powders to people who asked me constantly how Hester was, knowing that she would not be there when I got home. We had little news of her to go on; she wrote letters to Mother and included me in them, but they told us very little. We wrote back with all the news that we could think of, mostly about the garden, and Thomas's doings at school, and asked her questions that she never answered.

Veronica Braze began to frequent the shop. I grew used to seeing her tailored shape entering the doorway during the afternoon. She came nearly every day to buy something, and the conversation inevitably turned to Hester and David; her appetite for news of them seemed insatiable. 'Afternoon, Abbie. Lovely day today, isn't it. I suppose you'll have had post this week, won't you? Another letter from Hester, no doubt. Getting on all right, are they? I'll have a tin loaf today, Abbie. Enjoying their honeymoon with David's aunty are they? I'll have a dozen of those splits, too, look nice, they do. We're having a few friends from the Young Wives' Club to tea today. I'd be a member of course, if I was married.' She giggled and went red. 'Dave's wife would have joined, wouldn't she, if she'd been

78

living here in the village. What a pity they've moved so far away.'

'Not so far, really,' I said. 'It's not as if they've gone somewhere like Scotland or London.'

Veronica ran her hand along the counter and fingered it thoughtfully. 'Seen them, have you, since the wedding?'

'No,' I said, 'but Hester writes.'

'That's a nice dress you've got on today, Abbie. Almost makes you look a bit slimmer, it do. Happy, are they?'

'Why yes, I believe so,' I answered. I thought of Hester's rambling letters about the weather and the daffodils in the park, and her multitude of questions about the village and the garden at home; letters which told us absolutely nothing about her happiness and even less about David's. David had got a job, she wrote, selling vegetables in a shop in Truro, and liked it very much. She said after the country it was different living in a town (she supposed she should really say city) but she was a bit lonely and had made no friends yet. David had made a new friend, a young chap of same age who worked in a butcher's nearby. Such a huge chap it was a wonder he could get in at the door, but useful to get all that muscle behind a meat-axe. She was making me a pair of green gloves for Christmas, with white stars on the back of them, and a scarf for Lissie, also green. She hoped we were well at home and to tell Perran to thank the ringers for the peal, and give her love to us all, from Hester. It was written in her large, childish handwriting, with frequent crossings-out and an extraordinary way of spelling that was hers alone.

Mother had folded the letter and sighed, and looked at me with vague dissatisfaction. 'She sounds so homesick, Abbie, don't she?' She pinched her top lip thoughtfully. 'Do you suppose they're having enough to eat, my 'ansome?'

'I should think so,' I had said, laughing. 'Oh dear, Mother, you'd solve the whole world's troubles with a good square meal if you could!'

'And why not?' she asked indignantly, not seeing the funny side of it. 'There's need enough of good food in this world, with all those poor starving little children in foreign parts.'

'Mother,' I said, 'I'm perfectly sure they'd be getting enough to eat. Hester's a good cook – why, you've taught her almost all you know yourself, and if they run out of ideas they can always live on pasties and old vegetables.'

She had looked at me sideways, knowing that I was mocking her, but laughed with me, suddenly exploding into a girlish giggle that I hadn't heard for years, not since Hester had come to live with us. Father had heard us laughing in the kitchen, and had come in to make sure we hadn't been at his wine. Reassured, he shuffled absently out again and went back to tuning up his violin. He had been putting a new string on it and it kept slipping on the peg so that a very strange descending note would suddenly issue forth in the middle of a scale. Then Father would stop playing suddenly and click with irritation, and that had set Mother and me both off chuckling again. After a while we heard him flip-flapping up the brick path to his shed in the orchard to get a bit of peace. It was a happy moment. Looking back, a certain vague tension seemed to have lifted with Hester's departure but, although it was nice to be ourselves again, I sorely missed her and her sweet and odd ways.

Chapter Eight

THE BRIAR

I BECAME CONSCIOUS of Veronica staring at me. 'My dear life, Abbie, I don't believe you've been listening to a single word I've been saying, have you?'

'Sorry,' I said, 'I was miles away. What were you saying?'

'It's difficult to carry on a conversation when other people don't listen to you,' she said huffily, and sniffed. 'I'll have half a pound of butter while I'm here. I said that I'd heard as how Polly Tregulla thinks she might be expecting again, and Dawn only just turned eighteen months. I wouldn't think it was a good idea to have my babies so close together, would you, Abbie? It makes such hard work of bringing them up nice. All the extra nappies and things – like a production line in a factory. Now I shall plan mine properly, with a good gap between each one. Say two or three years, at least. Don't you agree, Abbie? Don't you think she's stupid to have another one so soon?'

'Seeing as how I'm not married and that it's a problem which doesn't in the least concern me at the moment, I really have no idea. I would have thought it was Polly's business, how and when she has her children, and no one else's.'

She gave me a look that was half spite, half pity. 'You're a funny girl, Abbie. You don't seem at all interested in getting married like most girls. Got yourself a boyfriend yet, have you?'

I sighed. 'Is there anything else you want, Veronica?'

'Yes,' she said, 'we're out of cornflakes. I would have thought you'd be a bit worried at not having a boyfriend at

81

nineteen, Abbie. You'll be left on the shelf if you don't look out.' She handed me a ten-shilling note. 'Are you planning to go over to Hester's soon? Find out how they're liking married life, and all that?'

'No,' I said shortly. 'And I told you, Veronica, we get letters.'

She raised her eyebrows and pursed her lips. 'Letters? From Hester, would that be? Or from Dave?'

'From Hester of course. Here's your change.'

She opened her purse and tipped the coins in. 'Much in the way of news, is there? I hear they're looking for a house to rent. I don't suppose they'll want to stay for long with Dave's aunty, now that Dave's found himself a job.'

'No,' I said. 'I imagine not.'

'Nice to have Dave for a brother-in-law is it, Abbie? I would have liked a brother. David's the next best thing to a brother to you now, I suppose, being your brother-in-law. But then dear me, I was forgetting. Hester isn't your sister exactly, is she?'

'No, she isn't,' I said, putting the splits into a paper bag and swinging it round to seal the top. 'She's my cousin, as well you know, Veronica.' I handed her the bag. 'So David isn't exactly my brother-in-law, is he? More a cousin-in-law; and as for brothers, I'm not exactly short of them, having two.'

She hesitated, seeming reluctant to go.

'Can I get you anything else?' I asked her.

'Um – well, I think I'll have a pot of that plum jam while I'm here. It'll go nice with the splits for the Young Wives' meeting.'

I knew her mother made her own jam, so it seemed odd that Veronica should be buying it, but I reached up for a jar and put it on the counter in front of her. 'Anything else?'

She put the money for it on the counter, and the jar into her basket. 'No, I don't think so.' She hesitated again, seemed about to go, and then said rather hurriedly, 'I suppose you're very fond of David, aren't you Abbie? Him being part of your family now.'

'Not particularly,' I said, in slight surprise. 'I've never really got to know him very well.'

'But you'll be seeing a lot more of him now – of them both now, won't you? When they come to stay, and times like that?'

I shrugged. 'Possibly.'

'I expect a lot of people were very disappointed when it was Hester he asked to marry him, don't you?'

I stared at her. 'How do you mean, disappointed?'

'Well – I think a lot of people were expecting him to ask someone else, don't you? Someone quite different, really. I don't know that David really loves Hester, do you? I've heard it was more a question of feeling sorry for her. I heard as how he was in love with someone quite different. I don't know exactly who was meant, of course; but someone quite different to Hester. Don't stare at me like that, Abbie, it was only something I heard. I might have been wrong of course.'

I suddenly remembered the charm-bracelet of a few years back, and the truth swept over me. I looked at her plump pink face, and sighed. 'No,' I said wearily, 'I happen to believe that David loves her very much. I doubt whether any chap would marry a girl out of pity. Sorry, Veronica.'

For a moment she went a deep red, and then she turned upon me a look of what looked suspiciously like hate. 'We know,' she said sweetly. 'We all know as how you were very disappointed yourself when he asked Hester instead of you, Abbie. Don't worry, mother and I were only saying this morning how upset you must have been; and we're all on your side, Abbie. We all understand.'

I stared at her in amazement, then gritted my teeth. I managed to say calmly, 'Not at all, Veronica. I was delighted for David when Hester said yes, as I happen to know her marrying him made him very happy. If you're suggesting that I had some sort of interest in David I'm afraid you've got it all wrong. He's very much in love with Hester, and she with him. I imagine that was why he asked her to marry him, and why she said yes. If he'd been in love with me, or anyone else for that matter, I imagine he would have asked them instead. And now, if there's nothing else that you want to buy, I'd be grateful if you'd let me get on. I've got some orders to pack, so I'm sure you'll understand.'

That evening after work, as I walked home through the village and past the station, my rage abated a little. I always enjoyed this walk home after work, and the summer air had brought people out into their gardens. I passed Veronica's house without a glance in its direction, and decided to forget the incident. It seemed a silly thing to be upset by a few spiteful words when there was so much quiet beauty in the warm world; the smells and sounds of home were all the balm I needed. I.turned into our lane as it ran past Joseph's cottage, but as usual there was no sign of him, in his garden pulling weeds or digging round his tobacco plants. I hardly ever saw him now. He seemed to have become more of a recluse than ever since the wedding. He was still there at church on Sundays, dimly present in his back seat behind the congregation; but he seldom spoke to me and never asked after Hester, even of Mother. On the odd occasion when I came across him in the village and we stopped to exchange the odd word it was always trivial remarks about the weather or the time of year; formal, meaningless affairs. He kept to himself in his little house up by the main road, presumably got his own meals, and kept his own counsel. The only person who really seemed to take any interest in what went on in his life was Mrs Blamey from the shop, who bought his eggs from him and delivered his bread, two loaves each week, on a Saturday. Father went up there occasionally to smoke a pipe with him and play a bit of music; but he never said if they had chatted at all, or what about.

And then one day, out of the blue, Mother asked him to supper. I never quite knew whether after all those years, she suddenly took it into her head that he needed a good meal cooked by a woman, or whether she was sorry for his loneliness; whatever the reason she asked him to supper on some pretext or other and this time, to our immense surprise, Joseph came.

He brought his pipe and arrived early, smoothing his

84

dark hair and shuffling in out of the summer rain with a little basket of eggs. He nodded to Mother and me, who were coming and going with plates and dishes, and sat down awkwardly on a chair wedged between the wall and the table where we ate all our meals. Living constantly on his own I suppose he was not used to conversation and the hubbub of family chatter, and seemed slightly at a loss. I thought perhaps he'd feel more at ease if left alone for a bit, but Mother had no such qualms.

'How are you, Joseph?' she asked him brightly. 'We don't seem to see much of you nowadays. All right, are you? You haven't been to a meal with us for ages. My dear life, it must be all of ten years.'

Joseph acknowledged this fact with a movement of his shapely head, nodded briefly, and was silent.

'Shy,' said Mother, mouthing words at me in the kitchen. 'Always was awful shy, was Joseph.'

'Oh?' I said. Privately it seemed to me to be less shyness than a disinclination to take part in the affairs of the human race, but I let it pass.

'Ask him if he likes pickle with his pie, will you, Abbie?' She drew the carving knife out of the kitchen drawer and began to slice. I went into them. They sat there, elbows on the table; Father drumming absently with his fingers upon the top, and Joseph looking vaguely discomforted, as if he really shouldn't have come at all. His eyes wandered round the room, at the low beams hung with pots and pans, and came to rest on the dark old dresser that had belonged to Mother's grandma, crammed with postcards, letters and mementos: the giant peg hanging on a nail, which Thomas had made to hold the bills, the blue china boot from Plymouth, the picture post-card of a sailing ship, the plaster-of-Paris squirrel that Lissie had made at school, and assorted vases with and without bunches of flowers that were to me as much a part of home as the people of my family. His eyes fell upon an envelope propped up against the jug from Falmouth, an envelope addressed in a large, childish hand. Mother, coming through from the kitchen,

85

saw his gaze fall, and swooped like a sparrow-hawk on a potential conversation.

'Letter from Hester,' she told him proudly, nodding towards it, and rummaging in one of the drawers for a table-cloth. 'Getting on lovely, they are; very happy, living over Truro.'

This information was received by Joseph as silently as if she had offered him an insult, but Mother went blithely on. 'David's got himself a job in a greengrocer's, and likes it, too. I expect he gets a bit of stuff left over at the end of the day to take home. Help Hester with the housekeeping a bit.'

This cosy picture of marital togetherness being at such variance with any possible way I could imagine Hester, I kept quiet. I stole a glance at Joseph. Such a blank, shuttered look had come over his face that I was tempted to effect some sort of a cutlery accident to shut Mother up. However, she rattled on innocently, 'You didn't come to the wedding, Joseph, did you, my 'ansome? You'd have enjoyed the wedding, wouldn't he, Abbie? Twas a lovely service, and Hester looked a picture in her dress with that hair of hers all gold and shiny.'

I shot Joseph a look of mute sympathy but he wasn't even looking in my direction. His face was shut and the blinds drawn down like the windows of the shops on early-closing day, and from his expression you could tell nothing at all. I thought desperately of ways to rescue him and, Mother threatening to launch into a detailed exposition upon Hester's domestic happiness, I took the only way out and dropped a plate.

It fell on to the stone floor of the kitchen with a resounding crash. The pieces rolled across the floor with glorious cacophony and lodged under the sink, the cupboard, and even the pantry door. Joseph leapt to his feet to come to my assistance and Father jerked back into life. Mother gave up rattling the cutlery and called out dolefully, 'Abbie? It don't seem like you to drop things, my 'ansome. You haven't burnt yourself, my love, have you?'

'No Mother,' I called out from the floor upon which I was

crouched, collecting pieces. 'Sorry about that. It was a cracked one, luckily.'

Joseph bent down to help me. His eye caught mine and the ghost of a grateful smile crossed his face, battling with the shuttered look. As we scrabbled about on the floor hunting for pieces of plate he grinned shyly at me, and I felt the china sacrifice had been worth while.

We all sat round the table for our supper: Mother, Father, Joseph, Lissie, Perran and me. Communication was difficult owing to Father's air of deep preoccupation, Joseph's natural reticence, Lissie's extreme youth, and Perran's adolescent reluctance to have his attention diverted from food. Suddenly Father looked up, frowned heavily at Mother and said, in tones of deep suspicion, 'Where's the lad to?'

We all looked at him, eating suspended for a moment. Mother sighed and said, 'Now Garfield, I told you this morning, didn't I? You don't listen to me, do you? He don't listen to me when I talk to him, Joseph. I told you, Garfield, Polly Tregulla's got a birthday party on for Toby this afternoon. Abbie, didn't I tell Father only this morning? I did tell you, Garfield. Now why else do you think Thomas went off wearing his best trousers at three o'clock in the afternoon and carrying a present?'

'A party, is it?' said Father. He coughed, and returned to his pie. 'Nice bit of pie, this. Have another bit of beetroot, Joseph? Plenty there.'

Joseph helped himself and after that the meal relapsed into silence once again. Mother opened her mouth to make another effort to get a conversation going, caught my eye and pleaded silently with me to back her up. 'Speaking of pie, Hester's a good little cook, isn't she, Abbie? I taught Hester almost all I know, so Abbie says.'

'Any more lettuce, Mother?' I asked her hurriedly. 'This is a very tasty bit of lettuce, Father. From the garden, is it?'

Father raised his eyes to stare at me with baffled scorn and I felt my face growing red. Mother hadn't bought a lettuce for more than twenty years. After a silent withering glance Father returned his eyes to his plate. Joseph munched steadily on, his eyes fixed upon the beetroot.

After a little while Mother was off again. 'Hester always did have a lovely hand for pastry,' she began thoughtfully; and I wondered desperately whether I should drop a tomato or a lump of mashed potato on to the floor this time. I had just decided in favour of the tomato as being less messy when Lissie and Perran began a muttered squabble over the salt, and this distracted Mother for a minute. I saw the chance to divert her from her subject and began to question Father frantically on change-ringing until both Perran and Father eyed me strangely and I fell quiet again, and gave it up.

After that the meal proceeded in relative silence except for the scraping of cutlery upon china, and the crunching of cucumber. At last Mother brought out a steaming jam roly-poly with custard to go with it, and there was much admiration of the pudding.

'I like a roly-poly pudding,' said Father to no one in particular. 'Hot custard, mind. The custard have got to be hot.'

'Oh, Lissie made the custard,' said Mother, beaming at her. 'Didn't you, my love? She's turning into a proper little cook, is my Lissie.'

I held my breath, afraid that this remark might herald another eulogy of Hester's cookery. 'David's got himself a job selling vegetables, you know, Joseph,' she began.

'How's your rhubarb doing this year, Joseph?' I asked recklessly, and was unexpectedly rewarded. A collection of crinkles gathered around his eyes until they creased into furrows and his eyes caught alight within, and Joseph smiled his rich and rare smile.

Mother saw it, and relaxed. Perran caught the end of it and gave up the salt to Lissie; and I basked in its warm radiance and wished with all my heart that I loved him and he loved me. It did cross my mind at that moment to wonder if this was Mother's little plan, but I dismissed it at once as being unworthy of her. Joseph was still watching me.

'Rhubarb's fine thanks, Abbie,' he said, nodding gravely. 'You must remind me to let you all have a bit when it's ready.'

'Why, thank you, Joseph,' said Mother, ladling custard. 'Now, who's ready for a bit of pudding? Perran? Abbie's still on her salad, I see. Yes, we have got a bit behind with the garden this year, what with Hester's wedding and that,' (I steeled myself to lose a radish or two but she passed on lightly) 'but Garfield's going to have a good go at it in the autumn.'

'Peas are doing well this year,' observed Father, looking up from a mouthful of custard. 'Make a nice drop of wine, do pea-pods.' This was conversation he understood, and warmed to his subject. 'Yes, pod-wine now, you can make a proper drop of wine with pea-pods.' He sipped his tea with enthusiasm. 'Tried a drop of pod-wine, have 'ee, Joseph? That's a good one, pod-wine. Not like your carrot wine, of course, not so dark, but good character all the same.'

Perran munched steadily, his eyes on his plate, and Mother chuckled, watching him. She loved a good appetite. 'That lad,' she said, 'the food he puts away!'

'Oh, leave 'en alone,' said Father good-naturedly. 'He's a growing lad.' He winked. 'Tenor rope stretching you, boy?'

Conscious of attention focused on him, Perran swallowed noisily and went red, and retreated lower into his pudding. Lissie wriggled and was excused and Mother and I made tea.

'Going all right, is it, Abbie?' she whispered to me in the kitchen over the steaming teapot. 'Did Joseph enjoy his supper, do you think? He seemed to like the pie.'

I had to know. 'Why did you ask him, Mother?'

She frowned and stirred the tealeaves in the pot, and gave me a frank look. 'I'm sorry for him, Abbie, and that's a fact. It seems to me he must lead a lonely, sad sort of life all on his own, with no one to talk to all year long, and only they old hens for company.'

'And his pipe,' I said.

'Yes, but what's a pipe, and a few chickens!' She shook her head and sighed woefully. 'He should have someone to look after him, cook his meals and wash his socks, and make cakes for him.'

'It seems to me that he just might like living on his own,' I said. 'Only a few months ago I thought you told me Joseph was a born bachelor.'

She frowned. 'Well now I'm sorry for him, Abbie, and that's a fact.' She put the lid on to the pot. 'He's a lovely chap, is Joseph. We used to see a lot of him when you and Liss was little; like one of the family, he was. Perhaps he do prefer his own company, but it's not right for anyone to be alone so much, and I'm beginning to think it would do 'en good to find himself a wife.'

'Mother,' I said guardedly, 'if your little plan for Joseph should by any chance include me . . .'

She glanced at me quickly, and whispered, 'No, Abbie?'

'Oh, no, Mother,' I said wearily, 'not me.'

'He do need a wife, Ab. And he's a lovely man. You could learn to love 'en, given time. You don't always have to start off loving a chap, you know, my 'ansome. Often tis a thing that grows with time, and living with the man, and doing things for him.'

A kind of breathless rage rose in my throat. 'Stop it, Mother!' I gasped. 'How dare you!'

She looked at me in hurt surprise. 'But I just meant that – I only thought . . .'

'Well, don't!' I whispered fiercely, on the verge of unexpected tears. She stared at me in amazement as I went on in a grim low voice, 'Maybe there was a wife for Joseph once; but it's too late now, Mother. She's married someone else. It's far too late.'

There was a rigid silence between us. I felt a sudden trembling fill my limbs as if my legs would fold beneath me, and my hand shook upon the cups.

Mother's lips were pursed together. She crossed to the pantry for the milk jug and began to lay the tray methodically, avoiding my eyes. I could hear the patter of rain beginning again on the plants outside the window, and a kind of breathlessness tightened my chest.

I carried in the tray of tea and bumped it loudly on the table, and the cups rattled on their saucers. Perran jumped. Father, abandoning the subject of carrot wine, turned startled eyes upon me. I did not look at Joseph.

Mother followed me in with the steaming teapot in one hand and the cosy in the other. She set the pot down on the teapot stand from Torquay, put the cosy upon it, and we took our places with silent motion.

'Sugar, Joseph?' She poured the tea and I passed it round. It was an even more silent ritual than the meal had been and I was glad to escape afterwards to the sink to wash the dishes. Mother followed me out. She put a contrite hand upon my arm. 'I'm sorry, my sweetheart,' she said. 'Why, you're shaking, girl. I didn't mean no harm, Abbie – twas only a passing thought.'

'It's all right, Mother,' I answered wearily, 'forget it. It was nothing. I'm not offended.'

She picked up a cloth and began to dry the plates. 'Sure you're not upset?'

'Quite sure,' I said. 'That was a proper supper, Mother. Joseph enjoyed it, that's for sure. You make a lovely pie.'

'Do I?' She sounded pleased. 'Abbie, just one thing. What did you mean about a wife for Joseph?'

'Nothing,' I said. 'Forget it.'

'But you said "There was a wife for Joseph once but it's too late now". What did you mean, Abbie?'

'Nothing,' I told her. 'Nothing at all.' But she pursued the subject and asked again, what did I mean? I shrugged. She glanced over her shoulder into the living room to satisfy herself that Father and Joseph were safely out of earshot. 'Did you mean Hester? Did you, Abbie?'

Perran came through into the kitchen. 'Any more tea in that pot?' he inquired cheerfully, 'I could do with a drop more.' He helped himself to milk and poured tea with the detachment of self-interest. 'I'm off now, Mother. Don't mind, do 'ee?'

91

She nodded absently. 'Ringing, are you?'

'George have got a peal organized for some visitors from somewhere. I said I'd go along.' He bent his growing height to kiss her on the cheek, buttoned his raincoat and was gone.

'And now, my lady,' said Mother firmly, turning back to me, 'I want a straight answer. Did you mean Hester?'

It seemed that there was to be no escape. I sighed and said, 'Yes, Hester.'

It was a while before she spoke. Then she gave a long sigh and laid down her cloth. 'I suppose I was foolish not to listen to you before, Abbie. You did try to warn me, didn't you? You did try.'

'Yes,' I said, 'I did try to warn you.'

'He do love her, don't he, Abbie.'

'Yes Mother, I believe he does.'

She was silent for a moment. 'I should have known it years ago, I suppose. The signs were all there.' She hesitated. 'Did you ever tell Hester?'

'No.' I shook my head. 'I never said a word.'

Mother said sombrely, 'Poor Joseph.' She stared out into the garden at the rain, now falling in relentless sheets across the cabbage patch and Father's carrot-tops, and sighed again. From the living room came the low buzz of desultory conversation, and the sweet acrid smell of tobacco. 'Ah well, perhaps it's just as well she don't know, Abbie.' She paused, and then she said thoughtfully, 'I wonder how things would have been if she had felt the same about him?'

There was a long silence. I followed her gaze out into the dripping garden and the trees beyond.

'Hester?' I said, and I dropped my voice. 'I hope for her sake that she never realizes it, but Hester has loved him for as long as I remember.'

Chapter Nine

THE FRUIT

IN SEPTEMBER WE had our fourth letter from Hester. It was addressed to me this time and I got it from the postman and read it sitting on my bed upstairs before Mother even knew of its arrival.

'Dear Abbie,' I read.
Thanks very mutch for your last letter, David is well and hope you are all well also at home we are haveing nice wether here – I wish you would come to see me Abbie – David is bisy with work, ringing a bit now and then he rang a peel with some chaps from Devon on a tour last week – I miss you Abbie and the others Doctor says I am to have a baby at Xmas – love from Hester

I sat on the side of my bed with her letter in my hands and blinked hard. I read it again, put it down, thought for a bit, picked it up again and read it through a third time with a growing sense of disbelief. Then I went down to Mother with it.

Mother took the letter from my outstretched hand and read it through and through again as I had done.

'Well!' she said at last, her plump face flushed. 'Well, my dear life and soul! En't that handsome? A baby she says; baby!' She looked at me uncertainly. 'I must go and tell your father right away. Garfield! Look at this here letter from Hester!' And she was gone, panting up the orchard path to the woodshed, apron strings flying, her bunched-up hair dangling wispy streamers from an unravelling bun. Father emerged irritably, bow in hand, to see what all the commotion was about.

'A letter to Abbie from Hester,' cried Mother. 'Look Garfield! She says she's to have a baby come Christmas – here, look! Tis here in black and white.' She shoved the quivering letter under Father's nose. He took it and read it, nodding 'Very nice,' and handed it back to her. He began to make adjustments to a string, frowning with fierce concentration as he turned a peg with meticulous care, head sideways, listening intently. Mother stared at him aghast, turned on her heel and returned to me, presumably for more satisfactory appraisal of the news. Father, with a shrug, withdrew to his shed, and after a few minutes we heard him beginning to labour hymns with the fanaticism of a broody hen. Like a mother with a child was Father with his violin. He once let me hold the neck of it and pull the bow across the awkward strings; they scraped and shrieked under my fingers until he snatched it out of my hands and began to stroke it tenderly, soothing it like you would a baby. Then he put it under his chin and began to play a quick tune, light and cheerful, as if to reassure it, the bow in Father's hands hopping and leaping over the strings with a mellow confidence all its own. I believe it meant almost more to him than did his children.

Mother could think of nothing else but Hester's coming baby and, once she was over the initial surprise, she was seized by a frenzy of joy. 'My first grandchild, Abbie,' she said, hugging the letter to her bosom and fairly dancing round the room. 'Oh, my dear life, the thought of it! I shall dearly love to have a grandchild. I'd hoped for this on the quiet at the wedding, but I never thought they'd oblige me so soon. Just think of it, Abbie! A dear little maid – or a boy, I suppose it could be, couldn't it – with maybe Hester's goldy hair and that sweet smile of hers. Oh my dear life, just think of it!'

It struck me afterwards as slightly odd that we should all think so naturally of Hester as one of our very own. She was, after all, only a cousin. Mother talked incessantly of her

94

coming grandchild, and yet, strangely, nobody troubled to point out that Mother would in fact only be a great-aunt, and that by marriage only. I felt in my own mind that I was going to be an aunty, and so did Lissie, which was an odd thing when you came to think of it.

Mother sent congratulations straight away, then heaps of advice and knitted garments by nearly every post. The living room was littered with scraps of baby-wool, little bundles of white and yellow knitting, and bootee patterns. Father, when he could detach his mind from the carrots, violin rosin and wine-yeasts, seemed fairly interested, and that was a lot for him. Lissie was quietly delighted, but practical as ever. 'Will Hester have the baby at home, do you think, Abbie?' she would ask. 'Or would it be in the hospital?'

'I don't know,' I replied. 'At home, I should imagine, now they've found a little house. I believe the nurse comes to your house to deliver the baby if the conditions are all right, and that's what the mother wants.'

It all made little difference to Perran's life, babies being so far removed from his sphere and experience as to be almost extra-terrestrial. Mother spent all her spare time sewing the scraps of knitting into little coats and socks and minute vests, and I was commissioned to take them all hot-foot to Truro, along with assorted pots of jam and bramble jelly, three jars of green tomato pickle, a tin of baby-powder, a yellowing shawl that had at various times been used for every one of us, a bunch of parsley, as many apples as I could carry and a set of ancient leather reins with bells along the front.

I got a Saturday off from the shop and set out on a golden day in early October. Summer had lingered late that year and although the lanes were full of swirling leaves, it was still quite warm. I carried my bulging bags out into the lane and kissed Mother goodbye at the gate.

'Now,' she said, 'have you got everything, my love? Have you put Lissie's shortbread down the side so it don't get shaken about too much? And Thomas's mirror? Don't let it

95

get broken, Abbie; it would break his heart. Spent ages, he did, on fitting it into the frame all nice and neat. Got it safe, have you, my love?'

'Yes, yes,' I reassured her, 'they're all safe. I've got the jam at the bottom of the basket, under the vests. Don't worry, they'll be all right.'

'Give her our dear love, Abbie, won't you,' she urged. 'Tell her to take care of my grandchild, and make sure she gets enough to eat. She don't have to eat for two, but eat sensibly, plenty of salad and stuff. Tell her a baby needs more than porridge to grow on. You know what Hester is like. Porridge, porridge, three times a day that girl would eat if you gave her leave.'

'Yes, Mother,' I promised, waving. Lissie, chin in hands, watched me enviously from an upstairs window, and returned a plump palm. Thomas's curly head bobbed up and down beside the living room curtains. He looked up absent-mindedly and gave me a brief wave.

It was good to be off on a trip and I sang as I walked down the lane to catch the train. The autumnal tints of tree and bushes swirled about my feet with the falling leaves and the warm air had a new freshness in it, hint of coming winter. I paused to rearrange my bags more comfortably, then picked up a fair speed, and walking quickly past the farm cottages I headed for the main road, which would take me to the station.

As I passed Joseph's cottage I saw him in the garden. He had his foot on a spade and was smoking his pipe with his back to the gate, absorbed in his digging. What looked like the beginnings of a bonfire smouldered away in a pile beside him, and amidst the wraiths of bonfire and tobacco smoke he looked vague and ethereal, a figure shrouded in cloud. He turned, hearing footsteps in the quiet lane, and saw me through the smoke. He raised a hand in greeting and then went back to his digging. I wondered if he had heard about Hester's baby, and if he would care. Perhaps I ought to tell him.

I stopped by the gate and carefully lowered my bags to

96

the ground. He turned again and peered through the smoke, surprised to see me stop. Politely, with an inquiring smile, he came towards me, looming up out of the smoke like a phantom assuming human form. He took his pipe from his mouth and gravely nodded to me. 'Morning Abbie. Off to town, are you?'

'Hello Joseph,' I said lamely, suddenly wondering what on earth I had got to say after all. I decided to let the moment take its own course, and then go. I would leave him to find out about the baby from Mother, Father or the vicar; anyone but me. I could not say it. 'No,' I said, 'I'm going over to Truro on the train.'

He nodded. 'Oh,' he said. He tapped his pipe out on the gate-post and the spent tobacco fluttered to the ground. 'To see Hester,' I told him. He nodded again. His eyes fell upon my bags. 'Taking her a few things from Mother,' I added awkwardly. I wondered whether he could see the contents from his angle.

'When's the big day, then?' he asked.

I swallowed. 'Big day?'

'When's it due? She's having a little one, isn't she?'

'Christmas,' I said. So he knew. There was a silence, awkward on my part, but not on Joseph's, I don't think. He had a quality of stillness about him so that silence hung about him always. With everyone else I'd ever known silence was a clumsy, embarrassing thing, a vacant gap between reassuring noises. With Joseph it was the reverse. It was speech that intruded. He was like the earth itself: profound, recondite. I had a sudden strange thought of Hester lying in the earth one day, safe in Joseph's arms; and, faint and unbidden, the memory came back to me of her extraordinary words that Christmas in the churchyard. I shook myself for being foolish, and dragged my attention back. Joseph was speaking to me, slowly, as he always did, with his warm voice. 'That was a proper supper your mother gave me the other week, Abbie. Tell her . . .' A chuckle crept into his voice, 'she do make a lovely pie.'

His kind grey eyes were gazing at me clearly, with

nothing to be read there but quietness and that rare quality of calm he had. Perhaps his turn of phrase was just coincidence, but hadn't I said those very words to Mother in the kitchen after supper: 'You make a lovely pie'?

'I'll tell her,' I said, in thinly-veiled confusion, and bent to pick up my bags. I turned to go, but he stopped me with a word.

'Abbie!' He paused, as if an idea had come to him, laid his pipe on the gate-post, and motioned me to wait. 'There's something here belongs to her. Perhaps you'd better take it to her for me.' He turned and went into the house, scraping his boots lightly on the step, and returned almost immediately with something in his hands. It was a smallish wooden object, and with it he had brought a paper-bag. I looked down at it in his fine, strong hands.

'For the kiddie,' he said, by way of explanation, but I needed none. I watched him put the object carefully into the paper-bag. He handed it to me, picked up his pipe and, with a brief wave, went back to his digging. And I went on my way.

Further up the road and out of sight, I took it out and looked at it. It was a baby's rattle: a lovely piece of workmanship, fashioned with skill and a good deal of hard work no doubt. It was made in pear-wood, with patterns round the handle and a smooth polished top, jointed in two places. Inside was something that jingled and chimed when it was moved or turned.

The day that had seemed so fresh and fine when I set out seemed sombre now, and the bright trees bent over in the lane and dropped their dead leaves and wept. I tucked the rattle in its paper-bag into the deep safety of my basket and stepped out into the road which would take me to the station. And all the way to Truro in the train, I cried.

Chapter Ten

THE THORN

I FOUND THE house without much difficulty: third in a row of narrow terraced cottages that elbowed each other for a place on either side of a narrow street which ran sharply downwards into another one: bleak, grey, low-roofed granite buildings with small blank windows and a front door which went straight up from the street. I stood before the door, my hands holding the handles of my bags and basket, and felt a strange flutter inside me, that could have been anxiety. I put the bags to the ground and knocked resolutely.

For a long time there was silence, then footsteps sounded somewhere within the house. A handle rattled, a scrape, and the door opened, and Hester stood there in the doorway.

We stared at each other for a while in disbelief, neither of us moving. Then she opened her mouth, and words came tumbling out. 'Oh, Abbie!' she cried, in a voice eager with joy. 'Oh, Abbie, you came! I never thought you really would. Oh, it's so good to see you!' Her hands pulled at me, clutched at my bags, and dragged me in through the door. 'When I got your letter telling me you were coming I was afraid you would change your mind. It's such a way on the train, and carrying all this stuff too! What is it? Oh, baby-clothes. What's this at the bottom of this one? Jam? Jam from Aunty Susan? Oh Abbie, look! Damson and plum and cherry!' Her hands rummaged in childish delight about the bag, feeling and guessing, and lifted out pots of Mother's jam, thick and dark, and resonant with the feel of home. I stood aside to look at her.

She was thinner, there was no doubt of that. The angle of her jaw was sharp against the dark stuff of her dress, and her wrists looked almost stick-like. Her tangled hair was piled up on her head in some confusion and her small hands snatched at bits of it and pushed it impatiently back up again as it fell from time to time about her ears. Her neck was thinner too, and the soft bloom of country air had gone. Only her swollen waist and the mound of clothes about her middle belied the thinness and made her seem like some badly made doll unevenly stuffed with sawdust. 'Hester!' I cried. 'Are you eating properly, child? You're so thin! You look as if you've been eating nothing at all for weeks. Oh Hester, Mother would have a fit!'

She gave me her smile, the quick fleeting one and, looking downwards, put her hands around her stomach. 'Thin?' she asked.

'Oh, I don't mean the baby,' I said quickly. 'But the rest of you. Look at your arms!'

'Yes,' she said briefly, 'I'm eating enough.' She leaned forward eagerly, 'Show me what you've brought from home. Oh Abbie, it's lovely to see you!'

'Where's David?' I asked her.

The briefest look of disquiet crossed her face. 'David? Oh, David's working. At the shop, of course.'

'Oh, of course,' I said. There was the merest pause. I looked around me at the room, for something to do.

'Do you like it?' she asked me. 'David was very lucky to get it so cheap. It isn't far from the shops. The station's quite near too, isn't it?'

'Yes,' I said, 'it's nice.' It seemed exactly that: plain, remarkably lacking in any sort of personality, and very, very clean. That much was obvious. It looked to me as if Hester must have spent all her time cleaning and polishing and scrubbing at it to make it shine with so much painful cleanliness. But it was a sort of empty shine, quite clinical; not at all the sort of cheerful disorder that we were used to at home.

'Let me make you some tea, Abbie,' she was saying

eagerly. 'I've longed and longed for you to come, you don't know how much. I planned to make you tea. You'll have something to eat, too, won't you? Some cake? I've made a bit of heavy-cake. It's such a long way on the train from home, too, you must be some tired. Sit yourself down, Abbie, while I put the kettle on. Oh, the lovely, lovely jam! It so reminds me of home. And apples, too? And what's this? Oh, knitting. And more knitting. And look at this, pickle! No, I won't look at any more of it until we have our tea.'

I began to feel a sense of vague unease. Hester was chattering away, it was true, but too rapidly, with a sort of brilliant desperation in her voice. Her eyes were bright, and she rushed restlessly about getting me a cup of tea, and cake, and asking me question after question about Mother and Thomas and Father and Lissie and home. She exclaimed endlessly over Mother's pots of jam and pickle, and Lissie's shortbread, and insisted on my eating a piece right away.

'And you too, Hester,' I said. 'You must try a piece, too. After all, Lissie sent it for you and David. You haven't even had your tea.'

'Not just now,' she said, brushing the shortbread aside with a wave of her hand. 'What else is there in your bags, Abbie? Oh, it's like Christmas!'

'Plenty of baby-clothes, bonnets and vests, and little knitted boots; and oh yes, Thomas has sent you a mirror with a frame that he made you. I hope it hasn't got smashed – he'd never forgive me if I'd broken it on the way here.'

She took the mirror from me and turned it over in her hands. 'It's beautiful!' she said breathlessly. 'Oh Abbie, it's lovely! Please tell Thomas it's the nicest mirror I've ever had.'

Then we began on the village. She wanted to know how the vicar was, and the shop, and Mrs Blamey, and the churchyard birds, and we had a long and frenzied (I thought) conversation about trivialities like the scratches on Thomas's knees. Every time the conversation seemed to show any sign of turning in her own direction she would deftly steer it away again until in desperation I stopped her headlong rush of chatter and asked her outright.

'And you, Hester – how are you?'

She began to look like a cornered animal. I was oddly reminded of poor Jacky all those years ago, crouching on its perch. Her hands grew restless and began to fiddle with the handle of the teapot, and she said with breathless haste, 'I don't want to talk about my doings, Abbie. I want to hear about home.'

'Well, you have heard,' I told her. 'You've heard already all there is to hear. Lanissick is really just the same as usual, exactly as it was when you left it last March, and no doubt exactly as it will be next year as well.'

'But I want to hear everything. Oh Abbie, I miss it so!' There was a low choke in her voice. I looked closely at her. This seemed to be a cry far nearer the truth than any of our conversation so far. Her anxious eyes looked up at me across the little room and pleaded silently. I risked the question.

'Aren't you happy, Hester?'

She gave that small tight little smile that I knew so well and looked down at her hands clenched together in her lap. She began to fiddle with her wedding ring, sliding it up and down the thin finger. 'Oh yes,' she said quickly, but that old closed-in look was back, 'David's very good to me. Quite wonderful, in fact.'

I thought of Joseph's words in the churchyard that evening before the wedding: 'David's a nice chap – he'll be good to her.' There was a clock on the narrow mantelshelf above the hearth; it dropped loud ticks into the silence. I waited for her to speak again. She didn't.

'And you're having a baby, Hester! That must make you very happy.'

She looked up at me, her thin face pale in the light from the small window, and caught her hands nervously together. She fidgeted with her fingers.

'Is David pleased?' I asked her gently.

She nodded.

'Are you frightened, Hester? Are you frightened of the birth?'

She looked quickly up at me and bit her lips until they went white, with small patches of blue between the teeth marks.

'It can't be that bad,' I said, with a bright attempt at reassurance. 'Mother had four babies; quite easily, I think. Why don't you ask her what it's like?'

Her thin cheeks filled suddenly with colour. 'Come home?' she asked me tremulously. 'Could I come home?'

'Well, yes,' I said, 'to see us. Couldn't you, Hester? Would David mind, do you think?'

She seemed not to have heard me. Her eyes were on the sky beyond the window and I wondered at the look of rapture on her face. Then she started, and looked down at her great mound of stomach, and said tonelessly, 'No – how could I? Not like this.'

'Would you like Mother to come here, to see you?' I asked her gently. 'Then you could talk about it, the birth and everything, with her.'

She looked up at me and said yes, but without much interest.

'But you do want to see her, don't you, Hester?' I pursued.

She nodded listlessly. Her eyes moved to the clock and a shadow seemed to cross her face. 'It's time,' she said.

I wondered for a moment if she meant it was time for me to go, but there was a sudden rattle at the door. Hester said, 'David', and the little drawn smile was back. She got slowly to her feet and crossed to the door to open it. David came into the room, shook hands with me, and gave me a boyish smile aching with earnestness.

'Hello Abigail. Nice to see you. It seems a long time, doesn't it.' His eyes fell tenderly upon Hester, and he flushed. 'And how do you think she's looking? Marvellous, isn't she. Married life suits her, don't you think? There's our proof, too!'

I saw Hester flinch, almost imperceptibly. David smiled again, and took off his jacket. He hung it up on a hook fixed to the back of the door, and waited. I wondered if Hester would offer to make him tea; it seemed inappropriate for me to do so.

'Kettle on the boil is it, petal?' He rubbed his hands together rather tensely. 'I'll make it, shall I? Have you made Abigail a cup? Oh yes, I see you have. I'll go and make my own.'

There seemed to be a very slight constraint between them, but I dismissed it as probable embarrassment at my presence. David went into the kitchen in search of tea, and Hester and I sat down again.

'He looks well,' I said brightly, after a pause.

'Yes,' she said. 'He keeps very well.'

The little clock on the mantelpiece ticked on. The sound of the kettle being filled came to us from the kitchen, then the quick small pop of a gas-flame, a muffled bump and scrape.

'David's put the kettle on,' Hester said lamely.

I nodded. The smell of gas drifted through to us. I tapped my fingers on my knees, and then looked down. For something to do I bent and rummaged through the basket by my feet, between the knitting and the parsley and the jam and vests, and brought out Joseph's present in its paper-bag.

'Here, Hester,' I said, 'I nearly forgot. Joseph sent you this.'

Her head shot up. Her eyes stared at me like great pools, for a moment deep with what looked like fear.

'Why Hester!' I said in concern. 'You've gone very white. Are you all right? Is it the baby, Hester? Shall I call David?'

She shivered, then took a deep breath. She said in a level tone, 'No. I'm quite all right.' She swallowed heavily. She held out her hand for the bag, and her fingers were shaking.

'Are you sure you're all right?' I asked her. 'You've gone a very funny colour.'

She nodded firmly. 'Just a twinge. What is it, Abbie, in the bag? What has Joseph sent me?'

104

'A rattle,' I told her. 'Oh Hester, it's beautiful. Take it out and see. It's for your baby.'

She put her trembling fingers into the bag and took the rattle out.

'Shake it!' I said eagerly. 'It makes a lovely noise.'

She did so, and the little bell rang inside it. Her face in the afternoon light coming through the window was set, rigid with pain. A curious misty look was in her eyes, a strange look of slight enchantment, as if she were listening to something far away. Then she said, very quietly to herself, as if she were quite alone, 'Oh God. Not that. Please not.'

Mother was avid for news when I got back. The train journey home was tiring, but more with the effort of planning what I would say to them all than anything else. I walked up the lane in the level evening light, my arms swinging without the laden bags I had set off with, but my steps heavy. It was only about eight in the evening but the curtains in all the cottage windows were drawn before their cosy lights, and the world seemed full of shade. For a Saturday evening it was very quiet. I went in through the cottage gate and Father, rubbing rosin on his violin bow, met me at the door.

'Well, Abbie,' he said, looking at me through his eyebrows, 'is it well with Hester?'

'Yes, Father,' I sighed, 'all well.'

Mother came rushing out, beaming. 'Did you see her, Abbie? Did you find the house? Did Hester give you tea?' She clucked over me like an anxious hen. 'My dear life, I don't give you a minute to get in first, do I! Perran? Perran! Oh, where's the lad to? Gone again. Well, Lissie, put the kettle on, my 'ansome, and make poor Abbie tea. And Thomas, get your drawings off that chair and let the poor girl sit down.'

When I had sat and drunk my tea and answered a few of Mother's questions, Father peered at me rather closely and asked, 'But is the child well?'

'As much as anyone could tell, I suppose, Father,' I answered with a half-laugh, 'for it's not supposed to be born until Christmas.'

He frowned at me. 'I don't mean the baby, and you know it, Abbie. I mean, is Hester well in herself?'

'She's well,' I answered carefully. 'She's thinner, but she's well.'

'Eating enough?' Mother asked me anxiously.

'I imagine so,' I told her, 'for they had supper while I was there and Hester had made pasties and a great stack of heavy-cake.'

'And the baby!' cried Mother. 'Is it definite?'

'Definite?' I had to laugh. 'If a great huge six-month stomach that jumps and kicks is anything to go by, then it's definite!' and they all laughed; and Mother beamed and put her big arms round me and hugged me in delight. Lissie looked envious, and Thomas cried, 'Abbie! Abbie, did you give her my mirror?'

'Yes I did, my poppet, and she said to thank you and to tell you that it was . . . the nicest one she's ever owned.'

Thomas's earnest face glowed, and Lissie brightened.

'Did she like my shortbread, Abbie? Did she think it as good as Mother's?'

'Yes, she did,' I said, 'to the last crumb!'

And they all went away satisfied.

Later, when we were alone, Mother asked the question I had been dreading. 'But is she happy, Abbie? Is Hester truly happy?'

I answered it the way I'd planned, the only way I could. 'She'd like to see you, Mother, very much. She's frightened of the pains when they come. She thinks that after four babies of your own you'd be able to tell her what to do.'

Mother glowed. 'She's like a daughter to me, do you know that, Abbie? She's as precious, almost, as a daughter of my own.'

'And a sister to me, Mother,' I answered soberly.

'Shall I go over and see her, do you think, my love? She can't get over here, and that's for sure.'

I sighed with relief, for the moment I'd dreaded was past. 'I'm sure she'd love you to,' I said. 'Why don't you go when she's nearer to her time?'

'Could you look after things here for a bit, if I stopped over? Father's meals and all that?'

'Of course,' I said. 'Lissie can help me with the cooking. You could go for a week, or more if you wanted to, and be there when the baby's born.'

In her delight she threw her arms about me and gave me another bear-hug. 'You're a dear daughter to me, Abbie, a dear, dear girl. Three daughters I've got, and that's a fact. Three lovely daughters, and all as precious to me as each other. So Hester and the dear baby's well. That's what I wanted to hear. I'm happy now.'

She went off into the kitchen to wash up the cups, and temporarily at least, I hoped, all her fears were reassured.

I could not escape so easily from Father. He stopped me at the corner of the staircase on my way up to bed, his hand upon my arm. He jerked his head towards the kitchen and lowered his voice. 'Now she's out of earshot, I want the truth. How is the girl?'

'The truth, Father?'

'Oh, you do know what I mean, Abbie. There's something isn't exactly right, I can tell. Oh, never mind your mother – she's so mazed by the thought to have a grandchild that she don't notice it. But I know you, Abbie. I've knowed you all your life. Out with it! There's something isn't right with Hester. What is it?'

'There's nothing wrong with her, Father.'

'Dammit girl, what's the matter with you? All this heaving and dodging and bobbing about. The truth, now! Isn't she happy with the fellow?'

'No, Father, I don't think she is.'

'The baby, is it? I hope tis only the baby. One of they women's complaints like blood-pressure, is it? What do the doctor say?'

'She's not ill, Father, just – not happy. She seems sort of hungry inside, somehow, and desperate for something.' I

107

hesitated. 'Perhaps, at a time like this, she needs her own mother.'

He shot me a warning look and began to cough, low in his throat.

'Father,' I said urgently, catching at the chance. 'What about her parents? I know her mother was your sister; but what about her father? Who was he?'

I regretted the question almost at once. A tightness had come over his face and his mouth had a grey, pinched look.

'I'm sorry, Father,' I stumbled on, 'but it seems to me that now we're old enough to understand it might be as well if we knew the truth. Was Hester a love-child? What harm could there be if she found out now? It might make certain things about her easier to understand.'

'I don't know who her father was,' he said, and his voice was slow and hard, and grated like ice on iron. 'I don't never want you to speak of this matter again, do you understand?' I dared not look at his face. 'Not to me, nor your mother, nor Liss, and certainly never to Hester. Tis something that was all over and done with years ago. Don't ever speak of it again.'

I turned to look at him, and was shocked to see his face. There was something there that I'd never seen before, a kind of haunted look, as if a moment long-dreaded had at last come to pass. There was weariness in it, and fear too, and suddenly he looked an old man. He sighed heavily, and passed his hand across his face. Then he said, more kindly, 'Don't ask me to tell you, Abbie. There's a great deal of pain in it; and there's some things past telling, even to a daughter. Tis best forgotten.'

He turned to go and then stopped, his hand on the door-knob, and turned back to me. 'She should have married him, Abbie. I'd have thought you'd have been able to make her see sense. Hester should have married him.'

'Him?' I echoed blankly. 'Him? Who, Father?'

'Why, Joseph, of course,' he said. 'She should have married Joseph. He's the only chap who could have saved her from herself. That boy – what's his name, David? He'll never do it.'

It struck me afterwards that it was a very odd thing to say about a son-in-law.

Chapter Eleven

THE WIND

THAT SUMMER LISSIE had had her fourteenth birthday and
Thomas his eleventh. Thomas was growing fast. From a
placid toddler, he was turning into a cheerful, curly-headed
youngster who sang in the church choir on Sundays and
lived in a world of his own. He was a solitary, creative child.
He seemed to have inherited Father's passion for beauty
but with Thomas it was drawing. He lived to draw. That
autumn Perran bought him a great thick pad of paper and
some drawing pencils and Thomas was lost to us from then.
Head down and pencil scribbling away, he drew everything
in sight, from flowers to pots of jam, Lissie when she'd sit for
him and Mother kneading dough.

We'd heard nothing from Hester and no news from
David so we presumed the lack of it was good. About this
time Mother began to get bad headaches and a flashing in
her eyes when she was tired. The doctor came and said it
was blood-pressure and that she must rest a lot, and so in
the end she didn't go to Truro for the baby's birth.

We wrote long letters to Hester, full of news of home,
such as there was. Mother wrote to tell her what to do about
the pains when they started, and what to get ready;
although privately I thought the district midwife would
have been more up-to-date with that kind of advice. Lissie
and I took over the household while Mother stayed in bed
and rested away the mornings and got up to potter about
when the headaches were not too bad.

Perran was seventeen now, and very tall; taller than
Father by a good few inches. He was much taken up with a
girl he'd met at work, Jennifer Ennory, a pretty, dark-

haired girl (he said) from the other side of our nearest town. Her father had a small bakery business with a shop, and took Perran on as a baker's apprentice. Jennifer worked behind the counter selling bread and splits and fancy cakes, and Perran bought himself a motor-bike and roared off on it to work there every morning.

Then, in mid-December, when the holly berries were glowing scarlet on the bush in the church field, we had our last letter from Hester. The postman brought it one morning, slipping on the ice in the lane and swearing softly under his breath and gripping the brakes of his bicycle. I took the letter up to Mother in her bed. She stayed there most mornings now until dinner-time. When we called her she would come down and eat a bit, but she was getting thinner and losing her rosy colour, and had begun to look older too.

'Look Mother!' I said brightly. 'Something to cheer you up. A letter from Hester.'

She took it from me and looked at the writing. ''Tis addressed to you, Abbie, not me. You'd better open it.'

And I did so, sitting there beside her on the bed. I read it through, silently at first, until Mother asked, 'Any news, is there? She hasn't had the babe early, has she? Abbie, is there news? Tell me!'

'No,' I answered. 'No news yet. But she doesn't think it will be long.' I put the letter down in my lap, considering what to tell Mother; for indeed it was the strangest letter I have ever had, and very short.

'Dear Abbie,' (it said).
Please come, You must be heir I cannt bear it if you dont come – I think the babies dead – please come – please come – love Hester.

'Can I read it?' Mother pleaded. 'I've no doubt she's getting really excited by now. Do she sound happy? Oh Abbie, I remember how I felt just before you were born: very chuffed and half-frightened and longing, afraid it wouldn't start and half-afraid it would.' She stared at me anxiously. 'You don't mind if I read it, do you, my love? You don't mind?'

'No Mother,' I said, 'I don't mind,' and I handed the letter to her.

She read it through slowly. Outside, although it was still morning, the wind began to get up from the hill and rattled the glass in the windows with a dry whispering ease. The flames in Mother's little bedroom grate danced up the chimney and threw off the smell of applewood, for we were burning the branches of a dead tree that Father had cut down. The room was very quiet. Thomas was at school and below us in the kitchen Lissie rattled saucepans as she went about the dinner. She was humming softly to herself and the sound came up through the floor-boards, gentle and half-muffled, like a bee.

Mother read the letter slowly, with her reading glasses on, and then laid it down thoughtfully, with a frown between her brows. 'Oh dear,' she said, 'oh dear, oh dear.' She looked up at me over the spectacles. 'What do she mean, Abbie? There's no word for me.'

'Just thoughtless,' I said, patting her hand. 'You know what women are like with their first baby – you told me yourself that you can think of nothing else at such a time.'

'But she sounds so desperate, Abbie,' said Mother, voicing my thoughts. 'Cold, and so strange, and so afraid. And that bit "I think the baby's dead" – why do you suppose she thinks that?'

'I expect she's just panicky,' I said, with more conviction than I felt. 'Perhaps the baby's not moving about as much as it was or something, and she's afraid it's stopped altogether.'

Mother squeezed my hand with relief. 'That's it – you're right! You're quite right. They do stop moving about just before the pains start. It comes back to me now.' She shook her head, as if to sort out her thoughts. 'One of us must go over there, Abbie, and stay with her until the babe is born. I dearly wanted to go myself, but I'm afraid it'll have to be you. Do you mind, my love?'

'Oh no,' I said, 'I don't mind, Mother. But can you cope without me here? What about the housework?'

'Oh, we'll be all right.' She paused, making plans. 'Thomas and Perran can help out with the cleaning for a bit – it'll do them good. Perran's a man now, and courting that girl Jennifer. He seems very set on her, don't he? Here, did you notice his face the other day when we were speaking about Hester's babe in front of him? Went quite red, he did. I think he's serious about her, Abbie. He's awful young, but he's level-headed, is Perran. I should like to see 'en settle down with some nice girl. Now, tell me, will Lissie mind about doing all the cooking, do you think?'

I said I was sure she wouldn't mind. She was a home-loving little thing, and loved nothing better than to potter about with food. In that she was certainly Mother's daughter.

I said, 'What about Thomas? Will he mind about my going?'

She laughed. 'Thomas wouldn't notice if the roof blew off and the house fell down about his ears.' She sighed. 'The boy's so dreamy, Abbie, sometimes I wonder what will become of him. He's so taken up with drawing pictures day and night that I wonder sometimes if he even knows his own name, or who we are.'

Then we both laughed, and I put away the letter, and went to tell Father in the woodshed what we had decided to do. Father grunted, put down his violin, wound down the bow, and came indoors to help us plan, which was a great thing for him to do in the middle of a piece.

When Perran came home that evening, cold but flushed from the sharp wind in his ears, we told him about the arrangements. Perran nodded and offered to give me a lift into Truro in the morning on the back of his bike to save the train fare.

'It's out of your way,' I said doubtfully. 'Are you sure? I don't want to make you late for work.'

He shrugged. 'That's all right, we'll leave a bit earlier. Cor – I'm some thirsty. Make us a cup of tea, Liss?'

'Here Abbie,' said Mother, 'you'll have to go up and see Mrs Blamey about the shop, won't you? Do you think she'll mind doing without you for a bit?'

I said I'd go and have a word with her after supper and that I didn't think she'd mind much as things were fairly quiet, being winter.

I packed my things in a small suitcase: washing things and enough clothes for a week or so, a few more bits and pieces for Hester, our Christmas presents for them both and one for the baby, and then I was ready.

'You'd better stay over Christmas if you have to,' Mother said. 'The baby might be late; first ones are, sometimes. Give Hester our dear love, and tell her to bring the baby home to see us as soon as she can, after. I want to see my first grandchild awful bad.'

It was only later that I remembered again that Hester was not actually her daughter, and only Father's niece.

That evening, on the way back from seeing Mrs Blamey, I went up to the church and sat in a pew all alone. It was cold in the soft gloom and I wrapped my collar up round my ears and sat thinking for a long while, moved by the silence. I'd never been very religious but somehow I felt a need for guidance and for something firm to hold on to in the days that lay ahead. It was as if I was going to have to handle something old and swift and fierce, that had stirred in the earth long ago, and had no name; a thing that, thrust aside and denied, had somehow grown fiercer and more turbulent because of denial, and the only name I could have put to it was love.

We set off in the morning. Perran wheeled out his motorbike, adjusted his goggles and buckled his helmet under his chin. He tied my battered suitcase on the back, shaking it vigorously to check that it was secure.

'I shall have to go very slow,' he said, 'on account of the roads are very slippery with ice. But I'm used to it, don't worry.'

I prayed that Mother wouldn't hear, or she might have

forbidden either of us to go at all. He showed me how to sit astride the saddle behind him, with my arms about his waist. I had a great feeling of safety with him in control up front and, as he jabbed the kick-start several times and a great cloud of roaring white smoke rose from the exhaust, a certain awe of the man who was my brother. He had a new air of assurance about him. We'd seen little enough of him lately, with him being so tied up with the bakery and Jennifer, and I realized with a sense of some surprise that he was almost a stranger to me.

I'd said goodbye to Mother in her bed, after breakfast. I told her not to worry and that I would send news as soon as I could before the baby's birth, and afterwards of course. While I was kissing her Lissie came in with steaming tea for her on a tray, and an egg and toast, and Mother said, 'See what lovely girls I've got?' and became a little weepy. We plumped up her pillows and patted her hands and cut the top off her egg for her, and Lissie buttered her toast.

I left them there, with Lissie sitting on the side of Mother's bed and making out a shopping list; with Mother nibbling the toast and Lissie saying, 'Flour, Mother? Salt? How about a drop of soup for dinner? I could make a nice soup from a few onions. And how are we off for cheese?' I left them to it. Thomas was still at the table in the living room crunching toast with an air of deep preoccupation; and Father, believe it or not, Father was at the sink.

'Washing up, Father?' I asked, for such a thing was unheard of. 'What's come over you?'

He grunted and turned to glower pleasantly at me, then gave his little dry cough and cleared his throat and a twinkle came into his eye. 'Get off with you,' he said. 'Off on your joy-ride, my girl. Got to keep the place tidy while you're gone, haven't I?'

From outside the back door Perran's muffled voice called out, 'Are you well wrapped-up, girl? It's icy cold out here.'

Father gave me a narrow look. 'You won't say nothing to Hester about – er, about the other business, will you, Ab?'

'The other business, Father?'

'About Joseph. Don't say a word, will you. Tis between you and me.'

'No Father, I won't say a word.' I pulled on my warmest gloves and as I bent forward to kiss him on his leathery cheek, his familiar smell of tweed and tobacco assailed me; and thus fortified, I went out into the cold morning.

We'd set off much earlier than we needed to, I thought, but we travelled slowly, for the roads were perilous with early frost, and Perran drove carefully and kept to the sides of the road.

Before reaching Truro we stopped off at a little café with gingham curtains half-way down the windows and checkered table-cloths and a warm atmosphere of steam and cigarette smoke, and Perran bought me tea. I sat at a table in front of a window dripping with condensation and watched him as he waited at the counter to be served by the woman behind it. He stood there in his leather jacket and helmet, with the goggles pushed back on top; a surprisingly alien figure. He brought the tea over and gave me a self-conscious grin as he bumped the thick white china down, and slopped the tea in the saucers.

'What are you staring at?' He pushed a cup towards me. 'I thought we'd have another bit of breakfast. Do you want a pastry or sommat to eat?'

'No thanks,' I said. 'I was thinking of the little chap you used to be just a few years ago. You're a man, Perran. I'd hardly noticed it before.'

He grinned and bent over his cup. 'No one at home's got thoughts for anyone but Hester,' he said matter-of-factly. He took a long sip of tea.

I frowned. 'And Mother,' I pointed out.

'Oh yes, Mother too, I suppose. But Hester mostly.'

I considered this.

'Right, aren't I, Ab?'

'I suppose you are. Do you mind that, Perran?'

'Mind it? What's there to mind? Tis the way things are, Abbie; always have been, since she came.' He said it quite without rancour and sniffed thoughtfully, his eyes roving round the hazy room. They fell appreciatively upon the woman as she served more tea, her rounded arm upon the tall urn-handle. His eyes returned to me. 'She should have married old Joseph, you know.' He said it quite casually, almost absently.

'Why on earth do you say that?' I asked.

He stared into his tea-cup and, picking up the spoon, began to stir it carefully. 'I saw David the other day.'

'Did you?'

'Rang a quarter of doubles with him. Nice bit of striking it was, too.' He paused, and then said guardedly, 'He isn't happy, Ab.'

I traced the margin of the checks on the cloth and scraped at them with my finger-nail. 'Oh?'

'We had quite a chat, Dave and I. He says there's sommat wrong.'

I took a deep breath. 'Wrong? With the baby? Hester says she thinks it's dead.'

'No. Not with the baby. The nurse-woman says the baby's fine. Sommat wrong with Hester's mind.'

A small hammer began to throb somewhere in my throat. 'What could be wrong?' I asked. 'She's having a baby, isn't she? No woman's in her right mind when she's pregnant.'

He gave me a sudden, boyish grin. 'And what would you know about it?'

I gave him tit for tat. 'And what would you?'

'Oh, enough. More than you think.' He brushed that aside. 'He thinks there's something wrong with Hester.'

'Oh?' I said carefully. 'Such as what?'

'A sort of wildness, Dave said. Oh, I know it sounds daft, but he's not a chap to fancy things, is he?'

'I don't know,' I said. 'I hardly know him really. What does he mean?'

Perran took another sip of tea. 'He says she's awful thin and a sort of desperate look comes in her eyes sometimes, like she's trapped and can't get out. He's awful worried, Abbie. He does love the girl.'

A silence fell between us. On the other side of the room there was a rise of laughter and a clink of cutlery. Someone shouted 'I never did!' and a good-humoured argument sprang up. Perran said, almost casually, 'Jen's pregnant.'

I closed my eyes. I wondered if I'd heard him properly. When I opened them again a low colour was in his face, so I knew I'd heard correctly. I licked my dry lips. 'You?'

He pushed his cup away irritably. 'Of course it's mine.'

'But Perran, is she sure? I believe you can be wrong about it sometimes.'

'Oh yes,' he said shortly, 'she's sure.'

'What will you do?'

'Marry her, of course.'

'Do you love her?'

'I believe so. And even if I didn't, it wouldn't make no odds. I'd still marry her.'

'She sounds nice, Perran. I'd like to meet her.'

'You'd like her, Abbie, and she'd like you, too. She's quite like you in a way. Not to look at, she's very dark-haired and thinnish, but in ways.'   .

I took this as a compliment. 'Have you told them at home?'

He laughed shortly. 'No, of course I haven't. What do you take me for? I'll get it all arranged first, the wedding and that, and then I'll tell 'em.'

There seemed no more to say on the subject.

'Perran,' I asked him, 'why did you say just now that Hester should have married Joseph?'

He groaned. 'Hester, Hester! Always bloody Hester!' He sighed heavily. 'Sorry, Ab. Never mind why.'

'No Perran, it's important. Please tell me.'

He shot me a curious little look. 'Well, you know the truth of it.'

'Know?' I asked him, 'Know what?'

He folded his black leather arms before him on the table and looked me straight in the eye. 'Yes,' he said, 'Dave's right. You'd know, if anyone would.'

'Just what am I supposed to know about?' I demanded.

His eyes were challenging. 'You know it's Joseph's baby, don't you?'

Chapter Twelve

THE BIRD

THE SMOKY ROOM swung round me several times, then
stabilized. I realized Perran was staring at me with alarm
and offering me a cigarette.

'Have one, Ab,' he was saying, 'you've gone awful green.
Have one; it'll help you.'

I gasped and shook my head. 'I never have, Perran. I'd
be sick.'

'Have one!' he said firmly; so I took one, and he struck a
match and held it out to me.

'I didn't know you smoked,' I said faintly, through the
haze. 'Mother wouldn't like it.'

'Mother?' he said. 'What's she got to do with it? Here, are
you all right now? Drag on it, Ab; go on.'

I took a nervous puff. It didn't do much, but it helped to
still my trembling hands. When I could speak again I
looked at him scornfully. 'You're wrong, Perran. You're
very, very wrong. You couldn't be more wrong.'

'Couldn't I?' He faced me across the table, arms before
him. 'It's what Dave thinks. He wanted me to ask you. He
said you'd know the truth of it.'

'Well, it's a dreadful lie!' I told him angrily. 'And David
of all people should know. Why didn't he ask me himself,
anyway?'

'Hush!' said Perran urgently. 'People will hear you.'

'I don't care!' I whispered fiercely. 'Oh Perran, you
shouldn't judge Hester by Jennifer's standards . . .' I broke
off, biting my lips hard. His eyes were glittering. 'Look, I'm
sorry Perran, but it's true. Just because you and Jennifer . . .'

'Go on.'

'Well, just because you and Jen don't – you and Jen did . . .'

He was watching me with half-closed eyes. Between the lids his eyes were like ice. He moved his hands towards the cigarette packet. 'Yes, all right. I asked for that, didn't I.' He took a cigarette and slowly applied a match to it. 'Look Abbie, let's get one thing straight. David thinks the baby's not his. I wouldn't know. He asked me to try and find out the truth.'

'From me?'

'Yes, from you. He reckoned you'd be honest at least, and give a straight answer. There's sommat going on that Dave can't make out, and he took the obvious way of it, that the baby isn't his. Hell, Abbie! Any chap would.'

A curious feeling gradually stole over me; a feeling that, in this seemingly well-ordered world, two people seeing the same situation could see it quite differently. And maybe both could be quite wrong.

'But why?' I asked him. 'Why on earth should it be Joseph's baby?'

'Because, my holy little sister, Joseph Chygowan's been soft on that girl for years, any fool can see. And don't tell me you didn't know that.'

'Oh yes,' I said wearily, 'that much I did know, at least.'

'Good,' he said. 'We've got something straight then, haven't we. Do she know the chap loves her?'

'No.'

'How do she feel about him?'

I shrugged, not knowing what to answer. I felt a strange reluctance to talk about Hester at all, and even more reluctance to talk about Joseph.

Perran peered shrewdly at me. 'Here, you're not gone on him, are you, Ab?'

'No,' I said crossly. 'Of course not.'

'Who is it, then? Who've you got your eye on?'

'Oh Perran, don't!' I said impatiently. 'There's nobody, nobody I want, not yet. There's more to life than falling in love with people all the time.'

'Who said anything about falling in love? You've got to get married some time. You're a nice-looking girl, Ab. How come you haven't found anyone yet? Drink your tea, and smoke properly. Fiddling around with it, you are. Take a good drag.'

'Won't you be late for work?' I asked him. I took another puff of the alien-tasting smoke, then stubbed the cigarette out.

'No,' he said briefly. 'Sam won't mind, anyroad.'

'Sam?'

'Jen's Dad. You haven't answered my question.'

'What question?'

'How come you aren't courting?'

I shrugged.

'I suppose you never meet anyone new, really, do you? You want to leave home, Ab. Get yourself a job somewhere.'

'I've got a job,' I told him.

'What? That old shop? That's not what I'd call a job. No, you want to get yourself a proper job up-country somewhere, or in town. Learn to type, or go nursing, or whatever girls do.'

'I'm perfectly happy at home, thank you,' I said. 'And anyway, I'm needed there, what with Mother being so poorly, and Lissie still at school.'

'Oh, you've got to break away some time; you can't stay at home for ever. You want to get yourself a husband and a little family of your own. It's what it's all about, Ab.'

'What is?'

'Oh, I dunno. Life. Having your own kids, bringing them up. Seeing them grow into new people. Getting a little place of your own; working for them, putting the food into their little gobs. See them toddling about, and calling out 'Dad' to you. That's the whole point of it all, Ab. If you don't marry and have little 'uns you go to your grave alone. Have kids, and you leave sommat of yourself behind. I'll tell you something, Ab, something I wouldn't want to tell no one else but Jen. I'm really dead chuffed about this kid of mine.

So's Jen. We're going to have a little lad and call him 'Andrew' or 'Philip', and when he's old enough, he's going to learn to ring. And he'll be bright, Ab. He'll be the youngest kid in the country to ring a full peal, you'll see. We'll have his name up on a board in the tower before he's eight.'

'Poor little chap. "First peal at five" I suppose it'll say, will it?'

He grinned sheepishly at me. 'No, "First peal of Spliced Surprise while still in nappies." You're laughing at me, Ab, but I tell you, this kid of mine is going to be something special, you wait and see. Then after a bit we'll have a little girl who looks like Jen, and when she've grown a bit, she can help look after the next one.'

'You've got it all planned, haven't you, Perran?'

'Well, you've got to, haven't you?' he said offhandedly. He pushed his cup away. 'Come on, I'd better get you to Hester's. Time's getting on. Don't mention nothing about my kid to them at home, will you? Sorry to spring it all on you, Ab. It's been a bit of a shock.'

I shrugged, and we stood up. 'It's all right,' I said. 'I feel I've got to know you better in half an hour than I've done in nearly eighteen years.'

He grinned at me. 'We haven't spoken much, really, for years, have we? I'm glad we had this chat. I'm glad it's Dave's baby too, for his sake. You're a nice kid, Abbie.'

'Kid?' I said, 'I'm nearly twenty. Older than you.'

'A kid,' he said, 'a twenty-year-old kid.'

I felt as if I'd grown up in an hour.

He dropped me off in Hester's narrow little street, and handed me the suitcase. 'Are you coming in?' I asked him.

'No, I won't come in.' He nodded towards the house. 'This one, is it? Give my regards to Dave.'

'And Hester?'

He gave me a sideways look through the goggles. 'Oh, all right, and Hester too, if it makes you happy.'

'Shall I say anything, if he asks me?'

'He won't ask you, not old Dave. I'll see him next week, anyhow. I'll tell him what you said.'

'Thanks for the tea, Perran. And the lift.'

He winked and gave me a shy grin. 'Pleasure.'

'Give my regards to Jennifer. I want to meet her soon.'

He gave me a brief wave, and the engine sprang back into life. Then he was off in a cloud of smoke into the cold morning; and I knocked on Hester's door.

David opened it this time. He held out his hand and shook mine warmly. 'Hello, Abigail! My, this is a surprise. A suitcase, too? Does that mean you can stay with us for a day or two?'

'If you'll have me,' I said, shaking his hand. He was wearing red slippers on his feet, with odd socks. He looked tired, slightly drawn, but sincere as ever, as if he had been taking lessons in charm. He stood aside and waved me into the little room. It looked exactly the same as before, just as painfully clean.

'Hester!' called David. 'Come here! You've got a visitor.'

A woman came through the kitchen doorway with a cloth in her hands; a small, thin woman with an enormous swollen mound of stomach, and marigold-coloured hair scraped back into a band at the back of her head. Her face filled with colour when she saw me, and she held out trembling hands. 'Oh Abbie,' she cried, 'you *have* come! I didn't really think you'd be able to.'

'Hello Hester,' I said, staring at her. I found it difficult to believe the change that advanced pregnancy had made in her. 'Of course I came. You asked me to.'

'We're very grateful, Abigail,' David was saying. 'Hester has missed you a lot. I've been a little worried about her lately. It would be marvellous if you really can stay for a few days.' His voice was warm and charming, the voice I remembered from the wedding. Hester was still staring at me in apparent disbelief. The ghost of a smile fled across her face. 'Can you really stay, Abbie?' she was saying. 'Can they manage without you at home? Oh, is it really true?

124

What about poor Aunty Susan being in bed? Can Lissie cope on her own?'

'I've brought a suitcase with some things in it,' I told them. 'I can stay for as long as you need me to.'

'Oh, that's wonderful!' she said, and indeed she did look overjoyed. David seemed genuinely sincere this time; he shook my hand again, several times, and I thought suddenly how nice he might really be, under the surface charm.

'Oh Abbie, this is all so marvellous,' Hester said. 'I can't believe it! You're really here again, and you're not going to rush away tonight, either. How did you get here so early? David hasn't even left yet.'

'Yes, I'm sorry,' I said, 'but Perran gave me a lift in on his motor-bike on his way to work. It was too good a chance to miss.'

'Perran did? How is dear Perran? He's working in a baker's, isn't he? And didn't you tell me in a letter that he had a girlfriend, too? What's her name? What's she like? Have you met her? Oh Abbie, it seems ages since you came last time; how I've longed to hear all the news from home! How long can you stay? Really? More than a week? That's wonderful, marvellous! How's Aunty Susan? How's Uncle Garfield? How's his violin? And dear Lissie, and little Thomas? David dear, is there tea for Abbie?'

He nodded and said yes, and gave me a warm smile almost like relief. Hester took me upstairs. She went ahead of me, her slight body mounting the narrow staircase with effort. Beside us as we ascended, the dull beige wallpaper was covered with sprigs of faded yellow roses, peeling and scratched here and there above the skirting. Forget-me-nots covered the walls of the landing. Hester led me into a tiny bedroom cold, austere and also painfully clean.

'I've had it ready for weeks,' she said, 'ever since Aunty wrote and said she would come over. But I'd much rather have you, really, although don't tell her. Will you be all right in here?'

I looked round the tiny room, at its narrow bed, and chest of drawers. 'Lovely,' I said. 'I'll be fine.'

'It's nice and clean,' she said proudly. 'I cleaned it again yesterday. There's no dust, you see? You needn't worry.'

'Worry? Bless you, I'm not likely to worry about a few specks of dust here and there. I'm not used to such spotlessness at home, Hester. You'll spoil me for going back. You must spend all your time cleaning!'

She nodded. 'Yes, I do. It helps.' Suddenly the tight little smile was back.

'Oh dear,' I said, 'what's wrong, Hester?'

There were footsteps on the stairs. David came in with a tray. He glanced quickly from one to the other of us and then said lightly, 'I thought you'd like the tea up here.' He edged the tray carefully on to the chest of drawers, then looked at his watch. He kissed Hester lightly on the cheek. 'I must go, or I'll be late. I'll see you tonight, Abigail. Take care of her for me.'

When he had gone, I looked at Hester. 'He seems happy.' I handed her a cup of tea.

'Yes,' she said tonelessly, 'he's good at that.'

Her mood of swift joy at seeing me seemed to be evaporating. There was a little silence. I looked down at the cup in my hands. We sipped for a while in silence.

'How's the baby?' I asked her at length.

'Oh, well enough, I imagine. It kicks a lot at night. I have trouble sleeping. I thought for a long time that it was dead.' She said it with a curious detachment.

'Mother says they do go quiet, just before the birth,' I told her brightly. She gave me a faint smile, as if to acknowledge my attempt at reassurance, and shrugged lightly. 'It doesn't really matter. I didn't want a baby, anyway.'

'Hester! How can you say such a dreadful thing! Your own baby, Hester! Of course you want it.'

'Oh, I expect I might like it when it gets here,' she said. 'But then, I don't really know, do I? I might hate it. I didn't ask for it to come. It just happened to me, without my permission. Things do seem to do that, don't they. Have

126

you noticed? Or perhaps they don't to you. I know what! If I don't like it when it comes, I'll give it to you, Abbie.' She got up laboriously and crossed over to the window. She stood looking out, with her back to me. 'What a cold, cold world. I think I like winter best of all. It doesn't pretend to be anything it isn't.'

'How do you mean, Hester?'

She shrugged. 'The summer's nice, when it pretends to be hot and sunny and kind; but with winter you know what's really there.'

I put my cup back on the tray, and hers too. She heard me put them down and turned to face me. 'Oh Abbie, you sounded so like Aunty Susan.'

'I didn't say anything.'

'No, you didn't need to. You just put down those cups with a sort of disapproving noise, which told me exactly what you thought of me.'

'How do you like her letters, all her advice?'

She laughed a little, but the laughter did not reach her eyes. 'Dear Aunty. Food and babies. Her great passions in life.'

'And jam, too,' I reminded her.

She chuckled, more naturally this time. 'Dear Abbie, how happy you all made me at home.'

'So you're still homesick, Hester?'

She nodded, with her back to me. 'Oh, David's very good to me, Abbie. Very, very good to me. He seems to love me very much. I really don't know why.'

'But you're not happy?'

She turned, and gave me the little tight smile. 'What is "happy"? Is anyone ever really happy?'

'I suppose so,' I said. 'I know I am, most of the time, anyway. It's a sort of peace; contentment with what you have, and what you're doing.'

'Like when we were younger? Oh yes, I felt quite peaceful then I suppose. I used to go and sit in the churchyard, under the trees, watching those great free birds coming and going in the sky. How I used to envy them; how I wanted to be one of them. Do you remember Jacky? I wonder if he's still up there now.'

'But that was years ago,' I said.

'Do you remember the day we went up in the tower after blackberrying?' she asked me. She turned again to the window, her hands upon the sill. 'I don't think I've ever been happy since that day.'

I shivered.

'Oh, poor Abbie!' she said, suddenly contrite, turning back to me. 'I'm sorry! I forgot you'd feel the cold up here. I'll take you downstairs, by the fire. You'll get warm again then. We'll make ourselves another cup of tea. Have you had breakfast? Would you like some porridge? I'm so sorry; I forgot how cold it is for you up here.'

I asked her curiously, 'Don't you feel cold, Hester?'

'Me?' She smiled softly to herself. 'Oh yes! I quite like the feeling; I forget that other people don't. It makes me feel nice and real.' She brightened. 'Oh Abbie, I'm so glad you came. Now we'll go downstairs. I've got lots and lots of questions to ask you about home. The vicar, now. Is he well? And Mrs Vicar? Remember how Perran used to call her Mrs Vicar when he was little? We'll have some more tea and then you can sit by the fire and tell me all about everything and everybody in Lanissick.'

Going down the stairs with the tray in my hands, hearing her happy voice, her laughter and her chatter, I could almost have believed that there was nothing wrong.

Chapter Thirteen

THE ROCKS

WE SPENT THE week before Christmas decorating the little room. David brought a tiny tree home from the shop and Hester and I hung it with small paper-chains that we had made out of coloured magazine pages. I went down to Woolworths and brought back some tinsel and a few glass-balls and we hung those on the tree as well. David brought home some holly and we pinned it round the room in little bunches with drawing pins stuck into the picture-rail. We put our few small parcels round the tree: two or three of theirs and the ones I had brought from home. The postman brought a few cards now and then: one from David's parents and one from his aunt in Bodmin, the latter rather a formal one of a severe wintry scene and the terse words 'Happy Christmas from Aunt Dorothy to David and Hester' inside. Hester put it aside with a defensive glint in her eye. I wondered about that look. There were a few cards from home, mostly made by Thomas but signed by everyone. There was also a card from Veronica Braze ('To Dave and Hester, all my love, Veronica') and a picture on the front of candles and a Bible lying open on an altar with a bunch of snow-covered mistletoe, which seemed an odd combination. Hester was delighted with all the ones from home.

'Look Abbie!' she said, holding up a large card. 'Here's one from Uncle Garfield. Do look! It's very clever.' Thomas had drawn a fat robin perched upon a bubbling wine jar. The ferment within the jar foamed up and down to form the letters 'Merry Christmas' and the inside said 'Merry Xmas to you' in Father's spidery handwriting. 'There's one from

Lissie, too,' she said eagerly. 'Put them up on the string, David, then we can see them properly.'

They never seemed to want to go out. Now and again David went off somewhere in the evening. Each morning he went off to work and each afternoon he returned at precisely the same time. I couldn't persuade Hester to go out at all, not even for a walk. Neither of them appeared to have any contact with the people in the houses on either side and nobody except the nurse called in to see them. Every other morning I went down the hill with Hester's basket to the shops for food, spending some of her money and some of my own, and David brought vegetables home at the end of the day. I once called at the greengrocer's where he worked serving great earthy mounds of brown potatoes and flame-coloured carrots with a streaked white apron round his middle and a capable air.

We planned each day's meals in great detail and when he came home David smiled and enjoyed our cooking, and I began to feel quite fond of him. Even his overwhelming sincerity became less of a strain. Quite often in the evenings he would go off ringing somewhere, while Hester and I sat round the little fire and talked about home. Once he came back and said that he'd seen Perran, and his face glowed all that evening; so I knew they'd had their chat, and he was reassured.

Hester was very large now and, I judged, without much experience in such matters, near to her time. The nurse came every few days to see her and tell her what to get ready, and what to look for to know that the whole process had begun. Hester would listen with a look of slight blankness upon her face and nod in appropriate places, as if it was nothing really to do with her but that she was paying attention out of politeness. When the nurse had gone off on her bicycle she would close the door with relief and say something like, 'Well, that's that for a bit longer, thank goodness,' as if the whole subject was really rather a nuisance. I once asked her whether the thought of labour still frightened her, but she turned upon me a gaze of such curious blankness, as if I had mentioned something indelicate or peculiar, that I never asked again; the whole subject of the birth seemed so extraordinarily trivial to her, so that I did wonder sometimes whether she realized what was about to happen to her.

Two days before Christmas I managed to get her to show me the things in their bedroom that she'd got for the baby. To my astonishment the nurse's list was complete. 'Why Hester,' I said, 'you must have been ready for months!'

'Oh yes,' she said carelessly, 'I had all this stuff ready last summer. A lot of it was given to me, and Aunty Susan sent all the clothes and nappies and things. I think a lot of it was yours when you were little. I should think there are at least twenty vests, counting the new ones. I could have twins without any worry.' Then she said quickly, 'Come on, we can't stand here looking at all this stuff all day. We've got that pie to make.' She pulled me out of the room and closed the door on it all – the piles of nappies and faded bibs and faintly familiar rompers and little threadbare dresses – and dragged me downstairs to make pastry. Dismissing my anxious questions about a cot with, 'Oh, don't worry. It can sleep in a drawer,' she turned to the far more important business of making apple pie.

But a little later that afternoon I found her in their bedroom, turning Joseph's wooden rattle over and over in her hands, and saying to herself in a strange low voice, 'Oh God, of God,' and the sing-song quality I loved to hear was gone. But when she turned and saw me she put it down hurriedly and her smile was instant. She quickly covered it all over with the curtain she used as a dust-sheet, and suggested making scones for tea. So we went down to the kitchen and while she soured the milk with lemon-juice and I collected flour, salt and margarine she chattered on about the jam we would have to go with them. 'Shall we open the plum this time, Abbie? I dearly love the plum. It has all those lovely great lumps of purple swimming about in it, doesn't it. Not the raspberry – that's a bit pippy for scones – and the strawberry ought to be saved because there aren't so many jars of it and I want to save it for after Christmas in case anyone comes to tea. I should think the plum would be exactly right, Abbie, wouldn't you? Yes, I think we ought to have the plum,' which all seemed an oddly elaborate conversation, just for jam.

She still ate very little. She tasted a few crumbs of everything we made with childlike pleasure, like a bird pecking at seeds, but she never seemed hungry. She cooked huge meals for David, but ate nothing of them herself; and we always had porridge for breakfast.

'I've never known such a one for porridge,' David said one morning. 'She's always the same, Abigail. It's all she ever really wants to eat. Was she like this at home?'

'Oh, Hester always did love porridge,' I told him. 'It was all she ever would eat at one time, especially when she was little.'

'Well, not me,' he said, standing up. 'I can't really stand the stuff. You're a good cook, Abigail, I must say. That was a remarkably good omelette. Finish yours up, Hester. You've got the baby to think of now.'

She pushed at her small piece with a fork. 'Really, I've had quite enough already.'

'Oh, come on, Hester! You've had nothing. I must be off now, or I'll be late, and I mustn't be late. Make her eat it up, Abigail, won't you? She seems to listen to what you say.'

I wished he'd call me Abbie. It would have made me feel so much more comfortable.

'Promise me you'll eat it, Hester? Come on now, no cheating. I want that son of mine well-covered when he arrives. And another bit, Hester! Look, it's nearly gone now. I must say, you two girls can certainly cook.'

Hester pushed her plate away. 'We had a good teacher, didn't we, Abbie? Aunty loves to cook, and feed people.'

'Oh yes,' I said, laughing. 'Food is her one great passion.'

David looked up suddenly. After I'd said it I felt vaguely embarrassed. It seemed somehow out of place to talk of passion in front of him, even if only of the culinary kind. He was so passionless.

Later, when he had gone to work and Hester and I were washing up the few plates and dishes in the scullery, she looked at me thoughtfully and said, 'I wish I was like you, Abbie.'

'Like me?' I said, astonished. 'Why? Whatever for?'

She put her head on one side, like a bird, and surveyed me. 'You're so solid, somehow.'

I laughed in mock-offence. 'I'm not that fat,' I said indignantly, 'just slightly over-normal. Mother's build.'

'No,' she said, 'I didn't mean that. I didn't mean your proportions. I meant solid and comforting and calm and never very troubled.'

'You make me sound like a Christmas pudding!' I said. 'But thanks all the same.'

'Do you suppose you'll want to get married, Abbie?' she asked later, as we sat by the fire cracking nuts to put on the cake when it was done. The late December light came in at the window from the pearly afternoon, soft and cold. We'd lit the fire after dinner. She made a pleasant picture sitting there on a low chair in front of it, walnuts balanced in a row along the top of her bulging middle, with the flames catching at echoing colours in her hair. I put my walnuts in a saucer, and we threw our empty shells into the fire. They caught light and cracked, and became suddenly alive.

'Dear me, I don't know,' I said. 'It depends if someone wants to marry me first, doesn't it? And if I love him back. Why?'

She leaned her head upon the chair back and looked into the fire. 'Oh, no reason, really. I just wondered how you felt about marrying, that's all.'

'Do you recommend it?' I asked lightly, and then at once regretted it. It seemed a question fraught with intrusion; but she didn't seem to notice. She smiled into the flames, more relaxed than I had seen her for days, and said thoughtfully, 'Well, I can't tell you much about the having babies side of it yet. I'll tell you in a month.'

I felt a slight tension in the air, probably entirely personal, that the other end of babies, the conception end, might come into view, so I said quickly. 'I'd like to have babies. That is, if my husband wanted them.'

'You'd want to be married first, then?'

'Oh, of course!'

She gave a little laugh, and two of the walnuts fell off her mound of stomach into the hearth. She said, 'Don't sound so offended. Dear Abbie, you're so shockable. It's part of your solidness,' and I was left wondering exactly what she meant.

'I don't see myself as too easily shocked, really.'

'No, you're not. Just beautifully conventional. It's very reassuring.' It was as if she had patted my hand, like we did with Mother at home when we wanted to soothe her. 'You're really very much like Aunty Susan, you know that, Abbie? Aunty without the apron.' And we both laughed easily.

'If the baby is a girl,' Hester mused, 'I should want it called "Elizabeth".'

'After Lissie?'

'Yes, sort of. And it would be easier for you, later on.'

'Easier for me?' I said in surprise. 'How do you mean?'

She smiled into the fire. 'Nothing. Just easier than if it was called "Abigail". I'd like it to be called after one of you.'

'I suppose there's always "Thomasina" or "Perrana", if you run short of ideas,' I said. 'Although isn't there a fish . . .?'

'Yes, a piranha. No. I don't like the sound of that. I don't want a child that might turn round and eat me away.'

I shuddered. 'Horrid thought. What if it's a boy? What would you call a boy?'

She gave me a sudden veiled look, like rocks under cloudy water, that was gone in a moment. She thought for a bit, and then said, 'I think I'd like to call him after my dear old grandfather in the churchyard at home.'

I stared at her until I remembered, and then we burst out laughing. 'Oh Hester,' I said. 'Poor baby! Isaac Bartholomew Penkevin? What a name!' and when David came in from the shop with a pound of parsnips and a battered cabbage under one arm, we were giggling like schoolgirls. I think, looking back, she seemed almost happier then than I'd ever seen her before.

Chapter Fourteen

THE BERRY

EARLY ON CHRISTMAS Eve our vicar called. He turned up on the doorstep, his gloves in his hands, with pink cheeks glowing from the cold. David had gone to answer the door. We heard low voices, and I recognized the ecclesiastical tones. I glanced at Hester. 'It's the vicar from home,' I whispered. 'No doubt paying you a neighbourly call. Do you want to see him? Shall I say you're too tired?'

She gave a quick smile and said no, it would be nice to see a harbinger of joy. There was the sound of a light step on the floor in the next room, and the click of the front door closing. Hester and I went through from the scullery.

The vicar was very seasonal, beaming and nodding and glowing in the little room, with the thin light of morning coming through the window from the street outside and shining on his satiny head when he took his hat off. David stood beside Hester with his arm about her shoulders and smiled his most handsome, most boyish smile. He shook hands warmly and said all the right things, and Hester stood beside him and smiled politely back.

'Well, well!' said the vicar, beaming rosily at her. 'How are you, my dear? My, you're looking well! Quite radiant. Isn't she radiant, David? And Abigail, too. How nice to see you, Abigail. And nice to see you too, David. We miss you in the belfry, my boy. Oh, I mean that, quite genuinely. The ringing has most noticeably deteriorated in your absence.'

'Do sit down, vicar. No, I'm sure it hasn't at all. They're doing very well without me, so I hear, although it's very kind of you to encourage me to think so. Do, please sit down. Shall I take your hat?'

'Thank you, my boy. Thank you.' He lowered himself gently into a chair. 'And when is the little one due to make his appearance, Mrs Penkevin? Dear me, that does sound strange, doesn't it. May I still call you Hester? Good, good. Next week? My, my! How the time does fly, doesn't it. It seems only yesterday that I was marrying the two of you young people.'

'It's very good of you to call, sir,' David was saying with a social ease I rather envied. 'Such a long way out of your way, too.'

'Not at all, not at all, my boy. As a matter of fact I had to come over to Truro on parochial business; a little matter of the diocese. Besides, I have been meaning to call upon you both for some time.' He gazed around him at the little room, tapping lightly on his knees with the fingers of each hand. 'My, my, this is pleasant. Quite a snug little home you have here. How lucky you are to have a view, Hester.' He nodded towards the small window where a distant slice of the great central spire of the cathedral rose narrowly between the gatepost and the next-door wall. 'Such a beautiful building, our cathedral. Beautiful, I always think.'

David cleared his throat. 'May I make you a cup of tea, sir?'

'How kind of you, my boy, how kind. Something to keep out the cold December wind? Yes, I should appreciate a cup of tea. Yes, tea would be very pleasant. Thank you.' He studied the floor with elaborate care for a few seconds and then looked at Hester. 'And how are you keeping, my dear? You look very well indeed, doesn't she, Abigail?'

I said that indeed she did. The vicar chatted blithely on, dropping little platitudes and bits of gentle humour into the air. After a while I noticed that Hester had begun to grow rather pale. I sat her down on the sofa and David brought her a cup of tea, which she drank eagerly. The vicar peered at her closely once or twice, so I hurriedly began to bombard him with questions about home, and almost everyone in the village. He sat back, beamed and nodded and grew jocular, and answered my questions genially; and once he said, 'By the way, Abigail, I hear your brother is planning to marry fairly soon. The young lady from town, isn't it? Splendid, splendid! Another family celebration for you all.' So I knew that Perran had told them about Jennifer.

'I believe the two young people wish to be married in our own church,' the vicar went on, 'which is very pleasant for us; and your parents too, Abigail. Ah, a cup of tea? Thank you, my boy. Just the thing to keep the winds at bay on such a cold morning. The young lady has only a father alive, so I believe; and there are no other children. Just the one daughter. Alice, is it? Dear me, no. Jennifer? Yes, of course, how foolish of me to forget. Her father is a ringer too, I believe, which makes it all the more pleasant. Possibly how young Perran met the family in the first place, no doubt, Abigail? Ah yes, I thought so.'

David came back with more tea, and the sugar bowl, and the vicar cast anxious glances at Hester. 'Are you all right, my dear? You seem very quiet. Does she not, Abigail?' He frowned at her in gentle concern.

'Yes,' I said, 'I think she feels quiet.'

'Oh!' he said, in some surprise. There was a little pause.

'How is your wife?' I asked brightly.

He blinked. 'My wife? Oh, very well, thank you. Very well indeed. Busy, of course, with all the festivities in hand. Christmas always comes upon us before we quite realize it, does it not, somehow? Yes, thank you, my boy. Two, if I may? Ah, thank you.' He stirred with care. 'Yes, my wife is very busy, as I'm sure your mother is too, Abigail. But there, dear me. I was forgetting – of course, she has to rest so much at the moment, has she not, on doctor's orders? Yes, and young Lissie being such a tower of strength while you are away, Abigail. Yes, yes. I believe they are all very well. And the little fellow, Thomas, is such a credit to us in the choir.'

He glanced benignly round the low room, sipping his tea. We shuffled our feet a bit, willing him to go, but reluctant to make it too obvious. 'You haven't your Christmas decorations up yet, I see, Hester. Oh, you have? Yes, very nice. I can see the little tree now, over there in the corner. Very jolly.'

At last he got up. 'Well, it has certainly been very pleasant seeing you all,' he said as we got to our feet. 'I'll give them your regards at home, shall I? Or rather, your love, I should say.' He shook hands with us all. 'I wish every one of you a very good Christmas, and hope the happy event goes well for you, my dear. Let us hope you will at least be able to enjoy celebrating Christmas first, shall we? I'll call upon you again, if I may, next time I'm in Truro, Hester. Have an enjoyable Christmas, my dear.'

I made Hester sit down, rather afraid she might fall down if I didn't. Her face was strained in the cold light and there were deep shadows under her eyes. The vicar shook hands all round once again. 'I know they would all send their regards to you from home. They seem to be keeping well so far, luckily, certainly in so far as I know.' And then he said, 'You've heard our sad news, of course, about poor Joseph?'

There was an extraordinary silence. Into it the little clock on the mantelpiece dropped idle sounds of tick and tock and rattled softly to itself as it turned the hour. The vicar looked from one to the other of us in gentle puzzlement and nobody knew quite what to say. Hester had gone very white. All colour had drained from her cheeks and she swayed a little on the sofa. Her eyes stared up at him, fixed unmovingly on his lips.

David said, as if with tremendous effort, 'And what exactly has happened to Joseph, vicar?' His voice sounded hoarse in the silence.

The vicar looked vaguely embarrassed. 'Dear me, you haven't heard about it, obviously. Such a shame. It seems so unfair. Poor Joseph worked so hard in his garden.'

I thought vaguely of hitting him but controlled myself.

David said, 'I think you'd better tell us,' in a tight level voice with a tone in it that I'd never heard before.

'Why, poor Joseph had a nasty little accident last week. A young cow from the field behind his cottage, a heifer I believe it was, got into his garden and trampled down his hen-house. Quite smashed it, I'm afraid, quite irreparably. One of his hens was killed in the mêlée, as it were. A nasty thing to happen, and in December, too. Dear me, you all look rather shocked. I hope I didn't alarm you all unduly?'

There was a little sighing sound. We all turned to look behind us. Hester, quite silently, had fallen sideways and slipped off the sofa on to the floor.

We carried her up the stairs together, David and I, and laid her down in the bed. David, with one look at her face, said grimly to me, 'Get rid of the old chap and then stay with her. I'm going for the doctor.' And then he was gone in a blast of cold air out into the street. I saw the vicar out.

'So sorry,' he was muttering. 'Dear me, perhaps I chose rather an ill moment to deliver my little piece of bad news. But I felt sure you'd like to hear all the little details from home. You are all rather fond of Joseph, so I believe. It seemed . . .'

'Yes, yes,' I said, 'of course we are. Don't worry, I think it's the baby.' I got his hat for him, and hustled him out. 'Of course you should have told us. I'm glad you did.' I'd got him as far as the door when he lowered his voice carefully, 'Is she well, Abigail? She's dreadfully thin, isn't she, my dear? And rather a strained look, I thought, about the eyes. Dear me, I hope the child is all right. And Hester, too.'

'Yes, yes,' I said. 'I hope so too.'

'So sorry if my little visit should have upset her,' he went on anxiously, turning his hat round and round in his hands. I clenched my teeth and prayed that he would hurry up and go. He lingered on the doorstep, and behind him in the cold December street a woman went past with a child, and peered curiously in at us. A page of newspaper, blown by the wind, fluttered out of the gutter and wrapped around his legs. 'I presume David has gone for the nurse, has he not?'

'For the doctor.'

'Yes, yes, of course. Very sensible. You don't feel that

perhaps,' he said, bending down to shake off the newspaper so that it continued on its way down the street, 'that perhaps I should not have mentioned the subject of accidents at such a time? My goodness, the sky looks remarkably laden. I think we are about to have a slight fall of snow. Dear, dear me. Perhaps not quite the right moment to bring up the subject of accidents . . .' And off he went into the bleak morning, holding his hat on with a gloved hand and muttering gently to himself, 'Oh dear, perhaps I should have refrained from mentioning . . .'

I sped upstairs to Hester.

My heart lurched at the change in her face. She lay looking up at me from the pillows, her face greener than ever. But she was smiling, a glowing, excited smile. All of a sudden her body began to heave, and she grabbed at my hand and dug her nails in hard.

'What is it?' I shook her arm. 'Is it the baby, Hester?'

After what seemed to me to be a long while she lay back and took a deep breath. 'Yes, it's the pains starting, I think. Don't worry, it'll be ages and ages yet. Hours, I expect.' She seemed extraordinarily calm. 'Aunty said it takes days and days with your first baby. Oh Abbie, I hope it isn't that long; but it is exciting, isn't it!'

'Very!' I said drily. 'Especially if they don't get here in time.'

She laughed, a joyous, light-hearted sound. 'Oh, of course they will. Get Aunty's letter – over on the chest of drawers. See what she says. Read it to me.'

I turned away to get the letter. I found it easily, Mother's squarish handwriting familiar as her face. I opened it and took it out, my hands trembling a little. ' "Dear Hester",' I began, and then she was clutching at me again. I held her hand and squeezed it while the spasm passed.

'Go on.' She took a deep breath. 'Read me what she says. The pain's going now. On the second page, about the breathing bit.'

I searched hurriedly among instructions for exercise and recipes for raspberry-leaf tea and the relief of heartburn and varicose veins and found a bit which started, 'When the pains begin'.

'I think I've got it!' I said in triumph. 'Listen: "When the pains begin my dear, do not go to bed at once but try to walk about as long as possible . . ." Oh Hester, perhaps you should get up?' My voice wavered doubtfully.

She laughed, joyously and loudly. 'Oh Abbie, I think I'm over that bit! Read on, further, where it starts about the bowls and papers.'

'Bowls?' I asked her. 'Are you sure?' I rummaged through several sheets of lined paper and found "get ready the bowls and newspapers". 'Hester,' I said, 'what bowls? Where are they? Where's all this newspaper she's talking about?'

'Oh, the nurse said she'd bring some special stuff,' said Hester through clenched teeth. 'I've only got those bath-towels over there. We'd better not touch those yet, not before she comes. Oh Abbie, here's another pain! Hold my hand!'

I held her hand and clenched my teeth for her, while her small body heaved about. She breathed heavily and swallowed a lot and once she looked at me a little strangely and said, 'Why Abbie, how nice of you to come!' as if I'd just arrived. I looked at her flushed cheeks and a slight panic began to rise in me. But almost immediately her face cleared and she looked at me in great delight and said again, 'Don't worry, it'll be ages yet!' in a voice of amazing calm.

A little later, when I thought she was dozing lightly, I went to the window to look for signs of David and the doctor, or the nurse coming up the road. I stood for several seconds looking out on the deserted street. Snow was beginning to fall and over on the distant skyline the low hills were obscured by bank upon bank of thick yellow-tinged cloud. I heard a little noise behind me from the bed. Turning, I saw that she was looking at me, staring up strangely from the pillow.

'What is it, Hester?' I asked her quickly. 'Another pain?'

At first I thought she hadn't heard me. Her eyes were oddly veiled, fixed on a point on the wall behind my head, and her lips were moving silently. And then in a strange distant voice she began to argue, as if with herself, very politely. 'No, no,' she said, 'I'm sorry! It's very important.'

I shook her arm gently. 'Hester! What is it? Have you got another pain? Hester, answer me!'

But she only said again, 'I'm sorry, but I must see him, just once more, before I leave,' in that strange little voice, like a dreamer talking to herself. 'Just once more. It's important. It's on the map. Just once, before I die.'

'Die, Hester?' I said, more briskly than I felt. 'You're not going to die! You're only having a baby. Don't be so silly.'

She gave me an odd look, as if I were a trespasser, and said irritably, 'Of course I am.' And then softly, as if to herself again, 'But not yet. Not for a little while. The baby first. There's the baby first, before I can leave.' Then, with a swift change of mood that was like the sun coming out, she laughed and said, 'Oh Abbie, it's so exciting!' and began to grit her teeth, so I knew another pain was coming.

Suddenly things began to happen with alarming speed. One minute she seemed to be lying there saying calmly, 'Don't worry, it'll be ages yet,' and the next minute she was heaving and thrashing about and biting her lips. 'Don't panic!' she said, in between gasps, 'I'm perfectly all right!'

'What do you know about it?' I shouted desperately at her. 'You've never had a baby before! Shouldn't I be getting things together, like scissors and hot water and soap and stuff?'

She threw me a look of glorious triumph, gritted her teeth, and dug her nails into my hand so hard that my fingers were bleeding. Then quite suddenly she stopped thrashing about and went very quiet and still. 'Oh Abbie,' she said, her eyes widening, 'I think you'd better have a look.'

My hands began to tremble violently. I threw back the bed-clothes and stared down, unable quite to believe my eyes. There, lying on the sheet between her knees, was a

143

small blue doll, and a long twisted whitish rope thing leading from its stomach into Hester. I gave a shriek and picked it up by its tiny blue feet and as I did so it gave a kind of splutter and began to wail irritably.

'Oh Hester! Hester, it's a baby! Hester, it's real!'

She gave a half-sob, and peered up at it in my hands in amazement. As we watched, the little creature rapidly changed colour all over and became a pinkish red. I grabbed a nearby shirt of David's that looked fairly clean, changed my mind, threw it aside, then grabbed the nurse's precious bath-towels and wrapped one round the baby.

'Aren't I supposed to cut the rope?' I asked her breathlessly.

She shrugged, her eyes dancing. 'I don't know anything about it!'

'Only producing one!' I gasped, and we stared at each other in disbelief, and then at the baby. Hester propped herself up on one elbow, and stared at it. 'Is it breathing?' she asked doubtfully. 'It looks awfully quiet. I think they're supposed to cry, aren't they?'

I peered at it closely, my legs trembling. I was suddenly finding it exceedingly difficult to remain standing. The baby gave a yawn of utter boredom and licked its minute lips with a miniature pink tongue.

'Yes, it's fine!' I shouted. 'Hester, it's lovely! It's gone off to sleep, I think. But it's perfectly all right! Here, hold it, look. It's lovely! It's a lovely, lovely baby! Oh Hester, I can't believe it. It's a marvellous baby!'

She took the towel-wrapped bundle in her hands. Downstairs the front door banged and two sets of heavy footsteps thundered up the stairs and halted, astounded in the doorway.

And thus, on Christmas Eve, in falling snow and holly bright with berries, Elizabeth Penkevin came into the world.

Chapter Fifteen

THE WOOD

I STAYED WITH them until the third week in January. Hester seemed remarkably well. The nurse came every day at first and taught her how to breastfeed the baby. For a week or two after the birth I said nothing about leaving, although I was beginning to worry about Mother again, for Lissie's letters were not as reassuring as I might have hoped. She wrote that Mother had become a great deal thinner in a short time, and that the doctor had advised the odd day spent completely in bed, although other than her blood-pressure he couldn't find anything wrong. There was talk of taking her to hospital for tests in a few months' time if she didn't pick up with the spring; and it all sounded faintly ominous despite the doctor's reassurance. Mother herself wrote a line or two to say we were not to worry in the least as Lissie and Father were coping well without me, and to stay as long as Hester needed me there, and to be sure not to let Hester lay the baby down on her back in case she was sick, and for Hester not to lift anything heavy straight after the birth or dreadful things might happen to her insides.

I wrote back to tell them all the news, and David wrote too. His parents came over once or twice with Jim to see the baby, but didn't stay long. They cooed and smiled at Elizabeth and said how like David as a baby she was. But there was a slight coolness in their attitude to Hester, and it puzzled me slightly at the time, although I don't think Hester noticed.

David's mother was very gushing. 'Oh, she's lovely, David, and so like you were at this age. Look at the dear little tufts of hair round the back here. Thank goodness

145

she's not a redhead. I was so afraid she might be, you know; so relieved to find she isn't. Ginger is such a dreadful colour. I think she's going to be your colour, David, with perhaps your grandmother's blue eyes. No, don't touch her, James. Hester wouldn't like it.' And she jiggled and bounced the little bundle about in her arms until it burped and a trickle of milk ran down the minute chin. 'Oh dear,' she said in slight displeasure. 'Take her, Hester, will you? I'm rather afraid she's going to be sick, and I don't really want the smell on my coat.'

David's father looked through the window and studied the road outside, as if the subject of babies might go away if it was ignored, and considered whether it was likely to snow again. James sat on the settee and scowled and kicked at the chair next to him with absent-minded aggression and made faces at the baby when he thought no one was looking. They left soon afterwards, and when Hester disappeared upstairs with Elizabeth, I told David I thought it was time I went home.

'Must you go, Abigail?' David asked me. 'It's been wonderful having you here. Hester is a different person when you're around.'

'I can't really believe that,' I told him, laughing.

'Yes, really, you have no idea how different. Must you go?'

'I really ought to, David, yet I'm so afraid of upsetting Hester's happiness at the moment. I'm also worried about Mother. Lissie didn't sound too happy in her last letter. I really think I ought to go. Would you like me to tell Hester?'

'I think it would be better coming from you,' he said.

And so, sitting on her bed a week after Christmas, I told her that I had decided to go home. She dismissed my carefully worded speech with a wave. 'Go home? No, of course you can't, Abbie. We want you here for – oh, I don't know, ages yet. But I can't think about that now. Look at Elizabeth. Don't you think she's the most marvellous thing that ever happened to anybody ever before? I thought I was happy once, long ago. But I was wrong, Abbie. I'm happy now. I'm so happy I could die! I didn't know it was possible to feel so happy . . .' And indeed, she did seem almost delirious with her joy.

But after the middle of January the weather turned suddenly milder, and I made up my mind. Hester was coping well with the baby and was very much absorbed in her own happiness. Every time it made a sound she picked the little creature up and held it to her, murmuring to it and whispering in its shell-like ears. A hundred times a day she would look at it lying asleep beside their bed in the drawer which served as a cot. She was radiant with joy. All the strange tension of the previous months seemed to have gone; and in my eagerness to see it so, I believed that she was happy at last.

I went home in melting slush, in time for Perran's wedding. I found Mother very much thinner, but desperately eager for all my news. Apparently she still stayed in bed each morning, and the rest seemed to have been doing her good. I sat on the side of her bed, while she caught at my hand and asked me ceaseless questions.

'When is she going to bring the baby to see me, Abbie?' she asked. 'I'm so gasping to see my grandchild, I can't wait much longer. Is David pleased? Does the babe take after him, do you think? He's a kind boy – he wrote to us after the birth telling us all about how you coped with it all. He's full of praise for you, my love. Said he don't know how they would have managed without you. He's a lovely chap, is David. I know he'll make Hester happy. Wasn't that thoughtful, Ab, don't you think, writing to tell us about the little dear? I wish that Hester could have dropped me a line or two as well, but there, I suppose she's awful busy with the baby, and couldn't spare the time.'

'I'm sure she'll write soon, Mother,' I told her, patting her hand. 'She sends her love, and a big kiss from the baby. Oh, it is good to be home again, although Lissie seems to have coped very well.'

'That girl has been an angel,' Mother told me proudly. 'She made Thomas tidy his room every morning before school. You know how awful untidy he can be. Well, Lissie went in there every morning to check it, and she wouldn't give him no breakfast until he'd put his night-clothes away and made his bed all proper, and tidied his table. Laugh? Father and I nearly split ourselves laughing on the quiet, to hear them at it. But we didn't dare let her hear us, she was some serious about it.' She sobered, looking closely at me. 'And you, my love. Here I am going on and on about what's been happening here, and you're the one with all the news. Come on now, I want to hear everything. Is the baby like her? Is the precious little child like my Hester? Here Abbie, fancy you being with her when the babe was born! My dear life, we never thought of that, did we? We never guessed that might happen. Were you frightened, my 'ansome, when it started?'

'Not frightened, Mother. I didn't realize what was happening until it was too late to be frightened.'

'What did the doctor say?' she asked me eagerly, eyes gleaming. 'Here, did he think you acted well, delivering the child alone? Dear life and soul, I wish it had been me. I'd have told her, Abbie! I'd have told her when to push, and when to hold still.'

I laughed. 'There wasn't much chance to tell her anything, Mother. She seemed to know what to do all on her own. Besides, it all happened so quick. One minute she was having pains, the next it was all over.'

'And the babe? Did it cry straight off? You smacked its little bottom, didn't you, Ab? That gets them crying straight away. I remember Lissie wouldn't cry at first, and the nurse had to give her a sound wallop to start her off. Perran now, he was born yelling, that boy. Such a loud holler, he had. I can't remember with you, my love. I was so mazed, you being my first; and tis all so long ago now. But what of the baby, Abbie? Is she auburn like my Hester?'

'No, not auburn. More fairish, I think. Like David. Very small and pretty, and a strong little thing. As for smacking her bottom – well, I didn't really need to. She started to breathe straight away. The doctor said we did the best thing in the circumstances; just kept her warm, and not tried to cut the cord. He said it was a very straightforward birth, no complications, and that Hester was very lucky to get it over with so quickly. Your instructions helped her a lot, Mother. We were reading them from your letter as the babe was being born.'

'Is that true, Abbie? My instructions to Hester? Well, fancy that, now. Reading them as the babe was born? Oh my dear life, that do make me feel glad, glad to have been of use. Almost like I was there. Did Hester find the breathing helped?'

'Very helpful, Mother. And the bit about not going to bed too soon, but walking about as long as possible. You've no idea how useful it all was to her. All your advice, it was all so helpful. I was glad of it too, not knowing what to expect.'

She sank back on the pillows, her face aglow. 'I'm glad of that, Abbie, awful glad. Perhaps it would have been a good idea to have gone through it with you, too, instead of only writing to Hester. I could have gone through it with you before you left with Perran, couldn't I? Told you what might happen. But no matter, you did just the right thing, my girl.'

'Did I, Mother?'

'Yes, you did. I told you, Abbie, you should have been a nurse. I told you that, didn't I! You've got an awful reassuring way with you, Abbie, when people do need you.'

'A solidness, Mother?'

'Solid? Yes, I suppose you could say solid. But calm and kind and quiet with it, and sort of efficient.'

'Hester says I'm very like you, Mother, so the credit is all yours.'

'Did Hester say that? Did she really? Oh Abbie, what three lovely girls I've got! And Lissie managing so well while you were away, too. And here Abbie, Veronica Braze have been here a hundred times a week, asking for news of Hester and them. Makes out she's awful friendly with Hester. Close as two pilchards you'd think they were, by her account. "Any news of my two dear friends yet?" she asks, coming up the path or poking her head over the gate. You know how she is, Ab, all pink and peering about. Quite a pest she was at times, with me being stuck here in bed. Liss dealt with her, though. "Veronica," she says to her, "don't trouble to keep coming here for news. I'll let you know the minute there is any. I'll come to your house and tell 'ee." She haven't been back since, although Liss did go and tell her, when we heard twas a little girl. Do you know, that girl's been like a mother to me? I don't believe Thomas has even noticed you've been gone, he's been that well-fed. Now you're back, how does Father look to you, Abbie? Do you find him looking well?'

'Yes, well, but tired, Mother, and very worried about you.'

'He has been worried, I must admit. He's had the worry of Hester as well as me. Oh, he don't say much, I know; but he do worry about things. He hasn't been playing his old fiddle as much as I like to see 'en do, not lately. Moping about the house, he's been, running up and down the stairs to me day and night. And ringing? He've hardly been up to church at all since Christmas. George wanted 'en for a peal of Triples a week or two back, but he wouldn't go. What do you think of that, Abbie? Have you ever known Father to refuse a peal before?'

'No,' I said, 'I don't think I ever have.'

'Very stubborn he was about it too. "No George," says he, "Susan do need me here with her, with our Abbie away. You'll have to get someone else. Get Harry to do it for 'ee." "Harry's ringing the four," says George. "I need you for trebling, Garfield." "Well, I can't do it," says Father. "You'll have to ring two bells, George, and take treble as well, or get someone else in." Very emphatic, he was, Abbie. He wouldn't budge. You should have heard him! Father can be awful stubborn at times.'

'Good for Father. And so what did they do?'

'Oh, Perran got a young chap over from Liskeard. Some ringing friend of his and Jen's Dad. Anyhow, they got the peal, so everyone was happy. But Father wouldn't budge. "My place is here with Susan," he said. And he stuck to it.'

'What was the peal for, Mother?' I asked her.

'Oh, some reason or other. When did George Pascoe ever need an excuse to ring a peal? He'd have Father up there every day to ring sommat, if he had his way. Nice young fellow though, Abbie.'

'Young fellow? George Pascoe?'

'No, my love, the young chap who came for the treble. Liss was very taken with him. Richard something. Didn't catch his other name. A good bit older than Perran, I believe he is. A friend of Jen's Dad. She's a nice girl, Abbie, is Jennifer. You'd like her. I do believe she'll make Perran very happy. Pity to start off like they are, but sometimes I think it don't matter very much in the long run, do you, my love? They've got the wedding all set for Saturday week up to church, and they're coming back along here for a bite to eat and a drop of Father's wine after. Liss is to be bridesmaid again, but tis only to be a very small family affair, things being as they are. You do know about their baby, don't you, Abbie? Perran says he told you before Christmas.'

'Yes, he did. Mother, were you very upset? Was Father?'

She shrugged, and gave me a rueful smile. 'These things happen, Abbie. They've happened before and they'll happen again, in this old world. And they'll be happy together, I know they will. Perran's a bright lad. He knows just where he's to, that boy. He's got it all worked out already. I don't never worry about my Perran. He do know exactly where he's going; always has.'

The following Saturday Perran and Jennifer Ennory were married very quietly by our vicar in the freezing church, with only a handful of us there. It seemed a marked contrast to the frantic preparations for Hester's wedding almost a year before. Yet in a strange way there was much more of a depth in it. Perran wore his wedding suit. Jennifer, slightly tubby round the waist, had on a quiet dress of cornflower blue. I liked Jennifer at first sight. She had dark brown eyes that darted everywhere, a quick tongue and ready humour. The church was almost empty: Jennifer's father had a family friend or two on their side, and just our family and Joseph on ours. In spite of the cold there was something there that had been strangely missing at Hester's wedding, and after the vicar had pronounced them man and wife I saw their hands seek out and reach for each other's when they thought that no one saw them. Joseph was best man, with a flower in his buttonhole. Being so few of us there, we all trooped in behind them when they went into the vestry to sign the register, with Father and Jennifer's father as witnesses; and I saw Perran look at Jennifer sideways and give her a quick intimate wink as if to say 'There, it's done, and I've got you now'; and Jennifer's face, up-turned to him, flashed open in the light from a window with a smile for him alone that could only be described as radiant.

Afterwards at home we had our small party, and the vicar came to swell the numbers. Lissie had made a cake for them, a lumpy shapeless heart with their names upon the top in pink icing, and it was elaborately admired. Lissie, with blushing pride, passed round the plates and we ate cheese and fish-paste sandwiches and drank their health with Father's carrot wine.

'The best one,' said Father proudly, nodding at his glassful, cheeks aglow. 'Good luck to you both, my son; you've chosen a good girl there.' The transient embarrassment which anyone might have felt pondering upon his particular choice of adjective was quickly masked by Thomas knocking over a small table with a plate of sandwiches upon it and treading on a cheese sandwich, turning everyone's attention to him.

Joseph, as best man, proposed a toast and went very red. Being such a silent man I think it took supreme courage to stand up at all in company, let alone speak to us, but he did it, flushing scarlet to the roots of his hair, and sat down very suddenly afterwards, even the tips of his rather well-shaped ears glowing from a mixture of embarrassment and wine. To cover it he nodded vigorously in the direction of the bride and groom, and we all turned to look at them.

And they looked happy, the two of them. Perran held her hand and put his arm about her with an obvious pride, and made a short speech. Jennifer in her cornflower-coloured dress flushed and her brown eyes darted about us all, like butterflies in the sun. Even when her slight thickening round the waist was lightly and jovially mentioned the glow did not leave her eyes, although at times it did seem to me that a slight defensiveness lurked at the back of them. Mother bustled about as she always used to do, and even if they noticed it, no one remarked upon her loss of weight. Perhaps it was Hester's absence that made the air a little lighter, or perhaps it was the wine, but we all relaxed and talked and laughed with easy familiarity in a way that we had not done for years.

The vicar stood talking to Lissie who, with eyes lowered and cheeks very red, cast little glances sideways at the cake from time to time, as if to reassure herself that it was disappearing with suitable speed. Thomas crawled silently about beneath the righted table, collecting bits of fallen sandwich, eating what was respectable and scattering the crumbs of what was not along the outside of the kitchen window-sill. Mother told him to close the window or we'd all catch pneumonia from the draught, and he did so; but for the rest of the party he sat with quiet concentration on the draining-board with his watered wine beside him and his pencil in his hand, drawing the birds that came to peck at the bits of cheese and squashed bread arranged along the sill. He'd hold his breath and frown if we came through to the kitchen for more wine or tea or bread and butter, for fear we should startle them away. Mother sighed and looked helplessly at me and said, 'What a lad, Abbie. Always drawing sommat,' in exasperated pride. 'Do you want more cake, my 'ansome?' she asked him, but he shook his head and frowned and waved her away. He bent over his paper and then looked up to peer more closely at the birds as they fluttered down to land on the sill outside, and I don't think he even heard her.

Mother was very busy, rushing about with plates and egg-cups (Father's pantry industry being rather short of such refinements as wine-glasses) and cups of tea.

'For goodness sake, Susan, sit down!' said Father, holding a ridiculously small sandwich in his huge hands and sipping enthusiastically at his wine. 'You've done nothing but run about after 'em all. Leave 'em be, and come and sit down.'

'In a moment, Garfield,' Mother called back over her shoulder. 'I'll just get Joseph another cup of tea. There now, I'm back again. Another bit of cake, Joseph? There you are, my 'ansome, I've brought you a drop more tea.'

Joseph, balancing a plate with wedding-cake upon it in one hand, an egg-cup in the other and a cup and saucer on one knee, smiled his self-conscious social smile, refused more cake, but accepted the tea. Mother shook the plate under his nose until I was afraid the slices of cake would fall off on to him with their own momentum; he surrendered and took one, and Mother beamed at him.

'Lovely cake, isn't it! Course, Hester's wedding was a much bigger affair, wasn't it, Abbie?' she said. 'Go on, Joseph, have another piece as well, my 'ansome. It'll save me coming back again. Tis such a pity she's not here for this one. Perran would have dearly liked her here; but it's so cold out, and the babe only a month old – another piece, Joseph? No? Oh dear yes, Perran was some disappointed, wasn't he, Abbie?'

Actually I thought Perran quite oblivious to the very existence of Hester on this day of all days, but I nodded to keep her happy. The blinds had come down in Joseph's face.

'You haven't seen Hester for a long time now, have you, Joseph?' Mother was saying. She shook the cake-plate at him again. 'Sure you won't have another piece? You'll get the chance soon, I shouldn't wonder. We're expecting her home soon on a visit. With the babe, of course, and David too, if the shop can spare him. Be nice, won't it, Ab, to have Hester home again?'

I smiled at her and said yes, it would, and why didn't she go and offer cake to the vicar who looked hungry, and she went bustling off. I knew that even if the vicar couldn't eat more cake Lissie would certainly oblige, being of an age to yearn for food. I was afraid she was beginning to look more than a little plump. Her rosy face shone at the sight of more cake, and when the vicar politely took another piece from the proffered plate, Lissie took one too.

'My dear, this is excellent!' the vicar said, munching heartily. 'Most excellent. What have you put in it? Butter? A slight touch of nutmeg? No? Ah, then it's the vanilla essence that gives it that depth of flavour. Am I correct? Ah, I thought so! And do I detect a trace of essence of lemon, too?' which was exactly the sort of conversation that Lissie adored.

Later, Father went to get his violin from the shed up in the orchard, and brought it into the living room. We cleared the centre of the room of chairs, and Father moved towards his favourite arm-chair, a hugely cumbersome piece of furniture with six-inch-wide armrests and a massive back with piping-cord and fringed braid all over it, sat on the arm of it, and tenderly took out his violin. Joseph applied a match to his pipe, leaned back, and watched him through the haze of smoke. Father took out a piece of soft cloth and began to polish the violin, turning it over in his hands; winding up the bow-screw and rubbing rosin on the hairs, a bit reluctant all of a sudden to play in front of us all.

'Oh, go on, Father,' begged Lissie. 'Do play something nice and happy, and then we can all dance.'

'Yes, please!' said Jennifer from the settee, where she and Perran sat, holding hands. 'I haven't heard you play yet, and I've got to get used to it some time, haven't I?'

There was a burst of laughter at this. Father shot a look at Perran, who said 'Come on Garfield, get on with it!' as one man to another, instead of as son to father, which made Father grin quietly to himself and pick up the bow.

The vicar nodded earnestly. 'Come Garfield, there should always be music at a wedding, should there not?'

'Yes do play, Father,' I said quietly in his ear. 'They didn't have the organ or the bells, so let them have a bit of music now. Play them a bit like you play on a spring morning in your shed.'

Father hesitated, cleared his throat and coughed his small embarrassed cough and looked shy, and I could see that he was longing to; but he looked up at Mother through his eyebrows and said gruffly, 'No, no; better not. It worries your mother. She don't like to hear me play.'

'Oh nonsense!' said Mother in a rush, all flustered. 'I love to hear the happy sound of it. Tis the sad, lamenting bits I can't abide, like the wind come roaring down from that old ancient windy hill behind the church – he always plays those bits up in the shed, vicar – but play a happy bit of a tune, Garfield. The piece like a bit of spring water in the mornings. The bit like the salad – you know, that bit I dearly love, like the lettuces growing, and all that,' and she sat down quite out of breath and overwhelmed at so long a speech with everybody looking at her, for she had really a shy little soul, had Mother, underneath all her upholstery.

So Father tuned his violin and picked up the notes from it with his fingers one by one, to check them for pitch. And we all leaned slightly forward in our chairs to listen. When he'd got the notes quite true he tucked the violin beneath his chin, picked up the bow, applied it to the strings and drew, by way of introduction before he began the proper piece, a long and cheerful sound from it like a light cascade of summer water. As he began to play in earnest, a vacant look crept across his face. It was as if Father's soul were not there at all, but somewhere else – among the pebbles of a river bed or flitting in the shallows – and I saw the vicar looking at him in surprise and raise his eyebrows quietly to himself as if in silent tribute to the music.

Jennifer's father sat back in the shadows and smiled benignly round upon us all. He was a roundish little man with the same dark darting eyes as Jennifer. He reminded me of a Father Christmas with his little tufts of fluffy white hair and a mellow look in his eye that I don't think was just Father's wine. I wondered, looking from him to Jennifer over on the sofa with Perran, what her mother had been like, and could guess that she had been a dark-haired woman, light and slim like Jennifer might well be without the bulge.

We waited for Thomas and Lissie to dance, but they were growing up and had gone suddenly very shy.

'Come along, you two young people,' nodded the vicar encouragingly above the music. 'It's up to you to start us off.'

But they grinned shyly and shook their heads, and no one seemed to mind. We just sat round listening to Father, and nodding our heads and tapping our feet in time with the changing rhythms. Perran and Jennifer sat and held hands in comfortable silence. I sat in my own quiet corner and looked secretly around the living room at the ten of us, at the nine faces I could see, and the ten bodies, and wondered if it would have been any different if Hester had been there as well. I tried to steal a look at Joseph when I thought no one was looking. Thomas had finished drawing birds and was busy lining up Joseph's spent matches into a pattern on the arm of a chair. Mother sat on the far side of the room by the kitchen door, her cheeks flushed and her eyes glowing with pride. Her face, thinner than I'd known it for years, but still round, and familiar as my hand, with the dear lines of it slightly deeper than I remembered prior to Christmas. Father was playing a piece of music with mountains in it now, great sweeps of sound full of summer and a little jig now and then of dancing-steps. The smell of roses was in the music, and new-mown hay. The faces round the room grew still and quiet, as if each one remembered something of his or her own, precious to themselves; and I stole my look at Joseph.

He was sitting back in the chair, pipe in his hand, his dark head against the frame, motionless, listening. As I watched, his eyes moved round the room until they came to rest on a little patch of floor before the stove where, so many years before, Mother had bathed the child Hester. As I watched his face it seemed to me that I saw before him a small girl, thin and slight, wearing a faded green dress, a girl with damp hair the colour of marigolds falling about her shoulders. She stood before him in the living room on that late autumn morning of Joseph's young manhood, straight and glowing as a fairy child newly come from the haunts of heaven, and held out her arms to him. And Joseph, as he had never done upon that distant morning, moved towards her and gathered her into his own arms and held her close against his breast. And for just a little while there was rapture in the world.

Father stopped suddenly with a scrape and flourish, and we all remained motionless for a few seconds, listening to echoes. And then suddenly there was talking, and a tide of laughter rippled round the room. Father put away the violin and bow and passed around another glass of wine, dandelion this time. Lissie passed around more cake, and Mother and I poured out more tea.

Lissie put down the cake-plate and went to sit on the floor at Jennifer's feet. Joseph looked up as she passed and gave her a quick shy grin. She flushed scarlet, and all the while she sat with Jennifer, swapping recipes for saffron-cake and bread and splits with all the self-assurance of a much-married woman, in her plump pink and goldness she looked more of a child than ever. Then they went on to the subject of babies, and I heard them discussing nappies, wind and push-chairs in low voices.

Lissie, aware of Joseph's proximity, tried to include him in their conversation, blushed and stumbled on her words, and cast him shy pink looks of adolescent reverence. And Joseph, like the kind and considerate man he was, smiled to himself, nodded when she turned to speak to him, and even answered occasionally.

The vicar took up a conversation with Jennifer's father, whom we had been invited to call Sam, and I heard them arguing good-naturedly about ringing, pleased to have a common interest. Father pricked up his ears, tucked his violin case safely under the sofa, and joined them. I heard them arguing about the relative merits of Grandsire and something called Plain Bob, and Father joining in to argue in favour of something called Stedman, which I think was something to do with ringing, but which sounded to me like a sort of sewing-machine.

'I'm a Grandsire man, myself,' Sam was saying with rosy enthusiasm. The vicar nodded sagely into his wine-glass (he'd been honoured with a wine-glass along with the happy couple, while the rest of us drank out of egg-cups and Father, at times, I noticed, out of a flower-vase) and said, 'Yes, but it's not the ideal basic method, you must surely agree there? Plain Bob is undoubtedly a more thorough grounding. Progress to Grandsire, certainly; but initially a good solid foundation of Plain Bob to set them on the straight and narrow, as it were.'

'Ah!' said Father eagerly. 'Stedman! Now, there's a method . . .'

'Plain Hunt,' Sam went on earnestly. 'We do start our lads off with Plain Hunt, and then go on to Grandsire.'

'Plain Hunt has its uses as an introduction, certainly; but it hardly merits consideration as a method, does it now?' said the vicar, somewhat severely. 'Tell me, do you go in for Cambridge much in your part of the world?'

'Stedman, now . . .' said Father hopefully.

'Not Cambridge,' said Sam. 'At least, not lately. But we did get a band together for a touch of Double Norwich about three weeks ago.'

The vicar raised his eyebrows and appeared deeply impressed. Father coughed pointedly. 'But Stedman, I always say . . .'

'Remarkable achievement!' said the vicar, sipping enthusiastically from his glass. 'Double Norwich, eh? Do you hear that, Garfield? I wonder if our lads could manage that, hum? Quite an idea, is it not? And tell me, Mr Ennory, have you much experience of London Surprise?'

Sam's eyes glowed like lamps in his rosy face. He nodded,

and the vicar nodded back and they were off, comparing things they called methods, and tossing mysterious words like "Warkworth" and "extents" and "Beverley" about, and I was lost. I wandered out to Mother, picking my way carefully across Thomas and his pencils, and found her in the kitchen cutting sandwiches.

'Not more food, Mother, surely!' I said. 'They've all had plenty to eat. You're never cutting more sandwiches for them, are you?'

She gave me a little sheepish smile and said no, these were for Perran and Jennifer to take home with them to their flat, there being plenty of food left, and did I like Jennifer? I said yes, very much, and was sure they would be happy together. She looked suddenly stricken, as though a distant memory had just occurred to her, and said to me in a low voice, 'Oh dear, Abbie! Perhaps I shouldn't have mentioned her to Joseph, do you think? Did he mind much, do you suppose, Ab? I was that pleased to see him talking so nice to Father and them, and being best man, and making his little speech and that, that I quite forgot what you told me that time – you know, his feeling for Hester. Did I go on a bit, do you think? And him perhaps missing her, too. Perhaps he'd like her to have been here with us? But then, perhaps he'd have been more shy if she'd have come, and not said anything at all . . .' Which was almost the first time I'd ever been aware of any perspicacity in Mother.

I wandered back to them in the living room and was met by such a warm atmosphere of talk, of Lissie's pink and gold blushes, and the smell of wine and Joseph's tobacco smoke, that fondness for them all overwhelmed me; and I felt a sudden aching sadness, like a memory going forwards instead of back, for somehow it came to me then that this might well be our last complete family gathering; and that, without Hester there, we were more relaxed than we had been for years.

After the wedding at the end of January the weather changed abruptly, and we huddled round the fire in a winter such as we'd not known for many years. Snow lay on the ground all through February, which was most unusual for us so far in the west. The bitter weather held us in an icy grip of spurious white peace. There had been no news from Hester for weeks now, and in the depths of our snow-bound world, what news could have got through anyway? For days and days the postman didn't call, the milk froze on the doorstep, and in the lanes dead birds fell at every turn, their poor frozen bodies lying stiff and ruffled on the ruin of last year's leaf. After the snow came hail and wind, sleeting off the old hill with icy vehemence, and after the hail more snow. March came before it thawed properly, and trickled down the lanes in soggy rivulets, and dripped with dreary persistence off the outhouse roof. Mother was very poorly. She had been failing slowly for some weeks and I think only the thought of seeing Hester's baby kept her going.

'Don't worry,' I would tell her a hundred times a day, 'when the warmer weather comes she'll bring the babe to see you, Mother. Don't you fret.'

'But Abbie,' Mother said wearily, 'I want to see them now.' She said it over and over again. 'The spring'll be too late. I want to see them now. Tell her to come, Abbie? She'll listen to you. Tell Hester I want to see my grandchild now. You could write to her, Abbie. Tell her now!'

'But Mother dear,' I argued helplessly, 'it's so cold. You wouldn't want the little thing to catch pneumonia, would you? It's freezing cold outside, and Hester would have to carry her all the way from the train. She'll come in the warmer weather, as soon as she can, you'll see.'

'You could ask Vicar to fetch her in his car,' pleaded Mother. 'Oh please, Abbie.'

'I don't like to ask him, Mother. He'd have offered if he thought it a good idea. Besides, you're very poorly at the moment. Let Hester bring the baby when you're stronger, in the spring. The doctor says your blood-pressure is getting better every day you rest, and excitement is the last thing you need. She'll come in the spring, Mother, don't you worry. Hester is longing to come home and show you the baby.'

But when the spring did come, and Hester brought the babe to see us, it was to Mother's funeral.

Chapter Sixteen

THE GROUND

SHE CAME WITH the baby in the vicar's car, on a day of limpid sunshine. She had put on a little weight and lost the thin desperate look, and was more beautiful than ever, with a sort of glowing radiance about her, a bloom of motherhood. The vicar dropped her off at the gate and waved cheerily as he drove off up the lane in his old battered car. Lissie heard her arrive. She sprang, red-eyed from crying, but agog to see the baby, to meet her at the gate. I looked from the living room window, and watched them coming up the path.

Hester, holding the small bundle and a large bag, glanced about her at the garden: a hungry, lingering look. Lissie bounced beside her, plump and rosy, the early sunshine catching in her yellow hair. She smiled eagerly at Hester and hung upon her arm, and tried to catch at the baby's little hands waving above the blanket. They came up the path together, their yellow and russet heads bent over the baby's green blanket, like a touch of autumn in the spring.

We sat Hester down on the sofa, the baby in her arms. She held the child out to Lissie, then looked around the living room in unconcealed delight.

'May I really hold her, Hester?' Lissie said breathlessly. 'Oh, she's beautiful! Elizabeth! You named her after me, didn't you? Oh Hester! Hester, she's so lovely. Come to Aunty Lissie, my pet.'

Her strong young arms lifted the bundle from Hester's and held it against her, murmuring softly. Hester looked about her, sighed, and her eyes met mine.

'Oh Abbie,' she said, 'it's good to be home.'

'It's nice to have you, Hester.'

'If only Aunty was here. Oh I'm so sorry not to have come before, so very, very sorry. Poor Aunty Susan. I had no idea she was so ill, Abbie, truly I didn't. Poor, poor Aunty.'

'How's David?' I asked her. 'He couldn't come with you, then?'

'No,' she said. 'The shop.'

I nodded. 'Good of the vicar to fetch you.'

'Yes, it was.' She paused, seemed about to say something, and then appeared to change her mind. 'Where's Uncle Garfield?'

'In his shed. He's always there these days. We'll tell him in a minute that you're here.'

'And Thomas?'

'Up at the Tregulla's with Toby. I didn't want him to come to the funeral. It seemed best not. He'll be back after tea. Perran and Jen are going straight up to church. No one else is coming. Father only wanted the family there.'

'What time is the – the service?' she asked lightly.

'Two o'clock.'

Lissie bent over the baby, making little clucking sounds. She looked up. 'Hester, can I take her coat off? She looks awful hot.'

Hester said yes, she could do what she liked, and followed me out into the kitchen. 'Abbie, I'm so sorry,' she said again. 'I feel so dreadful that I didn't come before. But I couldn't, could I? I had no way. . .'

'No Hester, of course you couldn't. Don't blame yourself. It couldn't be helped.' Then I said, more to myself than to her, 'The weather was much too cold. But she did so want to see you, and the baby.'

'Oh, I know, I know!' It was almost a wail. She played with her fingers. 'And I wanted to come, so badly. Oh, if only you knew how badly!'

'Must you go home tonight?' I asked her.

For a moment she said nothing. She looked at me as if to

164

gauge my thoughts, and then said carefully, 'I can stay the night if you'll let me.'

'Oh do, Hester, if you're sure David wouldn't mind,' I said. 'We'd love you to. We'll tell the vicar this afternoon that he needn't take you back. But what about the baby?'

'I'll put her in a drawer, like I do at home. I've brought all her – brought lots of things, clothes and nappies.' She looked at me eagerly, her eyes shining, 'I could stay for a bit, if that's all right. For quite a while, in fact.'

'But what about poor David?'

She shrugged. 'Oh, he's all right. He's happier without me, really. He won't care.'

I looked at her. 'There's nothing wrong, is there? Between you and David?'

'Wrong?' she said lightly. 'I don't think anything has ever been right, really.' She twirled away from me and towards the door. 'Come on,' she said, 'I want to see everything! The garden, the shed, the orchard – everything. Aunty, Uncle, the fence, even the dustbin. Everything!' Then she sobered. 'Oh Abbie, I'm so sorry! For a moment I forgot. It's like coming home to – to my childhood, and expecting everything to be the same. And of course it isn't. Aunty Susan isn't here!'

For a moment she looked like a frightened child about to cry. But Hester never cried. She pressed her lips together, then released them. 'Oh Abbie, I'm so sorry, so very, very sorry.'

I gave her a quick smile. 'It's not your fault, Hester. You mustn't keep on blaming yourself for not coming before. You couldn't help it.'

'No, I don't mean that.' She frowned. 'I mean, I'm sorry about being so happy to be home. I shouldn't be, when poor Aunty isn't here any more, but I can't help it. Oh, it's perfectly wonderful to be at home.'

'But Hester,' I said, 'surely Truro is home to you now, isn't it?'

She gave a short laugh. 'And David? David would be glad if I never went back.'

In the living room, baby Elizabeth set up a little grumbling noise, and Lissie shushed her soothingly. 'There, there, my poppet. Hungry, are you? Don't you fret, your mummy's not far away. Aunty Lissie has got you safe.'

'Come on, Abbie,' Hester said. 'I want to go outside. Let's go and find Uncle Garfield and tell him I'm here. Oh, I've so longed for this moment. Lissie's all right with the baby. Come on Abbie, please!' She danced ahead of me out of the door, like she used to in the old days when she couldn't wait to be out in the air, or up on the hill. I peeped into the living room to where Lissie was bent over the child. She looked up and gave me a breathless smile. 'Oh Abbie, I've never seen such a lovely baby! Isn't she beautiful? Have you see her little hands?'

'Are you happy with her for a moment while Hester and I go up to Father?'

She nodded, eyes shining, and bent back to the baby. 'Oh, of course I am.'

I followed Hester out into the sunshine. Somewhere at the back of my mind a small pulse of alarm flickered up, then died. We went up the path to Father's shed, and gently pushed open the door.

'Father,' I said hesitantly, 'here's Hester to see you. She's arrived, with the baby.'

For a moment I thought he hadn't heard. He sat upon his little stool in a corner, quite silently, looking at his violin. It lay on the workbench beside him, out of its case, and in the webby light from the window I saw his hands upon its strings, light and still. For a moment nothing happened, and then he slowly raised his shaggy head and looked from one to the other of us in bewilderment, and his eyes were dull and blank. And then he said, softly sorrowful, as if to himself more than to me, 'I can't play no more, Abbie. Tis no good. The music's gone from me.'

'Come, Father,' I said, catching at his hand, 'it's only for a moment. It'll come back, you'll see. Look, here's Hester, come to see us with her baby. Come inside now, there's a dear, and have something to eat before we go to church this afternoon.'

He looked from one to the other of us again, then stood up unwillingly. As he did so his sleeve caught in the waist of the violin beside him and it fell on to the earthy floor with a little empty clatter and hummed faintly to itself within the wood. I picked it up and dusted it off. 'There Father. Look, it's not broken, luckily.' I ran my fingers across the strings and plucked at them gingerly, so that the four notes jumped out at us from the silence and hung in the air. 'See Father, it's quite all right. Shall I put it in its case for you?'

Hester held the case open and I lowered the violin carefully into its ancient blue velvet bed, then unscrewed the bow as I had seen him do so many times. We closed the lid, and gently led him out of the shed. The April day had clouded over suddenly. As we dressed for church the sun went in, and we walked up the hill to Mother's funeral in the rain.

Tea was very quiet that evening, in spite of the unusual number of us. Perran and Jennifer stayed, both rather downcast and formal, although at one time I did find Jennifer in the bedroom with Lissie, bending over baby Elizabeth and chuckling as she smiled and waved her small hands at them and tried to catch their hair. Perran, in his wedding suit, coughed and cleared his throat occasionally with Father's little nervous habit, and he helped me clear the table after tea. Lissie munched sandwiches, her eyes on the table before her, yellow head bent. Father was quieter than anyone, and even forgot to cough.

Later, in the kitchen, Perran helped me wash the dishes. He seemed rather downcast. 'So,' he said heavily, 'That's that then, Ab.'

'Yes,' I answered. 'It seems to be. Poor Mother. She'd have loved to have been here with us this afternoon, wouldn't she? The family all together again, and with Hester and the baby too.'

He gave a short laugh and said yes, she would have done.

He wiped the plates with laboured care and laid them in a pile on the table. 'What will you do now?'

'Me? Why, carry on as usual, I suppose. I was going back to my job at the shop but Mother's death has changed all that. I shall have to stay home and look after them here. Lissie is too young to manage on her own, and besides, during the term time she's still at school.'

'Do you mind?' he asked me.

'No, of course I don't mind. It isn't really a question of minding or not minding, anyway. Father and the others need me here at home, so naturally this is where I shall be; at least until Lissie and Thomas grow up and leave home. We'll manage somehow – financially, I mean. Father's vegetables help a lot. I don't know what we'd do without them.'

'I'll send you a bit of money when I can, Ab, now and again. I know how difficult things are.' He paused. 'You must get out a bit more, too. You never meet anyone new, do you? You'll never marry at this rate.'

I stared at him. 'Marry?' I said. 'I'm not worried about marrying yet, Perran. I'm only too pleased I'm not married, to tell the truth. I don't know how I'll feel in ten years' time, mind you, but right now I'm perfectly happy. It was you who was so keen on marrying young, don't forget. I'm glad for you, Perran. Jen looks wonderfully happy, and you look well too. She must be looking after you all right.'

He chuckled to himself. 'Oh, she's doing a fine job. I got no complaints. But I worry about you, Ab. I don't like to see you wasting your life.'

'Perran, I'm not wasting my life. I'm very happy here at home. I have no wish to leave, to meet all these imaginary suitors you seem to think I ought to be meeting. I'm staying here at home for as long as I'm needed. For ever if that's the way things work out. If fate has got a husband for me lined up somewhere, then he'll have to come knocking on the door to look for me himself. I'm certainly not going out to search for him. And if he doesn't come I shan't mind much. I shall just spend the rest of my life getting older and greyer and thinner and knitting jumpers for all my hundreds of nephews and nieces and sighing a bit from time to time in wondering whether I would have liked things any different.'

He laughed to himself. 'Oh well,' he said, 'if you're happy. I suppose that's all that really matters.'

I handed him the bread-knife. 'Careful with that, it's sharp. How's the baking business?'

He chuckled again. 'Oh, well enough. Sam and I are taking on an extra chap. He's a ringer from up Liskeard way. He's a good chap, is Richard.' He paused. 'He'd do for you.'

I sighed, laughing in spite of myself. 'Oh shush, Perran, do! Here, give me that bread-knife. You'll cut yourself.'

'You can't have it,' he said, holding it high above his head so that his height made it impossible for me to reach it. 'You can't have it until you've promised to let me bring Richard over here to meet you. I fancy doing a spot of match-making. You and Richard'd suit each other proper, you would. Both stubborn as hell. Come on, Abbie, promise me you'll meet him? Promise you'll ask him to tea?'

'No Perran, I won't!'

'All right then, you can't have your bread-knife. We could do with a nice bread-knife at home, Jen and me. This is a good sharp one. Proper job, this is. Just the thing for Jen to slice up our bread with, for sandwiches and that. Come on Ab, you got to promise. If you want your bread-knife back you've got to have Richard as well. What do you say?'

'Oh Perran, give it here!' I began to giggle, trying to reach it, but he twisted and turned, holding it high out of reach.

'Choose!' he ordered. 'Richard and the bread-knife, or nothing. And don't you tickle me neither, girl. I know your little tricks, from old. There's to be no cheating. It's a fair choice. Have the knife back and you've got to have Richard too.' He brandished it in the air. 'You've only got to ask him to tea, Ab, with Jen and me. Is it a bargain? Promise, now?'

I could see the bread-knife waving perilously near the

light-flex. 'Oh, all right,' I said, laughing, 'but give it here, Perran. We don't want an accident. Come on, let me have it back.'

He waggled the knife higher. 'No so fast. We haven't discussed terms yet. We'll make it a Saturday, Abbie, and we'll have splits with jam and cream and – er, cake? A bit of Lissie's saffron, and a pasty or two to fill up the corners. I'll bring the splits and a loaf or two, and you can make the pasties. Richard likes a pasty. He'd like yours, Ab. Make a proper pasty, you do. A deal, is it? Right, you can have your bread-knife back now then.' He handed it back to me. 'When's the party to be, then? Got to be soon, before Jen gets too big to move. Come on now, when?'

Suddenly sobering, I looked at him. 'Not for a bit, Perran. Not until Father feels a bit better. He's taken all this about Mother very badly. I don't think we ought to plan any more parties for a while, do you?'

He looked suddenly grave. 'Sorry, Ab. For a moment I forgot. It don't really seem possible, do it? Just like she's out somewhere for the afternoon. Poor old Ma. Oh, dear life, I forgot for the minute.'

I put my hand on his arm. 'I know. It doesn't seem possible that she's gone for ever, does it? I suppose that's how it is when you've loved people. They're so much a part of you that they never really do just disappear. They're always still with you somewhere, in your mind.'

He nodded, silently. Then he shook himself quickly, as if to shake off a shadow, and looked at me. 'How's it going with Hester? Nice little baby. Looks like her, apart from the colouring.'

'She looks very well, don't you think?'

'Oh, she looks all right. But then, she always did. Nice looking girl, Hester; and that face of hers always did have a cloudy look. She don't take much notice of the kid, though, do she? I thought they was all over 'em when they were little. Jen's chuffed to hell about the thought of ours.'

I wondered exactly what he meant about Hester having a 'cloudy look'. I said slowly, 'Jen's a lovely girl. I like her very much, Perran. You said I would.' I paused, holding a plate up to drain. 'Do you really think Hester is offhand with the baby? She seems very fond of her, to me.'

'Well, she lets Liss do everything, don't she? I went in there just now and Lissie was changing its nappy or sommat with Jen, and they were chuckling to it and talking a bit, and Hester wasn't even there.'

'Well, at least she's feeding Elizabeth herself,' I retorted. 'No one can do that for her but Hester!'

'All right, spitfire!' He laughed good-humouredly. 'Dear old Ab, loyal as ever. I wouldn't like to be the one to lose your friendship, ever! Feeding it, is she? Properly, I mean, not with bottles and that? Good. Jen's going to do that with ours. I think a woman ought to. You got to give 'em the best start in life, and there's nothing better than that.'

'You seem to know a lot about it,' I told him.

'Oh, we've been to classes, Jen and me. Very progressive, we are.' He paused, and looked a bit hesitant and began to fiddle with the knives and forks, lining them up in meticulous formation as if all his concentration was on it, and then he looked up at me. 'Talking of Hester, what did you think of her news?'

'News?' I asked. 'What news?'

'Oh Gawd,' he said, 'you mean she hasn't told you?'

'Told me?' I asked him, and the little stabbing pulse of alarm flickered up again. 'Told me what, for heaven's sake?'

'Well, that he's left her, of course. I thought you'd know, Ab. David's left her. She's come back home to stay.'

Chapter Seventeen

THE FOREST

THAT EVENING WHEN they'd gone and Elizabeth had been put to bed, I tackled Hester. I said nothing at all while Lissie bathed the baby (under my eye) in the kitchen sink and Hester fed her (under Lissie's eye). They put her to sleep in a drawer, with a pillow for a mattress, and two of Mother's knitted blankets and the old yellow shawl around her, nice and snug.

'She went off to sleep like a lamb,' said Lissie to me afterwards, aglow with vicarious motherhood. 'I'll just wash out these nappies and hang them on the line before I take Father out. I think he ought to go out for a walk, Abbie, don't you? He's done nothing but sit up there in his shed this afternoon since we got back, all quiet and alone, apart from tea. He won't even play a tune or two. He just sits there staring. I'm awful worried. He ate his tea but he didn't really seem to know what he was doing, did he? Take him out for a bit, shall I? Get him to talk about Mother, perhaps. Do you think so, Abbie?'

'Yes, my pet, that's a good idea. It might help if you can get him to talk a bit. Besides, I want to talk to Hester. Where is she? And where's Thomas got to? Oh, here he is, behind me. Thomas, did you thank Toby's mother for having you?'

Thomas nodded. 'Ab, did Perran come? Did you go to church for Mother? Is it all over, Ab?'

I put my arm round his small shoulders. 'Yes, my pet, it is. I'm glad you didn't come, Thomas. It would only have upset you. It was much better not. There, there, don't cry, my darling, don't cry.'

I held my arms about him. After a while he looked up. 'It's all right, I've stopped now. Ab, did Hester come? Can I see her baby?'

I took his hand and led him into the bedroom where Elizabeth lay asleep in her drawer, small fists clasped beside her ears, her fingers curled in sleep. Thomas stared at her for a while, and then looked at me. 'Can I get my stuff, Ab?' I nodded and he dashed out, returning almost at once and with a concentration beyond his years, he settled down beside the baby with his books and pencils in his hand.

'You won't make any noises to wake her up, will you?' I asked him sternly. 'Or you'll have to come out of here, quick sharp.'

His eyes stayed on the baby's face and his hands leafed over the pages of his pad, but he turned his curly head, haloed with wild hair, in my direction, so I knew he'd heard. Quiet as a cat watching a bird was Thomas with a model to draw from, so I left him to it. I went downstairs to find Hester.

I found her in the orchard, deep in daffodils. The sight of her standing there beneath the trees startled me into silence. The words that I had planned to say melted away, and I could only stand and watch, reminded of the moments years ago when I used to come upon her thus, silent in the orchard. She must have heard me coming for she turned around with a wistful smile. 'Do you remember, Abbie, how we used to pick daffodils to put on the grave? And sometimes there were bluebells. We'd take them up there in great bunches, wouldn't we? And we'd put them on the grave.'

'You would, Hester,' I reminded her. 'He was your grandfather, remember?'

She smiled. For a moment I thought the lingering sun had suddenly come out upon the orchard; but it was only Hester smiling.

'Come in,' I said. 'I want to talk to you.'

She followed me back through the meady-coloured daffo-

173

dils, down to the cottage, and stopped me at the door. Her hand moved on the latch. 'Perran told you, didn't he,' she said.

'Yes Hester,' I said, 'he did. Why didn't you tell me? I would much rather have heard it from you.'

'I was afraid to tell you, Abbie. I was so very afraid.'

'Afraid?' I echoed. 'Whatever for? How could you be afraid of me, you silly girl?'

'Not afraid of you, Abbie. But afraid you might not let me stay if you knew the truth of it.'

'But Hester, of course I'd let you stay. This is your home; at least, it was.' I sighed. 'You'd better come inside and tell me all about it.'

We went into the living room, dim with evening. Lissie had picked primroses to cheer us up a little after the service, and they massed in velvety yellows in a bowl on our wide window-ledge. A wandering bumble-bee rattled angrily at the window-pane, seeing daylight and trying to escape. I moved Lissie's current knitting and sat Hester down. 'Now tell me,' I said.

'In a moment.' She sprang to the window after the bee, cupping her hand gently round its fat body.

'Careful! It'll sting you.'

She laughed gently, 'No, he won't.' She let it clamber round a finger, lifting itself upright with hairy L-shaped feet and pausing for a moment on her finger-tip. 'There,' she said, 'you're ready now. Off you go.' She saw it to the open window, and I was briefly reminded of the jackdaw all those years ago.

'Hester,' I said. 'Will you please come and tell me. Is it true?'

'Is what true?' she asked, her back to me. 'What did he tell you? Oh Abbie, I so love this time of evening!' She sobered. 'I wish Aunty Susan was here; I do miss her so.'

I waited, saying nothing, and presently she came and sat down opposite me, very calmly, in an armchair. 'Yes,' she said, 'It is true. David and I have parted.' She said it in a curiously pat way, very light, like a child reciting a lesson.

'But why, Hester? What on earth happened? What went wrong? You were so happy when I left you after Elizabeth.'

She shrugged her slight shoulders and caught her hands together in an old childish gesture. 'I don't know. It went all cold and lonely again almost straightaway. Almost as soon as you left.'

'But Hester, the house! What will he do? Where will he go?'

'Oh, David will stay there, I expect. Either that or go back to his mother's. She doesn't like me, Abbie. She never has done. She'll be glad I've gone. She would much rather have had Veronica for a daughter-in-law, you know. She told me so. I expect David will stay on in the house on his own.'

'But I thought that he had left you,' I said, puzzled. 'Perran said . . .'

'No.' She picked idly at a thread on her skirt. 'It's not quite like that, Abbie. The other way round.'

'You mean, you left him?'

'Yes, that's right,' She examined a finger-nail, avoiding my eyes.

'But why, Hester?' I asked. 'You said you were fond of him, and he loves you very much, you know he does. I thought you loved him, too.'

She gave me a strange, veiled look for a moment, and then said, 'Yes, I do love him, quite a lot. He was wonderfully patient.'

'Then what's wrong, Hester? Surely if you love him then your place is there with him.'

She looked at me. 'It seems so simple to you, doesn't it? Oh, I wish it was simple, really I do. If only you knew how much I wish it could be like that. But he's not real, Abbie. He isn't real. I'm not real. It's all so strange; it always has been.'

I picked up a strand of Lissie's wool and began to play idly with it, twisting it round my finger. 'Hester, I don't know exactly what you mean, I'm afraid. How can he not be real? Of course he's real! Like you are, and I am, and

Elizabeth. He helped to make Elizabeth, didn't he? And she's real enough, surely. So how can David not be real, for goodness sake?'

'Oh,' she said, in a voice that was almost a wail, 'you don't understand, do you? Nobody has, not ever, except – no, nobody. Let me stay here, Abbie? Just for a little while, please! Perhaps I'll go back to David, I promise I'll think about it, only just let me stay for a little bit first, a few weeks perhaps, and then I'll go away. But please let me stay here for a little while first. I've missed it so badly. I can't bear it if I can't be here.' There was an extraordinary anguish in her low voice. She clasped her hands in her lap, squeezing them together so that the knuckles went white. 'Just for a few weeks, Abbie; and then I promise I'll go away.'

'What about David?'

She didn't answer me. Her eyes were upon the window, suddenly wide with alarm. I turned my head around to see what was there, and caught the faint edge of a shadow passing the window. 'It's only Lissie coming back with Father,' I said.

She shook herself.

'Hester,' I said, 'you're shaking!' I put my hand on her forehead. She was quite cool, but trembling.

'It's nothing. Only a chill,' she said. 'For a moment I thought . . . oh, nothing. Look, here's Lissie with Uncle Garfield.' She stood up. 'Don't tell them, Abbie, promise? Not for a bit, anyway. Let me stay for a few days first?'

I threw aside the wool and sighed. 'All right,' I said.

The next morning Lissie and I set out for Polly Tregulla's to borrow a pram for Elizabeth. Their younger child was almost three, and Polly had offered to lend us the pram whenever Hester should be at home. We left Hester in the kitchen washing up the breakfast things, Elizabeth propped up on a pillow beside her in the wicker chair that had been Mother's, with a patchwork cushion on one side of her and Father's rolled-up cardigan on the other to prevent her from rolling off, and set off together. Lissie was humming gently to herself and we strolled along pleasantly in the morning sunshine, in no particular hurry. We came down the lane towards the village and the sun struck mellowly upon the slate cottage roofs. There was the smell of baking in the air and newly-washed clothes. And I thought how strange it was that my own mother could have been buried yesterday but the world could go on as normal, doing its washing and baking and worrying about paying its electricity bills, as if poor Mother had never even been born. I suppose that to anyone else she need not have been born; that all the stars and planets wheeling about the vast heavens would have blazed and turned and wheeled just the same whether she or we had been born to ponder upon them or not, but to Perran and Lissie and Thomas and me she was the cornerstone of our knowledge of this life and universe.

Sometimes it seems to me that it is upon the merest chance that we came into the world at all, for if my parents had not come together at that particular moment in which I was conceived, I would not have been created. Some other child would have come at some other moment in my place; but it would not have been me, and I should have missed existence altogether. Some other child might have been called Abigail, might still have looked like me with the same brownish hair and my freckles, but it would not have been me inside. And all in all, I was very glad that I had been made me, for it was a pleasant life with all those I loved about me and I was grateful to Mother for her bit of creation.

We reached Harry Tregulla's at the far end of the village. We went up a narrow lane between two rows of cottages, climbed the high steps, and knocked on the front door. It was opened by Toby, round of face, with Harry's same short nose. He looked at us without interest, sniffed, then called across his shoulder, 'It's Thomas's two sisters.' He frowned at us. 'Where's Thomas to?'

'At school, of course,' said Lissie scornfully. 'Why aren't you?'

Toby regarded us disdainfully, his jaws working, his hand in a small white bag. From time to time he withdrew his hand and conveyed it to his mouth. 'Why aren't you?'

'Never you mind,' retorted Lissie. 'We've come to see your mother.'

Toby sniffed again, and Polly shouldered past him. 'Who is it?' she asked. 'Oh Abbie, it's you. Come in, my 'ansome, do.' She peered at Toby. 'Here, you're not still eating sweets, are you? My dear soul, you don't never stop, do you. Come in, girls, it's nice to see you both. Here Abbie, I'm awful sorry about your mother. Lovely woman. Come about the pram, have you? I thought you had. When's Hester coming, then? Oh, she's here, is she? Toby, get on outside and look after Dawn in the garden, will you? And mind that cough of yours.'

She led us through the scullery behind the kitchen, where an enormous green mangle stood on a table. Beside it, and covered with cobwebs, stood a low, old-fashioned baby-carriage. 'Is it any good, Abbie?' she asked anxiously. 'You're very welcome to borrow it for Hester's babe, my 'ansome, if 'tis any good. Harry was going to clean it up a bit for you. It's been stuck here for two or three years now, ever since Dawn started walking. When did Hester come?'

'Yesterday,' I said. 'She's staying for a while.'

'Oh isn't that lovely for you all! Lovely girl, Hester. What's she called her baby? Elizabeth? Is that after you, Lissie? My dear life, I bet you just love to have that little baby in the house, don't you?' She detached the pram from its corner and bounced the handle up and down until clouds of dust flew off it. 'Can you give it a clean, Abbie? I wish I'd known, I'd have cleaned it myself for you.'

Lissie's eyes shone. She held the handle reverently and moved it up and down so that the pram rocked on its ancient springs and creaked. Polly nodded towards her and winked at me. 'Proper little mother, aren't you, Liss? How old are you now, my 'ansome? Fifteen, are you? My dear life, how time flies! I remember when you two girls was little things down here somewhere, holding on to your mother's skirts when I was carrying Toby. And look at him now! Dear soul, it makes you feel old, seeing the years pass so quick. Here Abbie, I'm some sorry about your Ma, my 'ansome. Sudden, wasn't it? We knew she hadn't been too well, of course, in bed and that, but we never realized twas so serious. How's Garfield taking it? Awful cut-up, is he? George Pascoe was thinking of a half-muffled peal for Susan, but Harry wondered if Garfield might take it badly, be upset and that. What do you think, Abbie?'

'Oh dear,' I said, 'I don't really know one way or the other. I don't think Father would even notice at the moment. I don't know what to say about that.'

'Oh well, perhaps t'would be better not. I'll tell Harry what you've said. He's awful sorry, Abbie. A lovely woman she was, your Ma. Everybody liked her. You just had the family to the funeral, did you? Did Joseph go?'

'No,' I told her. 'Father wanted just the six of us. Thanks for having Thomas, Polly. I think he would have been upset.'

'Yes, of course,' she said. 'He's never any trouble, that boy. I'll have Thomas any time. He had Toby and Dawn sitting on the floor in there, quiet as mice. Drawing them, he was, all afternoon. He's awful good, Abbie. I couldn't believe he'd done it when he showed the drawings to me. Here, come and have a look at them. He said I could keep them. Better than any old snaps, they are. Come and have a look.'

We found Hester cooking when we got back with the pram. Lissie had pushed it all the way home, up the lane and in at our gate, refusing any offers of help. She left it by the back door and we went into the kitchen to see Hester at the table making pastry. She looked up and gave us a little smile. 'I thought I'd make a pie for dinner.' She waved a hand towards the pantry. 'Uncle Garfield's in there, doing something with his wine. Did you borrow the pram from Harry's Polly?'

Lissie giggled. 'Oh Hester, you should see it! It's huge and very old and awful dirty. But I'm going to clean it up and put some scouring powder on it to get the white back, and it'll be lovely for taking Elizabeth out. Come and see it, Hester! Where's Elizabeth? Where's my baby to? Let her come and see it too.'

'She's upstairs asleep,' said Hester, wiping her hands on her apron. 'You shall get her when she wakes up, I promise. There was no post, Abbie, and nobody called.' She held out her hand to Lissie. 'Come and show me the pram. So you think it will be all right for Elizabeth's walks?'

Lissie took her out and I heard them laughing outside the door. I went upstairs to change my shoes, and peeped in at Elizabeth. She was fast asleep. I looked at her, remembering the moments of her hasty arrival, and her mouth contracted into a small pink line. She turned and whimpered in her sleep and stretched her fingers into small rose-coloured stars. I put a finger into a star and jiggled it gently, and ruthless tendrils of life curled about my finger and held on. Downstairs in the pantry beneath the bedroom Father shuffled invisibly, clinking wine-jars. I heard the back-door close, and then the sound of vigorous brushing beneath the window, and Lissie's muffled coughs.

I stood there for some time, my finger held firm in its stellate grip, while the sounds of home came in through the window and up through the floor. And gradually a certain curious rapture came upon me standing there, a kind of bliss of the everyday world; the sounds and smells of stirring life; the tide of breath within my lungs; the mysterious ecstasy of senses, sight and smell and touch, and the edge of hunger and of grief. I thought how strange it was that I did not mourn my mother buried yesterday, but relinquished her respectfully, and with a kind of trust. It was as if bliss came upon me standing there, a glimpse of something beyond reality, as if for just a second I had heard the whirr and tick of heaven, and the hum at the heart of the atom.

The baby struggled a little in her sleep. Downstairs the brushing started up again. There were footsteps, very light, upon the stairs. Hester peeped in.

'Still asleep,' I whispered.

She nodded. 'I've put the pie in the oven. She'll want a feed soon, but I promised Lissie she could come up and get her.'

I carefully withdrew my finger. 'I'll come and do the potatoes.'

'They're done,' she said. 'Everything's ready. Oh Abbie, it is good to be home!'

At the sound of her voice the baby opened blue eyes and screwed them up again at the light. She began to cry, little spluttering complaints in her throat, then smiled toothlessly, writhing with delight, when she saw Hester.

'You'd better tell Lissie that she's awake,' said Hester. 'I'll change her first, then Lissie can take her down. She's in the garden, cleaning the pram.'

As I went down the stairs in search of my sister I could smell the pie, and hear the potatoes bubbling on the stove. The memory of that moment in the bedroom when bliss had come to switch a light on in my world remained with me, and I thought how when it had come it was nothing but a distillation of everyday homely things, the sort of things that any woman might have around her, but held within it a shaft of pure radiance. And I thought, also, how strange it was that I had found my joy within another woman's baby's hand.

Thomas came in from school while I was laying the table. 'Look Abbie,' he told me proudly, holding up a battered volume, 'I've got a book! Teacher gave it to me to keep for my own. It's all about anamity, so I can see what goes on under people's skins; muscles and bones and things. She says it's important to know what happens underneath.'

'Anamity?' I asked him, laughing. 'Oh, you mean anatomy! Yes, I suppose it is important, if you want to draw everything in the right place. How lovely, Thomas. Wash your hands, my pet. Dinner won't be long. Hester is going to feed Elizabeth first, but you can start yours if you like.'

'No,' he said, 'I'll wait for you. I want to put this in my room. You won't take it away, Abbie, will you? You won't tidy round and get it lost? I don't want it to get lost.'

'No, I won't go in there at all,' I promised him. 'Mind you keep your room very tidy now, and then I won't have to. You've been much better lately. Now look, here's Lissie and Hester with the baby. Pop upstairs if you want to, and I'll call you when the dinner's ready.'

He was gone in a moment, rushing up the stairs to his bedroom, his coat, satchel and shoes scattered all over the living room like driftwood thrown up by a passing wave. I sighed, then chuckled a bit at the thought of Thomas poring over anatomy, and gathered them up into a heap on a chair. Lissie came in with Elizabeth in her arms. Hester took the baby from her, and Lissie went out again to the pram.

Hester settled down to give the child her dinner. She always fed the baby openly on the sofa in front of us. It was a thing of great beauty to see her unbuttoning her front and watch the bliss on the baby's small face as she sought and found the milk. Hester, richly maternal, bent over her, one white shoulder and the curve of breast above the baby's eager searching mouth.

'How does it feel,' I asked her shyly, 'to feed a baby, Hester?'

She looked up at me, her eyes dark-shadowed, mysterious with motherhood, and said softly, 'Oh, it feels like clouds feel, I should think, giving rain to thirsty earth.'

About her as she sat feeding her child, there fell a mellow silence. The baby suckled contentedly. Upstairs Thomas bumped softly as he moved about his room, and Father rattled in the pantry. On the window-sill a shaft of sunlight struck the bowl of Lissie's primroses with a golden glance and fell further, on to Hester's hair. Absorbed in her ancient task of womankind she leaned slightly forward, her body curved protectingly round the child, so that her rich hair fell over the baby in a luminous shadow. So, I thought, might Mary have leaned, feeding the infant Jesus on an April morning.

There was a sudden unexpected footfall on the step outside. A knock, and the door swung open. Hester, her shoulder curved about her child, looked up with hazy interest to see who came, and blinked a little in the sudden light. I looked up to see who trespassed upon glory at lunchtime on a weekday. And Joseph stood in the doorway.

With his hand upon the latch, his eyes fell upon Hester feeding her babe, upon auburn head softly raised above small yellow head; and his face was set with a terrible raw yearning. And Hester, looking up, saw Joseph standing there. Rich amber eyes met grey ones with a little sigh. Into both their faces there came a look of curious enchantment, as if in ancient recognition their two souls stooped low, and loomed, purple-shadowed and crepuscular, over the great dark forest of desire; as if their souls had thirsted for a thousand years, seeking a well-spring of water in the earth, and had come upon enough to shake the heart and, drinking, then be stilled.

Chapter Eighteen

THE EARTH

I THINK I was the first one to speak. Feeling foolish I said brightly to cover my embarrassment, 'Hello Joseph. Nice to see you.'

There was a brief silence, and then he seemed to recollect himself and pull his thoughts together with an effort. He turned his eyes away from Hester and seemed at rather a loss. I looked at his face and my heart contracted at the misery there.

'Sorry,' he was muttering to himself, 'I didn't mean to come. . .' He shook his head, as if to pull himself together. 'She's back with you. I – I didn't know.' His face was scarlet; a low tide of red suffused his skin, and beads of moisture stood along his lip. I looked from him to Hester. She had her head down low over the baby. Her lashes lay across her cheeks, shielding her eyes, but the hand that held the baby's blanket trembled like a branch when thunder threatens.

Joseph was staring at the floor. He raised an arm and lightly brushed it across his eyes. There was a scrape and a thud as the pantry door opened and Father emerged, sieve and piping in his hands. He stopped short when he saw Joseph. He nodded towards him, and Joseph nodded back, like two silent puppets on strings. I could have laughed at them if I hadn't seen the misery in Joseph's eyes, and the bleak look in Father's. Joseph turned to go. He put a bowl of brown eggs down on the table beside the sink, then hesitated for a moment. He stood there beside them, shuffling his feet awkwardly, looking as if he wanted to stay and go both at the same time. Father looked from one to the other of us, sensing some slight tension in the air, and said, 'Tea is there, Abbie?'

I nodded. 'Have a cup of tea with us, Joseph? We'll all have one.'

He nodded his head. There never was a more silent man than Joseph, I reflected in exasperation, filling the kettle at the sink. Hester had finished feeding her baby by now and deftly rebuttoned her blouse. She put Elizabeth over her shoulder and began to pat her back softly to bring up the wind, crooning gently to her in a special voice she kept for Elizabeth alone. When I turned again she had disappeared upstairs.

We drank our tea in silence. I tried once to talk to Joseph but his silence went deeper than words, I think, deep as the earth. I sorely missed Mother's presence and light chatter. Once Joseph said awkwardly, 'Sorry about your mother, Abbie,' and I glanced at Father. His face was heavy, set with a leaden look, and he began to talk jerkily to Joseph about the spring planting he was planning, the peas, leeks and beetroot and how much ground he was going to give to potatoes this year, as if to clear the thought of Mother from his mind.

Joseph drank his tea and thanked me, and got up to go. Hester had not reappeared. He went quickly and silently, stepping out of the door as if he was afraid something might detain him if he lingered, and I hardly had time to thank him for the eggs. I went with him to the gate. We said nothing as we walked up the path but as he paused his fingers trembled on the gate-post.

'Thank you for the eggs, Joseph,' I said, rather at a loss.

He nodded. 'Pleasure.' Then he said, 'She's back, then.'

'Yes,' I said, 'for a little while, on a visit. She gets very homesick over there in Truro. Do her good to have a holiday at home.' It was what I'd planned to say to anyone who asked, and it seemed a useful enough thing to say to Joseph. There was silence for a moment. Above us the light spring wind off the old hill caught in the trees and tossed the

185

bright infant leaves, and showered drops in spasms on our heads.

'Is she happy?' he asked me.

For answer I shrugged lightly. 'I don't know. I never know with Hester. I think she misses us a lot.'

He nodded, his eyes on the stones in the lane. 'Looks like another shower, Abbie.'

'Yes,' I said. 'It does.'

He lingered, seeming unwilling to go, and thanked me again for the tea. I glanced sideways at him. He turned and, looking at me full in the face for a moment, said, 'She couldn't have married me, Abbie.'

I knew not what to say. He took a piece of hawthorn, bright with flower, in his hands, then released it gently so that it swung back into the hedge with a little blossomy shudder. 'And anyway,' he said, 'it's too late now.' Then he turned on his heel and was off down the lane, turning only to wave me a brief goodbye.

I went back into the kitchen to dish up the dinner, conscious of a heaviness of heart that had not been there for weeks. Lissie came in from cleaning the pram, glowing with pride and hunger. Hester said very little. She made no reference at all to the extraordinary moment, but she was very quiet all through dinner. When Thomas came down from his bedroom and rushed up to her to tell her that his drawing of Elizabeth had been pinned up in a place of pride in the classroom she smiled and said she was delighted. And when Lissie pleaded to be allowed to take Elizabeth out for her first walk in the spotless pram that afternoon she nodded and said certainly. When I suggested going with them so that we could visit Mrs Blamey and show her the baby she smiled again. But the old enchanted look was back, and somewhere at the back of her eyes, behind the smiles and nods and acquiescences, was a new look of raw misery.

May came and went, and with it news from Perran. Jennifer was expecting twins, the doctor thought, and they were

186

both delighted at the prospect. She was keeping very well, but finding it difficult to get about much, being so big with two babies; but they would let us know the moment there was news, and for the moment they both sent their love to us all, and Jenny would be glad of any outgrown clothes that Hester could spare for the babies, money being rather short. Hester packed her up a multitude of little vests and nightdresses, shawls and bibs, and took them to the post-office in the pram.

'But Hester,' I said, 'won't you need them again one day? Perhaps. . .' I trailed off lamely. She looked at me with that curious pitying look I remembered and said, 'No Abbie, don't be silly. I shall never have another child.'

'But you don't know for sure,' I said, a little helplessly. 'You don't know what might happen. . .'

'Oh yes I do,' she said quietly, in a remote voice I had heard so often lately. 'I know exactly what will happen.' I shrugged, and let her post them off to Jennifer, who wrote back straight away to say how delighted she was to get them all. Jennifer wrote a cheerful letter, full of details of their arrangements for the twins, how excited they both were and Sam too; and that Perran sent his love and to tell me not to forget my promise about Richard.

'Promise?' said Lissie in surprise, putting down the letter. 'What did you promise him, Abbie? What did you promise him about Richard?'

'Oh nothing,' I said lightly. 'It was only a bit of fun, anyway. We were only joking. Perran wanted me to ask them here to tea with a friend of theirs.'

'The one who came before?'

'Why, yes,' I said. 'He came while I was away. Do you remember him, Lissie?'

Surprisingly, she went very red and said yes, she remembered him well, for Perran had brought him home after the peal and they'd had a cup of tea and he'd liked her chocolate cake a great deal, and had eaten three pieces.

'Then if Richard comes,' I told her, 'you must make another cake for him to sample. Perhaps a sponge or saffron the next time?' She laughed and blushed again and went off into the garden in search of Hester and the baby, covered in confusion. I put Jennifer's letter thoughtfully down on the dresser, and wrote back two or three days later to say that of course we'd like them all to come to tea, perhaps after the twins were born, and Father feeling a bit better.

Father was still worrying us. He had begun to complain of strange aches and pains now and again, of heaviness in his hands, and seemed very weary all the time. He still sat in the woodshed on his own for hours on end, but hardly ever tried to play his violin. Once or twice we heard him tuning it, and once a little feeble sound of music came winding down between the trees, but after it a sudden sliding note, then silence.

On a June morning heavy with the scent of blossom I took my shopping basket and set out with Thomas to walk the five miles or so across the footpath to our nearest town. We set off up the lane towards the hill ahead of us. All fair and innocent it looked, in the crystal light. We climbed the steep lane up towards the church, and met the vicar coming out of the vicarage gate.

'Good morning, Abigail!' he greeted me warmly, shaking hands. 'And young Thomas, too. No school this morning, Thomas? Oh no, of course, it's Saturday, how foolish of me. I see you are both off for a walk. How very pleasant. My, my, it really is a splendid morning, isn't it? It makes one feel quite glad to be alive under the Good Lord's heaven. How is your father, my dear?' He frowned and nodded thoughtfully. 'Still finding life a little difficult to come to terms with? Just a little better? Oh, I really am delighted to hear that. And Hester, of course, has no doubt returned to Truro by now? She has not? Dear me, dear me.' He hesitated. 'I wonder, Abigail – I wonder if you could spare me a few minutes of your time this morning. Perhaps you could pop back home with me for a moment. I will not detain you long. I – ah, I rather wanted to have a word or two with you about your young cousin.'

'Oh?' I said guardedly. 'Well, yes of course. Take the

basket, Thomas, and wait for me in the churchyard.'

'No, no,' he said, 'bring the young man with you. This little matter will not take more than a minute, I assure you. No doubt we can find him a chocolate biscuit or two to while away the time. You'd like that, wouldn't you, young man?' Thomas nodded politely, although he was not a boy greatly swayed by chocolate biscuits as a general rule. The vicar led us through the hall to the small room at the back of the house that he used as a study, and sat me down on a wooden chair so highly glazed with polish that I feared I might slide off it if I didn't concentrate, and offered chocolate biscuits from a tin.

'No thank you,' I said, 'although Thomas might. Wait outside, Thomas. You could go into the garden and draw the vicar's trees.'

The vicar blinked slightly, as if Thomas might possibly be contemplating drawing sap from tree-trunks with a knife, and then he brightened and said, 'Ah yes, of course. I hear you like to sketch, young man. Do you carry paper and pencils with you? Ah, I see that you do. Yes, yes, by all means go and sketch whatever takes your fancy. There is a fine old oak beside the south fence, a magnificent specimen several hundred years old; it would make an excellent subject.' He crossed to the window and stood looking out, then went on in his gentle, scholarly voice, 'My wife planted daffodils beneath it several years ago, and they are a perfect picture in the spring. They're over now, of course, but the roses are splendid at this time of year. Do you care for sketching flowers, Thomas? My wife is very proud of our pelargoniums. We have a magnificent display outside our kitchen window.' He waved through his little study window and I followed his eyes. 'My wife is out there now, weeding them. Why don't you go along and say good-morning to her?'

When Thomas had obeyed, munching chocolate biscuits, with his free hand cupped beneath them to catch stray crumbs, the vicar turned to me. 'Now,' he said brightly, 'how are you, my dear?'

'Me? I'm very well, thank you,' I said. I waited. He caught his hands together and walked up and down for a moment, as if unsure of how to begin.

'You wanted to ask me about Hester,' I told him helpfully.

'Ah yes,' he said carefully, 'Hester. Mrs Penkevin.'

I looked at my hands. 'Yes. Mrs Penkevin.'

'She – ah, she's still with you, then?'

'Yes,' I said, 'she's still with us.'

'Abigail,' said the vicar earnestly, 'may I speak to you frankly? I feel I've known you long enough to do so, my dear. I hesitate. I have an abhorrence of intrusion, but I feel in this case it is my duty to . . .' He made a fist with one hand and tapped it gently upon the other one, and peered thoughtfully out of the window. 'To – er, intervene in a situation which, I fear, is causing great unhappiness.'

'You mean, to David?'

'Yes, to young David.' He paused. 'Hester has been with you since April. It is now June. Tell me, Abigail, when is she intending to return to her husband?'

There was a little silence. 'I don't know,' I said. 'She's very happy with us. I don't think she wants to go back just yet.'

'But Abigail, she is his wife. She surely cannot intend to remain with you for much longer. Have you spoken to her about returning?'

'No. I thought she'd want to go back before now, but she hasn't mentioned it.'

'Forgive me, my dear, but yours does seem a somewhat casual attitude. Should you not be making some attempt to persuade her? Even to put some pressure upon her?'

'Pressure?' I asked him. 'What sort of pressure?'

He cleared his throat. 'Well really, child, you must surely know the kind of argument likely to appeal to her. Duty? Love? Their mutual happiness?'

'I don't think Hester was very happy with David,' I said awkwardly. There was another silence. He stood at the window, looking out, and rocking a little from his toes to his

190

heels, backwards and forwards. Then he said pensively, 'Her parents, Abigail. Who were they? Somehow I have never felt it my place to inquire from your father. I rather expected him to acquaint me with the basic facts when Hester first came to live with you some years ago, but he has never volunteered the information. Do you have any idea? Were they local folk? Do you remember them? Were they relatives, perhaps? I believe Hester is your father's niece, is she not?'

'Yes', I said, 'but I don't know much more. At least, I know who her mother was, but I never met her. I don't think Mother did, either. Her mother was Father's youngest sister.'

'And her father?'

'I've no idea at all. Father will never talk about him. I suppose she must have been illegitimate or something.'

He nodded thoughtfully, 'Quite so, quite so. No doubt you are probably right. She is a quite extraordinarily beautiful girl, Abigail. A fascinating child, but rather disturbing. I find her somewhat of an enigma. She has a curious air of tragedy about her, an oddly worrying quality that I cannot quite define.'

'Yes,' I said, 'I know what you mean. A sort of sadness.'

'A sadness, yes, but something more than that. I mean a strange quality of emptiness, as if some part of her were missing. Am I making sense to you? I wonder if I am imagining things. My wife tells me sometimes that I am becoming rather forgetful. My spectacles, for instance, seem rather elusive of late, as if they had a personality of their own and were wilfully avoiding me.' He chuckled. 'Encroaching old age, no doubt. It comes to us all. But I do not think I am unperceptive with people; quite the contrary, I find increasing age and experience leads one to see certain things more clearly. It is as if the faculty of insight becomes sharpened. The appearance one presents to the world becomes more rigid, routine becomes comforting and tradition precious.' He paused and tapped lightly on the window-sill, with his fingertips, looking out. 'But as life withdraws one's physical efficiency, it appears to substitute a certain capacity for clear-sightedness. It is a source of constant amazement to me how life continually surprises one. Forgive me, Abigail. How can I expect a child of twenty to understand? To return to Hester. She is not a happy young person.'

'No,' I said, 'she's not happy.'

'Does she wish to have the child baptized, do you know? I wonder that she has not mentioned the subject to me; but then, we do not often see her at church these days.'

'I – I think she finds it difficult to come, with the baby still so young.'

'Quite so,' he said. 'It must be very difficult, no doubt. But mention it to her, would you, Abigail? I should very much like to baptize Hester's little daughter.'

'Yes,' I said. 'I'll mention it to her.'

'And will you perhaps suggest to her that she gives her marriage vows a little thought? I hear that David has been most unhappy these past few months. Tell me, has he made any attempt to see her?'

'No, none at all. He never writes to her, not even to ask after the baby.'

'And she to him? No, I thought as much. But some effort is necessary on her part, Abigail, would you not agree? One cannot make a marriage in the sight of God and just walk out of it a few months later simply because one finds one prefers things as they were beforehand. I would be very grateful if you would have a word or two with Hester, my dear, grateful and reassured.' He hesitated, then said carefully, 'To be perfectly frank with you, I feel a little disappointed that she has not come to me herself. So often these little things can be straightened out with a word or two in the right direction. A question of setting one's feet back on the straight and narrow, as it were. So do speak to Hester about returning to David. Please assure her that I am here should she want somebody to confide in. I am almost always in. Ah yes, that reminds me, have you had news from your brother yet?'

'Perran? No, not yet. We expect to hear any day. You probably know Jennifer's expecting twins.'

'Twins! My dear, how simply splendid. Dear me, how delighted your mother would have been, poor soul. A most remarkable woman, your mother, Abigail. I expect you miss her sorely.'

'Yes, we do.'

'Yes, of course you do.' He sighed. 'Well, I must not detain you any longer, my dear. I shall be down to see your father tomorrow, as usual. I'm so glad to hear he is feeling just the slightest bit more cheerful. Please give him our regards in the meantime. Ah, I see your young brother found himself a subject! My wife, weeding in her wellingtons, it appears.' He waved through the window, and his wife looked up and waved back. He tapped on the glass and signalled to Thomas, and I waved too, indicating that I was ready to leave. The vicar shook my hand. 'Thank you, my dear,' he said earnestly, 'I feel considerably reassured now that we have had our little chat. I'm sure you can persuade Hester to return to David and her wifely duties, but in your own words, of course. Young people have their own jargon, naturally; we had our own in my day. One's elders seemed so hopelessly out of touch, so painfully old-fashioned . . .'

At the end of June we heard from Perran that Jennifer had had twin boys. They called them Philip and Thomas for their uncle; and it did seem a very strange thing to Thomas that he had both a niece and two nephews now. The babies were good weights, Jennifer wrote from hospital, and very well-behaved. The nurses said they never woke for feeding in the night, and she was hoping they would be the same at home. Father seemed to brighten a little at the news and for several days appeared more interested in life. He pottered about in the pantry with his wine, and went out more into the garden to dig and weed.

Hester was very subdued. She worked hard in the cottage, cleaning everything in sight, and doing endless washing. I tried several times to get her to talk to me about her plans but each time she only went very quiet, and a bleak look came into her eyes when I mentioned David. The vicar's request rang in my ears at night, and to salve my conscience I brought up the subject. She said she did not want the baby christened yet. Perhaps in a few months she would feel ready to think about it, but not yet.

'But Hester,' I said tentatively, 'what about David's wishes? Don't you think that he ought to be consulted?' I paused. 'When are you thinking of going back to him?'

I said it quite casually, but she jumped, and turned upon me eyes wide with what looked suspiciously like fear. 'Go back to him?' she echoed.

'Well yes,' I said, rather helplessly, 'don't you want to, Hester? Don't you miss him?'

She said nothing, so I took a deep breath and went on, 'He must miss Elizabeth dreadfully, and you even more. You've been here for three months now, and you said you only wanted to stay for a little while.'

'Do you want me to go away, Abbie?'

'Well no, of course not, we love having you here at home. But Hester, your place is with David. He's your husband, after all. You do love him, don't you?'

'Yes, I love him. But I can't go back to him – not yet, anyway.'

'But Hester, that doesn't make sense. Surely if you love him you must want to be with him?'

She shrugged. 'I suppose so.'

'Then why don't you write to him and tell him you want to go home? Ask him to come here on the train and fetch you and Elizabeth.'

She looked at me. 'You don't understand anything really, do you Abbie?'

I felt slapped, and rather breathless. I turned away, suddenly hurt.

'Oh Abbie,' she said immediately, 'I'm sorry! I'm so sorry, please forgive me. It's just that I can't go back. I can't bear it if I'm not here. Nothing is real with David. Can't you understand?'

194

'You said that before,' I answered in bewilderment. 'I don't understand what you mean about "realness". Everything is real. How can living with David be less real than living here with us?'

'I can't explain.'

'Is there something you haven't told me, Hester?'

She looked at me, her eyes wary. 'Like what?'

'Like David's parents. Was there a row?'

'No row, not exactly. But they don't like me, Abbie, if that's the sort of thing you mean. Still, I suppose that doesn't matter, thousands of people probably don't like their in-laws.'

'Do they know that David is living there without you?'

She shrugged again. 'I don't know. I imagine so.' She sighed. 'I wish he'd married Veronica Braze and left me alone.'

'But Hester, you didn't have to marry him. You accepted him happily enough at the time.'

'Yes,' she said, 'I know. That was before I realized.'

'Realized what?'

'Oh, nothing. Realized what it would mean. I thought everything would be all right with David, once we were married, that it would all be real. Don't you know what I mean, Abbie? I can't explain it any other way; there aren't any proper words. It's just a sort of nothingness all the time. Oh, I wish you understood, Abbie. I can talk to you more than to anyone else, but even you don't seem to know what I mean. Don't you ever feel that things aren't real?'

'No,' I said helplessly. 'Is it a sort of acting feeling, like people do when they're shy or frightened or something, and don't want anyone to realize? I suppose we all do that.'

She shook her head. 'No, it's not like that at all. It's – it's as if everything is a dream, and not really happening. As if I keep waiting to wake up all the time, and I never do.'

'Like a nightmare?'

'No, not particularly horrible. Just not real.'

'You said some things are real. What things?'

She hesitated, and caught her hands together. I looked

down at them, at the thin brown hands, at the gold band upon her finger. 'There are moments, that's all.'

'What sort of moments? You must try, Hester! You must try to tell me. It might help. Now come on, tell me. What moments have been real to you?'

She shivered, although the afternoon was warm. She took a deep breath. 'A long time ago I thought it was getting better. I got them quite a lot, the real times. Just for a few minutes, but quite often; sometimes even as much as once a week.'

I began to experience a slight sense of panic; this was something quite beyond me. 'Would it help to talk to the vicar?' I said at last. 'He wants you to go up there and talk to him whenever you want to confide in someone.'

She looked at me in astonishment. 'The vicar? Whatever for? He couldn't do anything, Abbie. Don't be silly!'

'Sorry,' I said shortly. 'But he's a lovely man, Hester, and very willing to help.'

She looked at me. 'To help?' she said. 'Help what? How horrible, Abbie! You've been discussing me with the vicar.'

'No I haven't, I promise you. He only wants you to know he's there if you should want to go and talk to him, about anything that's worrying you. And he asked me to tell you that he would be very pleased to christen Elizabeth if you wanted it done.'

'Well I don't,' she said abruptly.

'I didn't mean to offend you, Hester. I'm sorry.'

Quite unexpectedly, she smiled. 'Dear Abbie,' she said, 'you're trying so hard, aren't you? But there's nothing to worry about, really. Just promise me you won't try to make me go away before I'm ready to. I'll go one day, I promise you. One day when I find out.'

'Find out?' I asked her. 'Find out what?'

But she wouldn't answer me, and only said, 'I'll find out one day – one day soon. Sometimes I think it's very near. Sometimes I can almost hear it, like a voice calling me.'

'When do you hear it?' I asked her curiously.

'Oh, sometimes when the wind blows from the hill, I hear

it in the wind. It's strange, Abbie, very strange; but it's the only thing that is real, almost, and that ever has been.'

'You said "almost", Hester.'

'Yes, I said "almost".' She looked down.

'Do you hear it other times? Do you hear it in the church? I remember once in the empty church you said that you were listening, but there was nothing there that I could hear. Did you hear it then?'

She nodded. 'Yes, I often hear it in there. When it's empty. And in the churchyard, mostly in the winter, when it's cold. It's like a sort of music, Abbie. And yet it's not sound; it's almost like a scent inside my mind. I can't describe it any other way.'

She turned away from me and I watched her helplessly. 'It sometimes happens when I'm hungry, and often when I'm cold. But it's real, and wonderful when it happens. In a way, it's the only thing that ever has been real.' She paused, and then she said quietly, so quietly that I almost couldn't hear her, 'Sometimes I think it's getting nearer, and that I'll hear it quite clearly soon, like I did that once, long long ago.'

'When was that?' I asked her gently. 'When else did you hear it?'

'When he touched me. Once, when he put his hands on my arms, here.' She held her arms on either side. 'He made me so unhappy because he wouldn't speak to me then. I knew it would be too late if he didn't. The realness went away again straight afterwards.'

'He?' I asked, and then I remembered a patch of amber light touching the stone church floor in the fading dusk of childhood; and I remembered, too, the top of the tower, the ground perilously distant, and Joseph's hands upon her shoulders, and I said, 'Oh dear. Oh dear, I was afraid of that.'

'I don't think I've ever been happy since that day,' she said. 'It's much older than wanting to be his wife, or anything like that. It goes back and back, millions of years, until before the world began. It's terrible, Abbie.'

She turned back to face me, her hand against the light from the window so that I could not see her face. 'What he means to me is terrible. It's a dreadful tearing rawness that started a million years ago deep in the heart of a sun, and I shall never be free of it, not now, not ever. Even when I am dead I shall lie in his arms; and I would die, I know I would, if ever he should touch me again. He is the stuff of which I am made, and what I can't understand at all is why I cannot bear it.'

'Oh Hester,' I said helplessly, 'what can I say?'

'Nothing at all,' she answered. 'there's nothing to be said. There's nothing in this world that can mend it now, not ever, I know that. I love David very much, and I might have been happy with him if – if it hadn't been for that. As it is, I can never be free now.'

She smiled at me, turning slightly so that the light from the window fell across her cheek. 'But you have helped me, Abbie, much more than you know. All of you have helped me. Even Perran, even though he hates me.'

I stared at her. 'Perran?' I said amazed. 'Perran doesn't hate you, Hester. Whatever makes you think that?'

'Oh yes he does,' she said softly. 'He always has done. I knew it long ago. When you've lived with hate for all those years like I did as a child before I came to live with you, you recognize it when it's there. Poor Perran doesn't know he hates me, but he does.'

She sighed, and turned away again. 'Don't talk about my problem any more. It's a waste of time. But I'm glad you know the truth – at least, as much as I do, anyway. You're very dear to me, like a sister. And Aunty Susan was like a mother. I never knew a mother could be like that.' She smiled at me in the falling light. 'Thank you Abbie, for everything you've done. I couldn't possibly have had a better sister.'

That August, Thomas was twelve. Father made him a little easel out of wood, one that he could fold up and carry about with him. Lissie and I managed to scrape a little money together from the sale of Father's strawberries to buy him some paints. We bought water paints in five or six basic colours, and Perran sent a huge book of special painting paper as a present from the twins to their Uncle Thomas. Thomas set it all up in his little bedroom, the one that had been Perran's, and discovered painting. He'd always been a quiet boy, and never any trouble, and now he became almost invisible.

He still went to play with Toby Tregulla on occasions and Toby came to us for tea now and again, but there was a self-contained quality about Thomas that seemed to make him different from most other children. When Toby wanted to play robbers in the woods, Thomas was only interested in painting the trees. When Toby wanted to make catapults to fire at the wood-pigeons in the orchard, Thomas wanted to draw him whittling wood. When Toby wanted to go tadpoling or look for slow-worms on the hill, Thomas wanted to draw what they found, and only went with him on the condition that he could keep the creatures as models and let them go afterwards. It must have been very frustrating for Toby, and it was remarkable that any friendship flourished at all. They struck strange bargains with each other. Thomas agreed to swap his elf-bolt, and the stone with the hole in it, in exchange for half-an-hour of drawing Toby's bare feet. Thomas did Toby's homework for him several times in exchange for a whole hour of Toby's hands, held out before him to reveal the physiology of his knuckles, the chewed finger-nails, and even a wart or two. I once caught them in the outhouse, sitting side by side on the floor, with Toby groaning at having to wear a rubber-band round his wrist until the bloodvessels of his hand stood out like knotted string so that Thomas could draw his veins; and Thomas muttering, 'Keep still! How can I get it right if you don't keep still?' in intense irritation.

Our friendship with Joseph now seemed a very distant memory. Occasionally I would come across evidence of his presence in the lanes – clouds of his tobacco smoke rising in the still air and drifting away from where he'd been, like aromatic phantoms – but of Joseph himself there was rarely any sign. Occasionally, too, he'd send us eggs by way of Lissie, giving them to her as she passed his gate. Very occasionally he brought them himself, great pearly brown ones in a little basket, but he never came into the cottage at all and, by some mysterious method of his own, always managed to arrive when Hester was out with baby Elizabeth up on the hill behind the church, or visiting Polly Tregulla. Hester had become quite friendly with Polly. Polly's three-year-old would play for hours with little Elizabeth in the garden. I was glad for Hester to have a friend with whom she had something in common, even if it was only teething problems and rusks and nappy-rash. It was on one such October day when Hester was at Polly's that Joseph came, and this time he did come indoors. He brought, as usual, eggs. He came shouldering into the kitchen, wiping his feet self-consciously and glancing about as if to reassure himself that there was no one there but Thomas and me, although he must have known it, for he would have seen Hester and Lissie go off along the lane down to the cottages with Elizabeth in Polly's huge old pram not half-an-hour before.

'Well Joseph,' I said, 'come in, do! Will you stay for a cup of tea? There's only Thomas and me here. The others are out and Father's up in his shed. Do you want to see him? He's not playing or anything. Go up there, if you like.'

'No,' said Joseph, 'no Abbie, I won't go up there.'

Thomas looked up absently from his sketch-book and gave Joseph a brief grin. Joseph, equally silent, returned it. I sighed; it looked like being a somewhat laboured occasion. But in this I was to be proved wrong.

'Did you say yes to tea, Joseph?' I asked him.

He nodded. He sat down and put the eggs before him, pushing the basket carefully into the centre of the table. Thomas's eyes alighted upon them at once. He seized his pencil and pad and began to draw: the basketwork first, the intricacy of woven willow-cane, the frayed edges of the basket, the plaited border worn and battered; and, in contrast, above the wicker-work, the bland serenity of

smoothly contoured eggs, pearly and glistening, voluptuous of line. He worked swiftly and surely, his grubby
youthful hands holding the pencil and moving over the
paper with a confidence beyond his years. Joseph watched
him intently. Thomas worked his pencil about, flicking in
shadows here, a touch of depth there, building up the
shapes until the thing was finished and the pencil drawing
sat there on the paper, vigorous with a life all of its own. He
went to put the pad away and reach out for his tea, but
Joseph stopped him. He held out his hand and said firmly,
'Let me see it, Thomas?'

Thomas shrugged good-naturedly and passed the drawing over. He never minded being asked to show his work; he
never minded us ignoring it, either. It was the execution of
the thing that mattered to him. If Lissie admired a drawing
of washing hanging on the line, or Hester shrugged off a
sketch of Elizabeth's fat little body in the bath, it was all the
same to Thomas. I looked at his hands, small and brown on
the table before him, holding the pencil. I looked from them
to Joseph's hands holding the sketch-pad; the firm kindliness of them, the square, blunt nails. He was frowning at
the drawing. For one minute I was afraid that criticism
from Joseph of all people might, just this once, upset
Thomas. I glanced at him. His square, still-infant face, with
its smattering of freckles, was alive with anxiety, his mouth
tight-drawn along its length. I realized with some surprise
that Thomas cared what Joseph thought of his work.

For a long while Joseph said nothing. Then he looked up
and said quietly, 'I didn't know you liked to draw like this.'

Thomas looked down at the paper, flushed and nodded,
and then tucked the page away. He drank his tea, and then
went off with his sketch-pad into the garden, leaving Joseph
and me alone.

'Well, Abbie,' he said at length, then nothing else. Once
again I was aware of that strange facility of his for silence.
We sat there pleasantly, drinking our tea and saying nothing. I wondered what he thought about. From time to
time I glanced at him surreptitiously. A multitude of

subjects fled through my mind, and all of them impossible: Hester, Mother's death, Father, Perran, Thomas, but Hester uppermost. When he spoke at last, though it was not of Hester at all, nor of Mother, but instead he said musingly, with his eyes on the sky outside the window, 'I remember, Abbie, that little chap a baby tied into his chair.'

And I remembered, too, a day long ago at just this time of year, of dinner in the orchard under the trees. I said, 'You carried Lissie and me around on your shoulders, and Mother made you put us down for fear we'd hurt you.'

'They were happy days, Abbie,' he said, and I wondered then if they were the happiest days he had known; and realized with a sense of shock that they probably were.

'Eleven years ago,' I said.

He looked slightly startled. 'Only eleven? It seems to me like forty.' I wondered if he was remembering the day that Hester came. There was a long silence in the room. Around us the familiar things of home stood safe and square in their long-appointed places: the old blackwood dresser, the boot from Plymouth, the nail in the wall with the calendar of 'Colourful Scotland' hanging from it, the rag-work rug before the stove, the mugs and cups and plates along the dresser shelves, Father's wellingtons (that Lissie wore to pull rhubarb) under the sink, on the window-sill Thomas's school photograph and a bunch of nappy-pins. It must have seemed to Joseph, as it did then to me, that he was woven into the fabric of our home, part of the pattern of it, belonging to it, and yet with no rightful place; and suddenly I was seized with a quiet grievous pain that this dear man I loved just like a brother had no place here in our home because the girl he should have married had married someone else.

Up in the orchard I could hear Thomas singing to himself, a funny little made-up song in that self-absorbed way he had. Distant birdsong filtered in to us through the windows. A blackbird called from a tree of dying leaf, a late song, monotonous with purity. Across the silent room, empty of all the loved ones of our family, but full of their resonance, Mother, Father, Hester and the children we had been, young and old, baby and child, all gathered there accusingly. Invisible eyes looked at Joseph, who had not spoken when he should have done. And suddenly it all seemed to me a simple tragic matter of his silence and reserve. Silent as the earth was Joseph, the deep earth in which small things struggle, and a seed is born, and a dream may die in the darkness. And there in the kitchen, within the silent presence of all that I held dear, I could have wept for him.

Chapter Nineteen

THE STONE

NOVEMBER CAME, AND with it the last leaves of the year
died and fell into the quiet lanes, and were blown into piles
of soggy umber in the ditches. The wind from the old hill
blew all alone now, unaccompanied on stormy nights,
soughing down between the granite stones and whining
peevishly in at the gate. It rattled at the windows and
moaned under the kitchen door, carping dismally.

Father had begun to fail, imperceptibly at first, so that for
a long time only those of us close to him noticed. He rarely
mentioned Mother, but I think he missed her dreadfully;
her constant pottering presence in the kitchen and her
reassuring solidness. He had never shown much outward
affection for her as far back as I could remember, and
indeed seemed to go about his days ignoring her completely;
but she had been, I think, like an anchor of reassurance to
him in a world largely impatient with a man like Father.
His violin in the woodshed at the top of the orchard lay
silent in its battered case with no one to tune its strings and
they grew, like poor Father, slack and passionless, and went
slowly out of tune.

He sat for hours in his favourite chair before the fire
looking blankly into the flames all through that autumn,
while little Elizabeth learned to walk, and tottered about
and climbed up on his knee and played with his pocket-
watch, searching for it and holding it to her shell-like ears to
hear it tick. Father absently ruffled her fine yellow curls,
David's colour, not Hester's rich auburn, and let her comb
his hair at times; but his heart was not really with us.

In mid-November, after days and days of solid rain

sheeting from the hill and streaming endlessly down the windows, we had a visitor. He came on the train one Saturday after dinner, walking from the station on a day of dismal dampness: an older, thinner David, his youthful boyish smile replaced with something much more grim about his eyes. He spoke little to me at first; perhaps he blamed me for Hester's leaving him, in some peculiar rationale of his own. When I opened the door he came into the kitchen with rain upon his head and shoulders. He shook hands formally, but in his eyes was wariness, as if he suspected that we might be hiding Hester from him for some devious purpose of our own. Elizabeth looked at him for a moment and then clung, whimpering, to Lissie's skirt.

'Look, Elizabeth!' said Lissie brightly. She picked the child up and held her out to David. 'Here's your Daddy!'

'Hello Elizabeth,' said David. He held out his arms to take her from Lissie, but Elizabeth, her lower lip puckering, turned her curly head away and hid her face in Lissie's bosom, and would not even look at him. I saw the lines round David's mouth deepen, and a cold, bitter look began to lurk about his eyes. He did not reach for her again, and ignored her from then on.

He crossed to Father in his chair before the fire, and shook his hand. Father raised dull eyes and nodded to him vaguely, as if he was not certain who was there, and dropped his gaze back to the flames again. Thomas, suddenly very grown-up, was very formal and shook hands solemnly as if it were a social occasion, and answered politely when David asked him questions about school.

'Please sit down, David,' I said awkwardly, and he sat.

'Nasty weather,' said David.

'Yes,' I said eagerly, 'isn't it! We're having a job to get the nappies dry.' I thought of Hester in the garden with the nappies and wondered at what moment she might appear. 'It's been like this for days,' I said lamely.

David scarcely glanced at me. He drummed with testy fingers on the arm of his chair. 'Well now,' he said briskly, with a forced air, 'where is my wife?'

Lissie shot an anxious look at me. 'Um – in the garden, isn't she, Abbie?'

'In the rain?' asked David icily. 'Ah yes, of course, she would be. She does some peculiar things – I almost forgot her many eccentricities. How stupid of me not to remember.' He looked from one to the other of us in turn. We all sat mute as mice around the living room, staring anxiously at him and at each other, as if by some miraculous means Hester might suddenly materialize in front of us. Nobody knew quite what to say. I thought vaguely of offering tea, but dismissed it.

Elizabeth struggled a little in Lissie's arms. There was a chiming clink and a wooden thud, and on the floor lay Joseph's rattle, kicked off the sofa by Elizabeth's little foot. David turned to see what had caused the noise and saw it on the floor.

'Ah yes!' he said, in a voice that grated in my ears. 'Of course. How very stupid of me. I should have guessed, shouldn't I?'

We went on staring at him silently. He laughed, a short harsh sound, devoid of humour. 'What a fool you must all think me. Naturally she's not here. How extremely naïve of me to imagine that she would be.' He nodded towards Elizabeth in Lissie's arms. 'Tell me,' he said, 'why didn't she take that with her? Didn't Chygowan like the colour of its hair?'

I heard a gasp, and turned to look at Lissie. She was staring at him open-mouthed. Thomas blinked rapidly several times and frowned at him. Father went on staring into the fire, as if it were all nothing to do with him. I felt my hands begin to tremble.

'Just one minute,' I said firmly. 'Thomas, please go out into the garden and see if you can find Hester. Tell her David is here. Lissie, take Elizabeth upstairs. I won't have you talking like this in front of them, David.'

Thomas nodded and went out, but Lissie sat where she was, with Elizabeth in her arms. The baby patted small sticky hands on her hair and jiggled up and down.

'Lissie,' I repeated, 'please do as I tell you.'

'No, Abbie,' she said stubbornly, 'I won't go away. I want to hear what David has to say.'

'Let her stay,' said David grimly. 'It's time you let her grow up, Abigail. I'm disappointed in you. I thought you were on my side when you were with us at Christmas.'

'Side?' I said. 'Side? It isn't a question of sides. Hester isn't a child, David. It's up to her what she does. You don't blame me for things going wrong between the two of you, surely? I can't see what I can have had to do with it. Do you blame me, David? I should like to know.'

He looked at me. 'No. No, I suppose not. I'm sorry. Of course I don't blame you. I don't know what went wrong.' He slumped in the chair, his head in his hands, and seemed to thaw slightly. 'I loved her, Abigail. You know that. I thought I could make her happy, but I failed. Where did I go wrong?'

'Things might improve,' I said. 'Perhaps if you had another try?'

'Improve?' he echoed scornfully. 'Rubbish! Things will never improve with Hester. The closeness I'd hoped for, it just wasn't possible. She never gave me a thing of herself. I never knew what was going on in that strange mind of hers.'

'Yes,' I said, 'but that's Hester.'

'I thought I could change her,' he said. 'I was stupid enough to think I could. Perhaps you can't ever change people. But I tried, Abigail. I tried and tried, but it wasn't enough. She's flawed, do you know that? Flawed! It's as if she's empty inside all the time. She's so beautiful; I'd have done anything, do you know that? Anything!' He paused, and looked quickly up at me. 'Look Abigail, I've never asked any of you, but what do you know about her parents? You must know something; you're her cousin.'

I glanced at father. His eyes were closed and he appeared to be asleep. 'No, I don't,' I said, 'I never have.'

'But you must know the family history. Your father's her uncle, isn't he?'

'That's all I know,' I told him. 'Father won't ever talk about it. Did you ever ask her yourself?'

'Yes, I asked her once, before we were married. She just put that cold frozen look on her face, said she didn't know, and changed the subject. The only person she ever seemed to want around was you. What do you do that I don't? What are you that I'm not? A cousin! All right, more than just a cousin, almost a sister. But I'm her husband!' He sighed. 'When did she come to live with you?'

'When she was nine,' I told him. 'She was just the same then.'

'But I loved her, Abigail! Surely love should break down all barriers? She's my wife. We lived together. We slept together. But I hardly knew her. She was always like a stranger. Does anyone really understand her? Do you?'

I did not answer.

'No,' he went on bitterly. 'If you did you wouldn't tell me. I thought at one time perhaps there was someone else, that perhaps the child wasn't mine. You know I thought that, don't you? Perran asked you. Well apparently I was wrong. You say it is mine. Well, the woman never has been, apart from the physical sense. I've had enough of it. She made my life hell. It's so ruddy destructive loving a woman who never responds. Chygowan can have her, and welcome. Oh yes, didn't you know? The chap's been in love with her for years.'

'What makes you think that, David? Has he ever said so?'

'Him? You must be joking. He's a deep one, that bloke. But I remember, even years ago, the way he used to look at her. Once or twice I thought of telling her, but I didn't. I remember asking her what she thought of him once, before we were married. I asked her outright. And do you know what she said to me? "Who's he?" with that sort of vacant look in her eyes. "Who's Joseph?" as if she had never even heard of him! Hell, your family have known him for years, had him to meals and things in the past. Anyone would have thought the chap was invisible. I tell you, Abigail, it gave me the creeps.'

208

'Yes,' I said, 'she's always been like that about Joseph.'

'Well, I've had enough of her now. I would have taken her back if she had come to me in the summer and told me she was sorry, but she never did, and now it's too late. I've got someone else. My mother never liked Hester anyway. She warned me about her years ago, and she was right. Chygowan can have her, with my blessing. I don't want her any more.'

There was a sound from the kitchen and Hester stood there in the doorway, her arms full of damp nappies from the line. Her eyes swung round the living room, and came to stop on David's face. In his eyes looking back at here there blazed a look of raw hatred, shocking to see, with nothing in it at all of his youthful boyish charm, and I felt that I was seeing him for the very first time.

'So you think that Joseph wants me,' Hester said wearily. Her voice was low but every word was clear. 'How wrong you are, David. You always were wrong about so many things. You never understood. Nobody ever did, really. I'm sorry I made your life unhappy. You should have asked somebody else to marry you in the first place. It was a pity you asked me. Veronica would have made you a much better wife than me.'

'She does,' he said briefly. He stood up. 'Right,' he said, quite cheerily, as if that was all there was to be said. 'Now we've got the position straightened out, I'll be off. There's little point in my staying here any longer. I can see by all your faces that the sooner I go the better, for all of you.' He reached into an inside pocket and took out a little flat parcel, wrapped in silvery paper. 'I brought it a birthday present for next month,' he said, tossing the packet lightly on to the sofa. 'It's a book of nursery rhymes. You'd better have it, it's no good to me. I don't want to see the kid again. I'll be in touch, Hester, there'll be papers to sign and all that sort of thing. I expect you'd like to be free. I know I would.'

When he had gone, out into the rain, I went across to Father. He still sat there, dozing before the fire.

'Father?' I said. 'Don't worry, Father. David has gone now. Would you like some tea?' I shook his shoulder gently. 'Father, did you hear me? Would you like a cup of tea?'

He opened his eyes and slowly raised them to mine. 'What did the chap want, Abbie? Was it the Insurance man? I was feared he'd come soon for the money. I haven't got it, Abbie. Tis all gone, all the money. He seemed a strange sort of chap, Abbie, talking like that to Hester. Why isn't Joseph here? Joseph would have told 'en where to go. Oh dear, my head don't feel quite right.'

'It's all right, Father,' I told him gently. 'It's all right now. It wasn't the Insurance man, it was Hester's husband, bringing a little present for the baby.'

'Where's Joseph to?' he asked again. 'You'll have to send for 'en, Abbie. I can't sort it out no more.' And he bent his shaggy head and went to sleep.

Hester sank down on to the sofa, her arms still holding the nappies. Elizabeth toddled over to the parcel, patting it with baby hands, then dropped it on the floor. She wandered off, babbling to herself, in search of Joseph's rattle. There seemed nothing much to say.

Thomas pulled at my arm. 'Abbie, what did he want? Doesn't he love Hester any more? He seemed a bit horrid, Abbie. He thought that Hester had gone to live with Joseph, didn't he?'

I sighed. 'Yes, I suppose he did.'

Thomas looked puzzled. Then he said, 'Why, Abbie? Why did he think that?'

'I don't know, Thomas.'

'What did he mean, about the baby not being his? I heard him say it when I was in the kitchen. Elizabeth is Hester's baby, isn't she? How can she belong to anyone else?'

'Oh dear,' I said. 'Thomas, I'll explain one day. Take Elizabeth upstairs, will you, my poppet? I think Hester would like to be on her own for a little while.'

He nodded and went off, calling to Elizabeth. She trotted after him like a little shadow, jingling the rattle.

'Lissie,' I said, 'make us a cup of tea, could you? I wish we had some brandy in the house, but tea will have to do. I'm sorry you had to hear all that. How much of it did you understand?'

Lissie was staring at Hester. 'Quite a lot,' she said. 'Does Joseph love you, Hester, like he said?'

'Joseph?' said Hester, and the blank look was back. 'Oh no, Joseph doesn't love me. If Joseph loved me, wouldn't he have told me, all those years ago?'

'Lissie,' I asked her, 'are you going to make the tea? I'd love a cup of tea, and I'm sure Father and Hester would too.'

'Don't treat me like a child, Abbie,' she said unexpectedly. 'You heard what David said. I was talking to Hester.'

'Lissie darling,' I said wearily, 'I don't mean to treat you like a child. You aren't a child, anyway. I just want a cup of tea, that's all. I'll make it myself if you'd rather.'

'No,' she said, 'sit down. I'll make it. I just wanted Hester to know that – that I understand about her loving Joseph, if she does, because I know what it's like to – to love people. To miss them when they're not here, to want to wash their socks and darn their clothes, and look after them; and to feel glad and happy when they like your chocolate cake and eat three pieces of it.' She stopped and the colour rose in her face until it glowed crimson, then she gulped and ran into the kitchen to make the tea before we could utter a word. I watched her plump little figure filling the kettle and putting it on to boil, and wondered if I saw the future all mapped out for her.

Hester looked at me. 'That's that, then,' she said in a distant voice. 'Now I know where I am.' She shook herself. 'Sorry about that, Abbie. I hope it didn't upset Uncle Garfield.' She frowned and looked anxiously at Father. 'Abbie, is he all right, do you think? He seems very sleepy.'

I bent over Father and shook his shoulder. 'Father?' I said. 'Father! Can you hear me?' He gave a little snore and fell sideways in the chair, his eyes closed. I picked up one of his hands and released it. It fell back heavily into his lap. Then he stirred, opened one eye, and lifted up his head.

'Get Joseph,' he said in a leaden voice unlike his usual one. 'Get him.'

I looked at Hester in alarm. 'Father!' I said, shaking him gently. 'Wake up! Lissie is making you some tea. You'd like that, wouldn't you? Tea, Father? Cup of tea? Oh come on, Father, do wake up a bit!'

Father grunted heavily. Then he seemed to pick up a little. He straightened his head and said in a clearer voice, 'I got to see Joseph . . . my son . . . Perran, send for Perran . . . where's Joseph to?'

'But Father dear,' I said helplessly, 'who is it you want? Joseph or Perran?'

Father was muttering again, and we stooped to listen. 'Joseph,' he said firmly. 'Want Perran here. Got to know. Send for Joseph. Might be too late soon . . .'

'He seems so muddled,' I whispered to Hester. 'Does he want them both? Or does he mean Perran?'

We could make no sense of it, and after a while Father went to sleep again. We tucked a blanket round his knees, and drank our tea in worried silence.

Father spent the night in his chair, alternately waking and dozing and mumbling to himself. I slept fitfully beside him on the sofa, and in the morning we asked the doctor to call. A minor stroke, the doctor said, and nothing that a few days in bed wouldn't put right.

We couldn't hope to get Father up and down the stairs, so we made up a bed for him on the couch in the parlour, the little room we hardly ever used beside the front door. Thomas made up a fire with applewood to keep him warm, and the doctor said he'd send the district nurse round in the mornings to keep an eye on him and treat his pressure areas, whatever they were.

Father seemed quite contented in there. He slept a lot of the time. He seemed to want to eat very little, only soup from time to time, and needed a bit of help to drink it from a cup. Thomas sat in there for hours when he wasn't at school. He drew Father when he was asleep, and read to him when he was awake. I don't know how much of it

212

Father understood, but he seemed to be listening. I went in there once to hear Thomas, with a book upon his knee, struggling over the words: 'If you arrive in four five down without knowing whether to go in quick or slow, or knowing your course bell, note the bell you strike over at your first blow in fourths. If on leaving four five your first blow in thirds is over this bell make thirds and go in slow,' which sounded like nonsense to me; but Father was listening to the clear, young voice with a look of rapture on his face, and it seemed to comfort him. But half-way through December, when the rimy grass was stiff with frost along the lanes, Father worsened. And I sent urgently for Perran.

Chapter Twenty

THE HOLLY

PERRAN CAME ALONE, remote, responsible, a married man and now a father too. He came in from the back where he had left his motor-bike and nodded curtly to us all, as if he were a stranger. Perhaps it was anxiety, I thought, although it did seem more to me like rudeness, but I made him tea to warm him up, and he sat there at the table in his old place where he had sat for eighteen years since baby-hood, drinking the dark brown liquid and looking around him with a strange mixture of resentment and affection in his eyes. I made him drink the tea before I let him go into Father in the parlour. He helped himself absently to several rock-buns that I'd put before him on a plate, and munched steadily between the gulps. I saw from time to time that he eyed Hester sideways with hostility when she wasn't look-ing, and I hoped she hadn't noticed; but his eyes softened slightly when they fell on Lissie's plump little figure at the sink and fell, kindly I think, on me. He ignored baby Elizabeth. The atmosphere was very tense and after a while Hester, saying nothing, picked up Elizabeth and went out into the kitchen. I got up to go as well, having given up any hopes of pleasant conversation, but he said firmly and surprisingly, 'No, Ab. Sit down. I want to talk to you.'

I looked at him. He scowled at me, and reached for another bun. 'Go on, sit down. It's time we had this out.'

'Oh?' I asked him. 'Had what out?' I sat down again and waited.

He bit into the bun and munched steadily. 'I was right, you see.'

'Right?' I asked. 'About what? About Father?'

'No,' he growled. 'Don't be so bloody innocent with me, Ab. You know quite well what I mean. I mean her!' The venom in his voice shocked me a little, but I put it down to anxiety about Father, and excused him. I think my very mildness irritated him. He sat there heavily, slumped in his chair with his elbows on the table, glowering in the direction of the kitchen, where we could hear low murmurs of their voices and the baby's little gabbles as they dried the dishes.

'Perran,' I said in a low voice, 'leave her alone. She's unhappy enough, anyway, without you getting at her too.'

'She's unhappy?' he retorted scornfully. 'And what about her husband, I'd like to know! What about Dave, then? What about him? He's a different chap altogether from the chap I knew. Have you seen him lately?'

'Yes,' I said wearily, 'he came last month.'

The muscles of his jaw flexed. 'That bloody girl! I could wring her neck. There's been nothing but trouble in this house ever since she came here all them years ago. Nobody's had any time for anyone else but her. Is dear Hester happy? Is dear Hester eating enough? Is dear Hester warm enough in her bed at night? Bloody hell, she isn't even one of us, and she had more of Mother's time than all the rest of us put together.'

'Perran!' I said sharply. 'That is not true, and you know it. And please stop swearing in this house, if you don't mind. There's poor Father dying in there, and Mother hardly buried. If all you can do is sit there hating poor Hester for some imaginary thing she can't help at all and never could, then you'd better go away again as quickly as you came and not come back in a hurry. I wanted to ask you all sorts of pleasant things: to have a little chat about old times perhaps, to ask you all about Jen and the twins, all the little things they do now they're six months old. Who do they take after? Do they look like you, or Jen? Do they look very alike? What colour is their hair? Are they little and dark like Jen, or are they going to be tall like you? When are you going to bring them to see us? All these, and other

215

questions too, I was going to ask you. I was hoping for a pleasant talk about old times, and new times as well. Wouldn't you like to hear the news about Thomas?'

He stared at me, his jaws slowly munching on the bun, while I went on and on; on and on, it seemed to me, the words poured out of me, and he watched me in amazement.

'What about Thomas?' he demanded. 'He's all right, isn't he?'

'Of course he's all right,' I said. 'Wouldn't I have let you know straight away if he wasn't? But do you know about his Art School? What Joseph and the vicar did for him? Do you want to hear about it, or would you perhaps rather rage on and on about Hester? Thomas is going to Art School. He's brilliant, Perran. Joseph got the vicar to see the Principal or whatever he's called. I wouldn't have known what to say to him, but the vicar went with Thomas for an interview, seeing Father was too ill. And it was Joseph who set all that in motion. Offered to pay for all his books and pencils and all those kind of things, Joseph did! Perhaps you'd like to have a go at Joseph next? You seem to hate our family, and Joseph's the next best thing to family after all these years. Imagine Joseph, and the little bit of money he must have to manage on, wanting to do something like that for Thomas.'

He went on staring at me, his mouth still now. 'Joseph wanted to do that?'

'Yes, he did. He recognized Thomas's talent when none of us did. It's all due to Joseph. Thomas starts next term at the Art School and the chap said he would take him a year early as his standard is so high.'

'That's good,' he said grudgingly. 'Good old kid. He'll do all right for himself. Be famous one day, I shouldn't wonder.'

'It's nice to know you think so,' I retorted. 'And what about Jennifer and the twins? What have you got to tell me about them? That is, if you can talk calmly and sensibly without getting angry again.'

He shrugged, and resumed his munching. 'Not much to tell. They're good little kids – not very alike. One's a bit like

216

you to look at; that's Philip. The other one's got more of a squashy nose, a bit like Mother used to look in those snaps of her as a baby. Tam's darkish. We call him Tam, although of course his name's Thomas, after his uncle. Philip ent quite so dark. They don't do much except yell for food, of course, but they're only little kids yet.'

'And Jennifer copes with them all right, does she?'

'Oh yes,' he said, with a trace of pride, 'she's good at coping with things, Jen is. Made a good choice there, I did. A proper wife, Jen is.' He glowered towards the kitchen and I clenched my hands beneath the table to feel the tension creeping back. 'Not like some I could mention.'

I took a deep breath. 'You don't understand anything, Perran, so drop the subject.'

It was entirely the wrong thing to say. I could tell that immediately by the way the muscles of his jaw went hard again, but I carried on. 'All right, so she has left David, and I'm sorry for him. But try to see Hester's side, just for a minute. She's very unhappy, dreadfully unhappy, can't you see that? I don't know why, but she is. There's something gone terribly wrong somewhere between them, but at least it's better to try and help them sort it out instead of just shouting around and hating her. You don't get anywhere like that.'

I glanced at him fearfully. He was breathing heavily, the muscles of his jaw jumping and flexing. Then he smiled to himself, a grim smile, almost one of satisfaction, and said in a low harsh voice, 'But I was right, wasn't I? I said she'd come back here to stop for good, and she has. That little kid of hers never sees its father, do it? I ask you now, Abbie, when did David see it last? What's its name, Elizabeth?' He glowered at me, still munching steadily. 'Not since Mother died, was it?'

'No,' I said, 'you're wrong. He saw Elizabeth last month.'

'Last month? Last month! What sort of good is that? Last month? That's the first time, then, since it was a few weeks old! Do she think Dave don't care? Do she write to him? Do she let 'en know about the kid? How many teeth has it got? Is it walking yet? Does it talk? Do it say "Mamma"? I bloody well bet it don't say "Dadda"!'

There was utter silence. I looked across the table into the kitchen. Hester stood quite motionless beside a frozen Lissie. The baby in her arms looked reproachfully across her shoulder towards us, and her lower lip began to tremble. Perran shoved his chair roughly backwards and banged his tea-cup down into the saucer, nearly wrenching off its handle. 'Well, I've had enough of you forever sticking up for her. She married the bloke and she's got his child, his so you tell me. So why don't she go and live with him? The poor chap's been living in that house all on his own for months; it's no wonder he's taken up with Veronica Braze now. He should have had the sense to marry her in the first place. She would have made Dave a damn sight happier. Pity he didn't ask Veronica in the first place, if you ask me, instead of bloody Hester!'

I stared at him aghast. I hardly recognized my brother. There was a hollow silence, which seemed to go on and on and on. Dimly I realized that Lissie at the sink was shaking silently with tears. Hester stood beside her like a rock, hardly seeming to breathe. I could not see their faces as they had their backs to us. The dreadful silence went on and on until I felt I might scream, just to break it. Nobody moved.

Perran continued to stare into his tea-cup for a few moments, breathing heavily. Then he threw the half-finished bun on to the plate, and with a rough thrust of his chair he was out of it and crashing through the hall to Father. I looked at the mangled bun upon its plate; the currants and sultanas scattered about the pretty, mocking pattern. I stared and stared at it, feeling sick, feeling dizzy. All I could see were the broken scattered crumbs about the worn pink pattern of Mother's wedding china, ancient with washing-up and faded with use.

After a while I got up and went out into the kitchen. I put my arms round Lissie's shoulders and patted her helplessly. Hester stood staring blankly out into the garden, her face quite expressionless. 'Come on,' I said gently, leading her back into the living room. 'Come and sit down, my pet. Don't take any notice of him, Hester. He doesn't know what he's saying. He's worried and angry and upset about Father. He says the first thing that comes into his mind. Don't take any notice at all. Look, here's Elizabeth. Give her a cuddle. She's upset too, and frightened of all the shouting. Here, take her.' But she wouldn't. She allowed herself to be led and sat down in a chair, but her eyes were blank, and when Lissie tried to put Elizabeth into her arms she didn't move. The baby struggled a little and clung to Lissie, and in the end Lissie took her out into the garden.

After about half an hour Perran came back again. I heard his footsteps by the stairs and steadied myself, taking deep breaths to calm my hands. He came into the living room, slowly and quietly this time, moving carefully as if he might shatter something if he moved too fast. Hester didn't move. I looked up at him as he came towards us, and there was a curious gleam at the back of his eyes, a kind of triumph. He came towards us and stopped, looming over us as we sat together on the sofa.

'Abbie?' he said. 'Out, girl!'

I sprang to my feet. 'Oh don't, Perran! Leave her alone! You've done enough damage for one day. Can't you leave her alone?'

He gave me a level look. 'I've seen Father,' he said, and his voice was quite calm. 'I've seen Father and I've talked with him. Now I want to talk to Hester. You needn't worry, Ab, I only want to talk to her.'

I looked at Hester. She sat quite motionless on the sofa, her hands clasped together in her lap, staring blankly at the floor. 'If you want to talk to her, carry on,' I said, 'but I'll stay here to listen.'

'No,' he said, almost kindly, 'leave us alone, Ab. Go next door to Father. I want to talk to Hester on her own. The shouting's over. I got nothing to shout about now. But I want to talk to her, and I don't want you to hear. Go in to Father, Abbie. He wants to see you. He wants to pee, or sommat. Go on. I've promised I won't shout at her no more.'

I looked from one to the other of them, Hester so still and silent, my brother, calm now, and authoritative. 'What shall I do, Hester? Do you want to hear what he's got to say? Do you want me to stay?'

She moved her eyes round to look at us both, and gave a little sigh. 'No Abbie, you go. If Perran has something he wants to talk to me about, then he'd better do so. Go and see to Uncle Garfield if he needs you. I'll be quite all right.'

So I left them there together in the living room, and I went next door to Father.

Father was very trembly. He caught at my hands as I went towards the bed, and held on to them tightly.

'Are you all right, Father?' I asked him.

'Oh yes, Abbie,' he said, 'I'm all right now, my girl, now I've seen the lad.'

'Can I get you anything? Perran said you wanted something. Do you want your bottle?'

'No,' he said. 'No, I don't want nothing. I got all I want now. I'm happy now I've seen the boy.'

'Did he tell you about the twins, Father? He says they're fine little chaps, and look like Mother when she was small.'

'Oh yes,' he said, still holding on to my hands, 'yes, he told me. I'm glad I've seen 'en, Abbie. You did right to send for 'en to come. I feel a lot better now I've seen the lad. He's doing all right, is Perran. I liked that girl Jen. Take good care of him, she will. He's a wise old gentleman up there, Abbie. Do you know that, my girl? A sharp old gentleman, who do know exactly what He's doing with all His plans and schemes for all our lives.' He sighed and patted my hand, 'His ways are strange sometimes, and awful bitter often, but you got to trust to His method. We might not know just what He's got in mind, but the path is there all right. He calls your bobs and singles in their rightful order and you got to dodge or make places, snap lead or go in slow; win or lose, you got to obey His calling. But it do all make sense when your touch here is finished and you come

220

into rounds and you can see the method He've had in mind crystal clear in the light. We can't see it here, for we've got our noses too close to the ropes. But up there we'll see it, make no doubt.'

'Will we, Father? I'm glad of that.'

'A great Lord, He is, Abbie. A great Lord of might and coincidence, who do know exactly what He's about.'

'Coincidence, Father?'

'Yes, my maid, coincidence. You don't surely doubt it wasn't part of His plan for those little chaps of Perran's to come along, do 'ee? Unwanted they were at first, I don't doubt. Brought the lad up a bit short, I believe. But tis all worked out proper now. He've got His plans for every one of us, He have. You got to trust Him, though.' He peered sternly at me, and forgot to cough. 'You trust 'en, don't you, Abbie? I've brought you up to trust Him, haven't I? I believed I had.'

'I don't know, Father. I suppose so. But wasn't Hester unwanted?'

'All part of His plan for something, is Hester, make no doubt. That I'm sure of, sure as I lay here now. I can't tell exactly what His plan were creating the girl when – when, well, never mind that bit; but create her He did, and He must have had a purpose. He had a purpose for Thomas now, didn't He? Joseph tells me the lad's a genius, and knowing I've helped give a genius to this here world do make me feel awful happy laying here.' He sighed again, 'I'm happy about all my children. Tis only Hester I'm not happy about. But I have to tell myself to trust the old chap to know what He's up to. Everything do work to a purpose in His pattern, and don't 'ee ever forget it.'

'No Father,' I said meekly. 'I won't forget it.'

'I'm tired now, and I'm going to have a little sleep. I'm glad the boy came, Abbie. Some glad you sent for 'en; but I'm going to have my sleep now. I shan't want no dinner, my 'ansome, so you leave me be.'

'All right, Father,' I said, patting his hand. 'Are your pillows right?'

'Yes, yes,' he said. 'You leave me be, now. You been a dear daughter to me, Abbie. I couldn't have wished for a better. Tis only Hester I'm not happy about, and Hester never was my child. Perran's a good lad. I'm happy now I've seen my son Perran.'

To my surprise Perran was alone downstairs.

'Where's Hester?' I asked him.

He gave me a strange look, a quick glance, and then looked away immediately and started to collect up his gloves and helmet. 'She went outside,' he said briefly. 'I've got to get back, Ab. Got to be on my way now.'

'That's very sudden,' I told him in surprise. 'I imagined you'd stay to supper.'

'No,' he said. 'Best not. Jen's on her own with the twins. I've got to get off home.'

'What did you say to Hester?'

He shrugged. 'Nothing much. Just a few home truths, a bit of straight talking. Sommat she ought to have heard way back. Well, I'm off, Ab. Take care of Father.' He strapped his helmet into place and pulled on his gloves. 'I'll be in touch.' He jerked his head. 'Let me know if there's any change in there, won't you?'

'Yes,' I said, 'of course.'

He hesitated, then sniffed a bit, as if in doubt about something, and drummed with his gloved fingers on the table.

'What is it, Perran?' I asked coldly. His eyes came round to look at me at last, a slight defensiveness lurking behind them, and what might have been shame.

'Sorry, Ab,' he said.

'Oh well, it's done now, isn't it?'

There was surely nothing in the words to make his head jump up the way it did, but he began to look thoroughly uncomfortable. Suddenly it seemed he couldn't wait to be away. I saw him off at the gate. 'Aren't you going to say goodbye to Hester and Lissie?'

'No,' he answered. 'I've said enough for one day. I'll be off now, Ab. See you some time.'

'Goodbye Perran. Give our love to Jen.'

'Right,' he said, with a rather forced brightness. 'Right, I'll do that. Right.' He kicked the starter and was off, out of the gate and down the lane, not even turning to wave. I heard the sound of the engine long after the view of it had disappeared, winding in and out of the leaf-bare trees like a disembodied bumble-bee, and slowly dying in the distance. I stood there beside the gate, looking down the empty lane, for several minutes. The smell of woodsmoke was in the air, and the scent of ice, heralding snow. The wind was beginning to rise in the December air, and up on the old hill I knew that it would be about between the ancient stones, mysteriously alive. I shivered, calling to Thomas. He loomed up in the dusk beside me, a small, grey figure vague with gloom. 'You'd better come in now,' I told him. 'It's getting cold.'

'Abbie,' he said, 'come and see Hester. She's been sick.'

'Sick!' I said, astonished. 'Sick? She was all right earlier.'

'Well, she's been sick,' he said.

'Thomas! Why was she sick? Where's Lissie? Where's Elizabeth?'

'Lissie's got Elizabeth inside. It's all right, Abbie. The baby's all right, but I don't think Hester is. Come and see her, Abbie? I don't think she's very well.'

'Where is she?' I asked him, suddenly afraid. 'Has she gone upstairs?'

He shook his curly head. 'No, she's in the outhouse.'

'The outhouse! Whatever for? Why didn't she go to bed? Oh Thomas, has there been an accident?'

'No,' he said, 'I don't think so. She just talked to Perran when you were with Father, and then she went outside. I found her being sick in the garden, and then she went into the outhouse. Oh Abbie, it wasn't like an ordinary sickness. I was frightened. She was awful sick and looked all funny, sort of speckled and muddy. Come and see her, Abbie. You'll know what to do.'

I followed him round the path towards the garden at the

back, my legs trembling. Hester was rarely ill. A small hammer of alarm began to beat in my chest. Thomas led me over to the outhouse door and pushed it gently open. It was very dim inside and the window let in little of the fading light. I peered round in the gloom, trying to make out shapes. The gardening fork and spade stood up against the cobwebbed bricks as they had always done, along with jam-jars filled with old paint-brushes, rusted and bristle-bare, soaking in ancient turpentine and oily, stagnant water. There was a small convulsive movement in the corner opposite the door, a choking noise. Followed by Thomas I moved carefully over towards it, picking my way between the hoe and the rake and empty seedling boxes, and bent down beside the figure crouching there. The acid smell of vomit rose to my nostrils. My stomach heaved.

I shook myself. 'Hester!' I said urgently. 'Are you all right? Whatever's wrong? Thomas says that you've been sick. What is it, Hester?'

There was no movement from the crouching form. I looked up. 'Thomas, go and turn back Hester's bed and put the kettle on for a hot-water-bottle. We'd better get her to bed. Tell Lissie to look after Elizabeth and go in to Father if he calls. Can you do the bottle? Don't burn yourself with the water when it boils, will you, and be careful to turn the gas off again. Run along and do it for me now.'

When he had turned and gone, I pulled gently at her arm. 'Hester, get up, my poppet. You can't stay here.' Her arm was trembling and her body shook. She went to push me away, but her hand was trembling so much she pushed at empty air, and not even in my direction. 'Come on, my love,' I said. 'You must come in! Have you got the 'flu? Come on, I want to get you upstairs and into bed. You'll have to help me, Hester! I can't lift you up alone.'

Still she did not move. 'Hester, please!' I urged. 'Come on; you must come inside.' I pulled at her arm again, trying to lift her up. Then suddenly, she spoke.

'Go away, Abbie,' she said, quite clearly, in a curious little voice. 'I'm not ill, not ill at all. I just want to be left

224

alone. Abbie, please go away and leave me on my own.'

'But you can't stay here like this! Whatever is it? Are you crying?'

She shook her head in the gloom. 'Just go away,' she said. 'I don't want anybody near me.'

I considered it for a moment, quite seriously. 'No,' I said, 'I can't do that. You must come in with me. You ought to be in bed. You've been sick. If you're not ill now you should at least be in the warm, or you most certainly will be. Please Hester, now!'

She drew a shuddering breath, a long gasp that seemed to come out of her whole body. Then, quite suddenly, she stood up and allowed me to lead her out of the outhouse and into the dim evening. We stood for a moment outside the kitchen. The lights were on inside, shining out of the windows and making the cottage look as cosy and safe as the church on Christmas Eve. Hester stood on the edge of the light so that for the first time I could see her face. Her lips were deathly pale. Around the corners of her nose were small blue patches like half-moons, as if she had stopped breathing for a space, and hardly had begun again. She stood like a wall of white silence, looking towards the light. Then suddenly she gave herself a little shake, her eyes dilated strangely, and she turned and looked at me. 'So that's it,' she said softly, 'that's it. At last I know.' Then she turned and went from me, through the back door and into the kitchen, as if I wasn't even there.

It snowed in the night, the first fall of winter. I slept very little. Lissie dozed easily beside me, Thomas was quiet in his little room above the pantry. We'd given Hester Mother and Father's room as Father was downstairs, and she slept in there with baby Elizabeth. Whether she slept or not I could not tell, but shortly before dawn Elizabeth awoke and whimpered a little. We heard the muffled sound through the wall between. I lay for a moment, puzzling over the strange, pale light reflecting from the ceiling, then closed my eyes and dozed again. A little later I heard Lissie creep from the bed, moving gently so as not to wake me, and pad out on to the landing. I heard her go into Hester's room. She came back almost at once, with Elizabeth in her arms. She brought her into bed; the small body cuddled down between us and the rounded limbs, cold as ice, grew slowly warmer. At last the child relaxed. Her curly head against my neck, her feet on Lissie's middle soaking up the warmth, she fell into soft baby slumber. My heart ached full with love for her, and tightened at the thought of Hester, who now slept there alone.

'Did Hester mind?' I whispered above the curls.

Lissie shook her head. 'She's fast asleep, I think. She never moved.' She said she'd whispered to her once but Hester never stirred, not even when Elizabeth cried, but lay still in the semi-darkness with her head turned to the wall, so that she knew she was asleep.

I lay awake with Elizabeth's hair tickling my cheek and her small breath rising and falling against my ear, while Lissie dropped back into sleep. I lay and listened for the usual sounds of winter dawn, for the birds beginning to rustle and twitter in the trees outside my window. It was a sound I dearly loved to hear in spring-time when the birds began their tumult: querulous at first with anxious twitterings and then, one echoing another, rising slowly to a pitch of fluid clamour, until the world was awash with the frenzied purity of sound, like disembodied spirits hammering at the gates of morning. But the December dawn was curiously silent. I lay there in the strange, dim hour on the edge of wakening, and almost didn't hear the little noise.

At first I thought that I'd imagined it. The soft creak of a floor-board, a scratching like a rasp, the subdued scrape of the sash, Hester opening her window. I relaxed, but the creak came again. Another rustle, a distant thud, then silence. I waited for the creak of springs to tell me that she had got back into bed. It did not come. I lay there in the growing light, conscious of tension in my limbs.

Lissie and Elizabeth slept on, oblivious. There was

silence from Thomas's little room and no sound below from Father. I slipped out of my side of the bed, shivering in the cold.

The room before my eyes was empty. The drawer which still served as Elizabeth's bed was in its usual place, the blankets rumpled and the little hollow in the middle cold to my hand. Hester's bed-clothes were folded neatly back; her clothes were gone, and her shoes too. The window was open, the sash high. I sighed, and slid it down, shutting out the icy air. So she'd gone for a walk in the snowy dawn, and had not wanted to disturb the rest of us by going out through the kitchen. Pulling an old dressing-gown of Mother's close about me, I sat down on the side of the bed.

I sat there for a good few minutes, playing thoughtfully with my fingers. She would have gone up to the old hill, walking alone through the snow. She had made no attempt to waken me. She had wanted to be alone.

I sat on the side of Mother's bed while the light grew in the room, staring at the dark mirror of the wardrobe reflecting the window greenishly in familiar reverse. Then I got up and crossed to the window, looking out upon the snow. She might, of course, have gone down towards the cottages; but I knew that although in her place my feet would have taken me down the lane, I was almost certain that Hester's would have taken her up. I went back into my bedroom and dressed quickly, grabbing my clothes as quietly as I could.

It was icy by the gate. About me the trees held still with early silence. On the ground there were footprints in the thin snow, leading up the lane. So now I had my answer. She had chosen the hill.

I followed the footprints up the lane, scanning the hill ahead of me for some movement of her figure or sign of her bright hair. The mound lay still and brooding in the distance, mottled with patchy snow. The cold rasped on my bare hands. I stood for a moment breathing heavily, wishing I'd had the foresight to wear gloves.

There was a crunching sound behind me and I turned with relief, expecting to see her. Joseph plodded up the lane towards me, muffled in his old brown duffle-coat and wellingtons, pipe in his mouth, puffing thoughtfully. He nodded to me. 'Off for a walk?'

'No,' I said. 'I'm looking for Hester.'

'Oh? Lost her, have you?'

'Yes. You haven't seen her, have you?'

He shook his head. 'Where's the child?'

'Asleep,' I said, 'with Lissie, in her bed.'

'Oh, she'll be all right up there on her own,' he said reflectively, and his words left clouds in the air. 'She do love that old hill, Hester do.'

'But I'm worried, Joseph. Perran came yesterday to see Father. They had a talk, Perran and Hester. I don't know what he said to her. She went into the garden afterwards and was sick several times. What could he have said? Oh Joseph, I'm worried.'

He looked suddenly alarmed, and looked quickly at me. Then he said, 'No. Don't worry, Abbie. He wouldn't have told her that.'

'What? What do you know that I don't? Did Father ever tell you anything?'

'Oh, Garfield told me years ago,' he said grimly. 'I've known it all along.'

'What? Tell me, Joseph.'

'If you don't know, then I won't tell you, Abbie,' he said stubbornly. ''Twas long ago, and Garfield told me as a confidence. I hope your brother didn't tell her, for tis a thing best not to know. I wouldn't want her to know that, not Hester.'

'You love her, Joseph, don't you?'

He sighed. 'Oh yes,' he said, quite easily, 'always have. But that don't make it no better for her.'

We had reached the lych-gate by now. To my surprise the footprints, instead of going past and up towards the hill, led into the churchyard. We followed them round to Isaac Bartholomew's grave. They stopped beside it and then led off again, round the path to the church field. They stopped at the gate, and then went on down the field towards the big holly bush at the side.

'Holly!' I said triumphantly. 'She went to pick holly. Hester!' I called hopefully. 'Hester! Where are you?'

There was no answering call. A few rooks wheeled in the empty sky above us, croaking dismally. We peered at the ground together. There were footprints coming back up the field again. They crossed the path and went into the church.

Relief broke over me like a wave. 'Thank goodness,' I said. 'She's in the church, of course! I should have guessed it all along. Oh Joseph, I'm so sorry to alarm you. I might have guessed she'd be in there. There aren't any footprints coming out again, so she must still be in there. Joseph? Joseph, what is it? What's the matter?'

His face had a grey look. 'The door,' he said, 'the door.'

'It's open, look!' I said. 'It's quite all right. Look, she's gone inside. She isn't in the porch. Don't worry, she'll be safe in there.'

His voice seemed to come from a great distance. 'The door,' he said again, 'the door. They don't keep it locked no more, not now.'

I stared back at him, feeling the blood drain from my face.

Chapter Twenty-one

THE TREE

WE FOUND HER on the ground beneath the tower. By the wall she lay, where so long ago Perran and I had found poor Jacky; like a broken toy against the snow, looking about her in bewilderment, whiter than white against the grey stone and the pale world. Her eyes moved, and fell on Joseph's face.

She turned her head towards him, and they looked at one another. And Joseph bent down, reached out, and touched her cheek.

I had the strange thought that in all the years we'd known him Joseph, to my knowledge, had never once deliberately reached out and touched another human being, except Hester. I thought of how he'd picked the child Hester up in his young arms and carried her upstairs on the night that she had arrived. Then again, his arms about her here in the churchyard, how he had held her to his heart when she had fallen against him. But never before had either of them reached out and touched the other until now. And Joseph had put out his hand deliberately, and touched her cheek. And then I remembered her words.

We took her from the churchyard, Joseph and I. He scooped her up in his arms with a smattering of snow and carried her light form, like a grey winter bird, cold and pale. The holly she had picked was still grasped tightly in her hand. One of the stiff, dark leaves had broken off and fallen between them, caught between her arm and Joseph's wrist, and made a scratch on both their skins, so that two small streaks of red met and ran across her arm. Hester, looking down, saw what had happened, and into her face came a look of extraordinary release. She smiled: a lovely smile, quite glorious. She raised her hand, letting it fall on the back of his neck. She lifted up her face to his and, pulling his head down gently, kissed his mouth.

We brought her home and laid her in my mother's bed, Joseph and I; and all the while he carried her down the lane their eyes never left each other's. I sent Lissie, poor startled Lissie, to Polly's with baby Elizabeth, and Thomas for the vicar. The snow was falling again, thick and fast this time, and I sorely doubted they would get through in time.

I washed her poor, bruised body clean of mud and snow, and covered her with blankets, and all the time it was as if I wasn't even there. Then suddenly those eyes of hers found mine, as if she'd just become aware of me, and my heart stood still at the colour of her face. She said quite calmly with a kind of quiet delight, 'I'm dying, Abbie. You know that, don't you,' as if we were having an afternoon conversation by the fireside over a cup of tea.

'Of course you're not, Hester,' I said shakily.

She sighed and said wearily, 'Don't be silly,' as if I were a nice but rather tedious child. After a little while her eyelids closed, and I thought she had fallen asleep. I sat beside her on Mother's bed, on the old patchwork counterpane that had been Mother's wedding present from her own mother, with its once-rich reds and greens and blues almost blended into one with years and years of laundering, and underneath which no doubt we'd all four of us been conceived; and it passed through my mind in that strange lengthy hour, unreal with pallid daylight from the snow, to wonder in what distant bed Hester had been conceived, and whether her mother had loved the man. For it seemed to me, having no experience of my own to draw upon, a deep mysterious thing, this meeting of a man and woman in their bodies; a thing with a dark power of its own, to be used for good or ill. I looked at Hester's waxy face and at the gold ring upon her wedding finger and knew she must have known it in all its secret mystery, for Elizabeth's existence was living proof of that; and I wondered if she'd liked it, and whether I would like it too, if ever it came to be that I should know it.

I held her hand and sat there still beside her, smoothing the rich hair away from her forehead and watching her face. Strangely enough I felt no desire to cry, no sadness whatsoever. Something of a profound and serious reality was taking place, and I knew with a curious certainty that Joseph would not bring the doctor in time, and that Thomas would find the vicar out, and that I would be alone with Hester when it happened. And I was glad that I was with her and no one else about, not even Joseph. For I was well aware of what was happening; I had no doubt of it at all.

After a while she opened her eyes and smiled at me, and in the strangest way it was for a moment Mother lying there on the pillow and smiling at me with Hester's eyes.

'You mustn't worry, Abbie,' she said softly. 'You won't be upset, will you, promise? You'll look after Elizabeth for me, won't you? You'll bring her up for me? Don't tell her about my parents. Just say that I was your cousin, and that we were very close.'

'Of course, darling,' I said gently.

'It was such joy when she was born, Abbie. So real, just for a moment. I've never known what it was to feel like a proper person, but I did then, just for a while. But it went away again soon afterwards. Everything else was just that awful strangeness all the time. But at least now I know why. Oh Abbie, I'm so glad Perran told me, can you see that? You must forgive him, promise me?'

'Perran?' I said. 'Forgive Perran?'

'Yes,' she said. 'Uncle Garfield told him, of course. He made Perran promise not to tell me, but he did. It upset me dreadfully at first, that's why I was sick. No Abbie, you mustn't mind. I'm glad he told me, very, very glad. It explains everything. If only you could see how much it helps.'

She sighed a little and gave me a shaky smile, 'No, you

232

don't know about it, do you. I can see that. Perran didn't tell you. Surely you've guessed by now?'

'Guessed?' I asked her blankly. 'You love Joseph, I knew that long ago. What else is there to realize?'

'Why,' she said in a little rambling voice, 'about my mother, of course, and how I came to be born. It explains everything. I've always felt as if there was a piece of me missing inside, as if I'd been made by accident, not properly as other people are.'

She sighed. 'When I was younger I used to wonder if perhaps I was the result of my mother being raped or something. She hated me so much, and I never knew why.'

'Oh Hester . . .'

'I told you Perran hated me. I was right, you see. He'd never have told me if he hadn't hated me. Don't worry, I'm quite used to it.' She gave a little chuckle, 'In a way it makes me feel at home. He was killed in the War, of course. He left their family and went away to fight, and never came back. I expect they were quite relieved.'

She turned her face towards the window. 'Oh Abbie, look, it's snowing! What a lovely moment this is. Do you know, when I jumped off the tower just now, I thought how God probably wouldn't mind a bit that I did it, because he couldn't really have meant me to be born in the first place, could he? I must have been a sort of mistake. Perhaps the angels were looking the other way for a moment and forgot to concentrate, and I happened.'

'Hester,' I said helplessly, 'I don't know what you mean . . .'

'It's him I feel so sorry for,' she went on softly. 'He must have hated himself so much afterwards. My grandfather. My real one, of course; I don't mean the one in the churchyard. My father. Abbie, I'm the result of what's called incest, haven't you guessed that yet? My grandfather was my own father. I'm not properly made like other people are, with proper parents. I'm not a real person.'

I stared at her aghast. And years and years of clouds rolled over memory and swirled like snowflakes in my

233

brain. I just kept staring at her wordlessly; and all that I could do for her was hold her hand.

After a little while she seemed to go to sleep again. I crossed the room and stood by the window, looking out upon the wintry garden and the hill beyond, remembering. Her obsession with the grave; the reason she was steeped in sorrow and could never be free of it; her curious feeling that nothing in life was real. Low and murmurous came back the memories, and beat like wings about my mind. I stared out of the window, seeing only the falling wall of snow.

And I thought also, looking out, that every one of us has this odd heresy of life within us in hidden measure, but our love of self disguises it. But Hester had been born without her portion of self-love. David had tried to understand, and had failed. Possibly only Joseph had ever understood, and Joseph had let her go.

After a while she murmured, 'Take care of Joseph's child for me.' I looked at her for a moment, baffled; wondering if at this late hour I still had judged her wrong. Then she said 'No Abbie,' very slowly and softly, 'don't worry, my so-solid Abbie. Her father truly is David, but Elizabeth is Joseph's child.' And the strangest smile played about her lips, a secret, mysterious smile like a little pain. And then she said, 'Oh but I shall lie with him, Abbie. I shall lie with him in the dark earth, when I am dead.'

And a little while later, with her hand tight-closed about the holly leaf, she died.

Now, in the late spring sunshine, I walk up the lane. Beneath the trees there are bluebells, carpeting the ground. I turn into the deserted churchyard with my flowers: a few daffodils from the orchard to put on Mother's grave. Father likes me to do that for him. Hester lies beside her as she has done now for several years. The birds still nest above them both in every flurried spring. I stoop to arrange my flowers.

After a little while a shadow falls across the world. I look up, wondering, across the golden evening. He looks tired, older too; the lines of his face deeper-etched than I remember.

'Well Abbie,' he says at last. 'Here you are.'

I struggle to stand. My mouth is dry. I can scarcely breathe. I am standing under a roofless sky, and light breaks all around.

'Are you well?' he asks.

'Well enough,' I mumble through stiff lips.

'And the child?'

A small breeze moves about us from the fields, and stirs the grass by our feet. 'Well too,' I manage to reply. 'It's been a long time, Joseph.'

'Not so long, Abbie,' he says slowly. 'Nothing really.'

Above us in the sky rooks call at the evening and the air is full of blossom. In the distance a dog barks, and the trees are heavy with windy noise.

'Tell me about them,' he says. 'How's Garfield keeping?'

I shrug. 'What's there to tell? Father's very doddery. Sits by the fire most evenings. Or else we get him to bed and read him Lissie's letters. Her oldest boy is having violin lessons. Father dearly likes to hear about that.'

He smiles to himself. 'No doubt of that. And Perran?'

'Keeping well. Comes to see us from time to time. The twins are fine lads now, tall and strong. Thomas . . .' I pause. 'Oh Joseph, why?'

He shakes his head.

'But all this time, Joseph! In all this time you've not been near us once, never once come to see Father.'

'Oh, I've had my reasons.'

'Reasons? What reason could you of all people have for staying away? It's sorely grieved Father, though he never mentions it, not now. After Hester died he dearly wanted to see you, to talk to you, but you never came.'

'No.'

'You could have come to see him, Joseph. It wouldn't have hurt you, not just once.'

'There's nothing I could have said to Garfield. Twas better not.' He pauses, his eyes on distant fields, and then

235

relents. 'There are questions he would have asked me, Abbie. Questions I couldn't have answered. Better this way.'

In spite of all my vigilance a tear creeps down my cheek. He says nothing, but puts up a hand and gently wipes away my tear. It is the tenderness that breaks my heart; the silence I can bear.

'What is it?' he asks me. 'Don't you cry. Twas all over, all the pain and trouble, many years ago. Don't you grieve.'

'But it's you!' I cry brokenly. 'You, Joseph. You have nothing, nothing at all. No family. No children. Nothing but lonely, empty years.'

And Joseph looks at me across the level light, my lovely Joseph, and he says to me, 'No family, Abbie? But don't you know who I am?'

'You?' I ask him blankly. 'You? Why Joseph, who else could you be?'

He gives a smile. A little shaky smile, as if his thoughts go far far back, into a past that I know nothing of; years and years before I was even born. And when he speaks it is as if his words are practised, long-anticipated. 'I'm Garfield's son, Abbie. He's my father. Don't ever tell him; it would break his heart to know it now, after all that's happened. Twas a quick love affair one summer when Garfield and my mother were very young. I've always known the truth of it. My mother married shortly afterward, and Garfield never guessed.' He sighs. 'And knowing too about Hester's parents being as they were, how could I have married her? I couldn't have done that, Abbie. It wouldn't have been right.'

The small breeze swings about us from the fields and then is gone. A million years rise up and die, and lie like shards about my feet. 'No,' I say to him. 'No. I see that you couldn't.'

'And as for family,' he says, as soft as summer wind, 'I've had a family all my life, though they knew nothing of it. I've had their kindness and their trust. I've had my work, and memories, one or two. And I've had a sister of my own, straight and strong, true as a tree. A precious sister you've been to me, Abbie, and I've loved you dearly for it all these many years. Love is a very strange thing. It don't seem to matter how it comes to you, or what the moral rightness of it, the power of it is there all the same, coming to you through the dark. I've felt it in the wind at night, and in the daytime too; in between birdsong and thunder, under winter. You've been sending it to me all my life almost, and it's held me, in the troubled times, like the fierce loving beat of angel-wings.'

Then for a long time he says nothing more, and the little breeze that had crept about us fifteen minutes earlier, before the world was old, moves round about us with a sigh. He looks at me across the arch of evening, and the rich warmth of his smile falls full upon me. And then he softly says, 'For the wood is life to the leaf, Abbie. But the soul of the tree is the sun.'